D0297547

3 0116 01766532 2

Praise for Alan Judd

'Funny, exciting and sad, as well as revealing . . .
Its clarity and pertinence demand our attention
in a way which not many novels do'
New Statesman

'Funny, intelligent and frightening'
The Sunday Times

'Rivetingly accurate . . .'
Observer

'Deserves all the attention it can get'
Times Literary Supplement

'Alan Judd writes exceedingly well'
Evening Standard

'Twisty, accomplished and engaging'
Kirkus

'This espionage thriller is a standout'
Publishers Weekly

'Judd is a masterful storyteller, with an intricate
knowledge of his subject and a sure
command of suspense'
Daily Telegraph

'Judd keeps plot and action centre-stage . . . he has written
a novel perfect for brightening up a drizzly winter Sunday'
Mail on Sunday

ALAN JUDD

UNCOMMON ENEMY

SIMON &
SCHUSTER

London · New York · Sydney · Toronto · New Delhi

A CBS COMPANY

First published by Simon & Schuster UK Ltd, 2012
A CBS COMPANY

Copyright © Alan Judd, 2012

This book is copyright under the Berne Convention.
No reproduction without permission.
All rights reserved.

The right of Alan Judd to be identified as author of this work has
been asserted by him in accordance with sections 77 and
78 of the Copyright, Designs and Patents Act, 1988.

1 3 5 7 9 10 8 6 4 2

Simon & Schuster UK Ltd
1st floor
222 Gray's Inn Road
London WC1X 8HB

www.simonandschuster.co.uk

Simon & Schuster Australia, Sydney
Simon & Schuster India, New Delhi

A CIP catalogue record for this book
is available from the British Library

Hardback ISBN: 978-0-74327-566-8
Ebook ISBN: 978-1-84983-274-8

This book is a work of fiction. Names, characters, places and incidents
are either a product of the author's imagination or are used
fictitiously. Any resemblance to actual people living or
dead, events or locales is entirely coincidental.

Typeset by M Rules
Printed and bound by CPI Group (UK) Ltd, Croydon CR0 4YY

To William and Caroline Waldegrave

1

After the lock turned in the door Charles Thorough-good leaned against the cream brick wall and looked around his cell. There was a wooden bedstead bolted to the tiled floor, with a green plastic mattress and matching rectangular pillow. Above it, close to the ceiling, was a narrow window with frosted glass so thick that the iron bars outside were faint shadows. To his left, behind a low brick wall, was a stainless steel lavatory bowl with no seat or paper. Set high in the wall above the door was a camera and in the ceiling a single bright bulb behind a wire mesh.

He took it all in but his thoughts were elsewhere. He had been parted from his possessions, stripped of belt, shoelaces, watch. They were searching his two properties and two cars and confiscating his papers, computers, mobile phone, passport, diary, old address books – anything they thought they wanted. Yet, deprived of liberty and locked in a police cell, he felt strangely free. It wasn't the heady, transitory sense of liberation that shock can bring, nor the removal of the daily burden of choice. Rather, he relished this abrupt solitude because it freed him to consider what had brought him here, and why it felt so apt. It was as if this was where the current of his life had long been flowing, towards a reckoning he had yet to fathom. But one thing shone through it all: betrayal.

He walked over to the bed, propped the plastic pillow against the wall and sat. The camera above the door hadn't moved and it was hard to tell how much it could see – the toilet, for instance. He wondered how long it would be before he had to use it. They had permitted him to pee when they had arrested him at his London flat that morning, but he wasn't sure what time that was. The wall clock in what he had already learned to call the custody suite had said six-fifteen a.m. when they brought him in. Searching, recording, form-filling, questions about keys, access to his house in Scotland and his cars, photographing, fingerprinting and taking his DNA had gone on for some time, but he had no idea for how long.

Nor had he any idea how long they would hold him. He assumed he would be released on police bail later that day, after interview. No-one had said as much but he couldn't believe that the ostensible reason for his arrest – suspicion of breaking the Official Secrets Act – would merit refusal of bail. He hadn't broken the OSA, anyway, so far as he knew. The two arresting officers were considerate, given the circumstances, and he had cooperated fully. That was a lesson he had learned long before in the old MI6. Whether or not you had anything to hide – and on espionage operations, under alias, breaking the law in foreign countries, you usually did – you made no trouble. You were the innocent abroad: naïve, anxious, bewildered, keen to help, unthreatening, trying to make them relax with you, persuading them they had the wrong man.

He had volunteered to the search team where his cars and keys were, how to find the spare mobile hidden in one of them, how the spare keys to his Scottish house had to be felt for in the angle of the rafter in the shed that housed the old Land Rover, and that it probably wasn't locked anyway. During the photographing, finger-printing and the DNA mouth swab he was patient and obliging, taking an interest in procedures and asking questions they were pleased to answer. Officials, he knew, enjoyed explaining. In return they had handled him gently, mentioned breakfast, allowed him to take a book and reading glasses into the cell and had not handcuffed him, unlike the prisoner brought in afterwards. They were concerned that he did not want a lawyer.

It helped, of course, that he had nothing to hide, at least so far as the charge was concerned. He could think of no secrets he had supposedly caused to be published. But there were other matters, related matters he was still trying to work out, which he was determined to keep back. Above all was his growing sense that the major themes of his adult life had started with one person, Sarah; long ago they had radiated outwards from her and now were leading back to her. It was like the slow revelation of an architectural or musical harmony of which he had long had an inchoate awareness. He welcomed it, but the consequences were unclear.

The book they had allowed him – after one of the officers had opened and shaken it – was *Jane Eyre*. He had been shamed into reading it by Rebecca, the former MI6 secretary in whose Durham house he had stayed on his way south a few weeks previously. With the licence of past intimacy, she had scolded him for not reading more of the other half of humanity.

In fact, what had now happened went directly back to Rebecca rather than to Sarah. Or, more precisely, to David Horam, her journalist partner and author of the article that had led to Charles's arrest. Charles had skimmed it the day it came out, but only because he knew the writer. It was a comment piece, typical of a Sunday paper that could neither ignore the events of the week nor find anything new to say. David's subject was the afternoon bombing of a cinema in Birmingham, in which a young man had been killed and two people slightly injured. The bomb had gone off in the gents and the victim, whose remains were unidentified, was thought to have been the bomber. It wasn't clear whether he had intended to kill himself or whether the cinema had in fact been his target. There wasn't much of him left; no-one had noticed whether he carried a bag and the usual indication that a suicide belt had been worn – an intact head – was unavailable. The device was packed with nails, like some that Charles remembered from the streets of Belfast, decades before.

Despite media speculation that it was the work either of al-Qaeda or of a lone-wolf sympathiser, there was nothing to link it to any particular group or cause. There had been no claim, it was not part of a coordinated attack and there seemed no obvious reason why a half-empty cinema showing a film about struggling New York musicians should have been the target, unless it was significant that the director was Jewish.

David's article called for more resources to combat terrorism, proposed that legal structures should be modernised to cope with the evolving threat and ended with a paragraph on the problems of surveillance, which

quoted figures from an unidentified security source on the
number of staff needed to watch someone round the clock.
The SIA – the new Single Intelligence Agency, by which
Charles had been temporarily re-employed – should,
Charles assumed, have been pleased with it. It was sup-
portive, unlike other articles in the same paper written by
someone called James Wytham during the past year. They
were well-informed pieces quoting from leaked documents,
albeit vitiated by implausible conspiracy theories and carp-
ing assumptions of wrongdoing. They had damaged the
SIA because the factual truths meant that the implausibil-
ities and assumptions were taken as equally true. There had
been questions in Parliament, media demands for shake-
ups and calls for the retirement of Charles's friend and
mentor, Sir Matthew Abrahams. He was the SIA's first
head and before that had been the last chief of MI6. Charles
could not believe that Matthew had anything to do with his
arrest, or even knew of it. He would, as soon as Charles was
free to tell him.

He opened Rebecca's copy of *Jane Eyre*, thinking he
should have brought Koestler's *Darkness at Noon*. That
seminal evocation of communist tyranny began, he remembered, with the cell door closing on Rubashov, loyal servant
of the Party that was about to devour him. Rubashov leaned
against the wall as Charles had done, then lit a cigarette

while he considered his position. Presumably that would be a further offence here.

He pictured his ancient Penguin Modern Classics copy on the bottom shelf of his rooftop flat in the Boltons, not far from London's Brompton Road. The cover was a detail from Francis Bacon's *Man in Blue*; a seated, faceless man, a bureaucrat, the sort who, with a stroke of his pen, would have legitimised Rubashov's betrayal after years of pitiless loyalty to a rationalist illusion.

But any comparison of himself with Koestler's hero was ludicrously presumptuous. Rubashov's beliefs had been chiselled out of suffering and hard thinking; Charles had merely imbibed his from the comfortable social and intellectual world that had nurtured him. After university he had joined the army, after that MI6. Patriotism, though it was unfashionable to express it, ran deep and he had willingly risked his life for his country. He had been generous, he hoped, in friendship; but his public generosity was limited by dislike of the crowd, mistrust of theory and by the easy assumption that, above subsistence level, there was not much that should be done for mankind as a whole. He thought the urge to improve the human condition was too often dangerously close to the urge to control. Born into a generation that prided itself on wanting to change the world, he had only ever wanted to join it, to feel part of it.

The desire to be of some service to the state had been strong in him. It still was. That why he had agreed to come back. And it had led him to a police cell.

There was a rattle of keys and the door opened. A plump policeman with a farmer's red face looked solemnly at him. 'Fancy a spot of breakfast?'

The word made him hungry.

The policeman beckoned conspiratorially. 'Sit and eat it in reception if you like. Watch 'em all come in. More interesting than sitting here.'

They sat on a bench against the wall in reception. The clock showed twenty to nine. It was reassuring to know the time again, like a glimpse of headland to a sailor in a sea-mist. A man in civilian clothes brought Charles a fried breakfast on a tray, with a mug of tea for the policeman. He wondered how long you had to be a guest of Her Majesty before you were provided with toothbrush and paste.

The policeman looked at Charles's breakfast. 'Same as what we have, that is. Same kitchen.'

Charles, his mouth full, nodded his appreciation.

The outer door was banged open by two broad, squat men with shaven heads and no necks, both wearing jeans and leather jackets. One was black, the other possibly Turkish. Between them they half-dragged, half-carried a pale young man in handcuffs, shoving him onto the other bench. One went to the desk while the other stood along-side their prisoner, still gripping his upper arm. The young man's features were thin, his expression resentful, almost bitter. It was easy to imagine him as vicious. The middle-aged burgher in Charles, reassured to see such robust enforcers of the law, ceased worrying about toothpaste.

His policeman nudged him. 'People say it's a real education, watching what comes through here.'

Later the policeman took his tray away and left him alone. More prisoners were brought in, all young and generally cosmopolitan. One attractive young woman, who looked Eastern European, was addressed with fatherly familiarity by the custody sergeant.

'Seen you here before, haven't I?' he said as he took her details. 'Not your first time, is it? And I told you before what I'm telling you now. Pack it in, stop it, don't do it any more. If you do you'll keep getting arrested and one day you'll find yourself in prison and you won't like it. It's no life, I'll tell you that for nothing. There's lots of other things a girl like you can do. Go and do them.'

The handcuffed young man was processed as Charles had been, but with his captors watchful on either side of him. He struggled when first being searched but then sullenly cooperated until taken down the corridor to the cells, when he began shouting until the cell door slammed shut on him.

Then one of Charles's arresting officers appeared, the taller one, a man of about thirty with sandy hair and freckles, wearing a light grey suit. He looked reassuringly bureaucratic, Charles thought. He could deal with bureaucrats.

'Searches are going well. They've nearly finished your flat. I don't think the neighbours are aware.'

'Thanks.'

'Not much chance of neighbours poking their noses in at the Scottish house, I gather.'

Charles's house on the north-west coast was yards from the sea, sheltered by a rocky outcrop at the edge of a bay facing the Summer Isles. His nearest neighbour was a modernised croft across the bay, the holiday home of a well-known television journalist. Perhaps he would be accused of leaking to him next. There were half a dozen other dwellings scattered at intervals along the unmade track leading to the bay.

'They'll know,' he said. 'They notice everything up there. So little happens.'

The house was white-walled, red-roofed, built in the 1970s, practical, spacious and almost weather-proof. He loved it for half the year, provided he could escape to London whenever he wanted. He wasn't lonely there – he had persuaded himself he never felt lonely – but recently he had been tempted to escape more often. He told himself that had to do with the book he was writing rather than the place.

'They let themselves in easy enough,' continued the policeman. 'It wasn't locked, like you said. But they'll use the spare keys to lock it when they leave.'

'There's no need up there.'

'Until it happens. You should lock it.'

'I know.'

The policeman sat. 'They've done your car, too. I've never seen one of those. 1968, isn't it?'

They discussed his car. It struck him as he spoke that he might have chosen such a rare and idiosyncratic breed partly because it symbolised something of the very national culture that was now disowning him. He obligingly went through what the Bristol cost to run, what he'd paid for it, what it was worth. They then considered whether the policeman should replace his Honda.

The policeman lowered his voice. 'You know it's going to take a while, all this? It'll be this afternoon before we interview you. Are you sure you don't want legal representation? Your service would pay for it, they told us. They've got a list of lawyers they trust. Unless you've got your own?'

Charles had only ever used lawyers for conveyancing. He didn't think he needed one now. He was confident that he had no case to answer, and a lawyer might only prolong the process by arguing. 'I'm happy to answer whatever you ask. If I think I would like legal advice, I'll let you know.'

Later, when left alone again, he wanted to pee. He approached the custody sergeant, suggesting he return to his cell to do it so that no-one need escort him.

'That's a help. I see you're getting the hang of this place.'

Someone closed the cell door on him while he was peeing into the steel bowl. He waited a while before pressing the red button on the wall, then waited a longer while for the peephole cover to slide back.

'What do you want?'

It was not the friendly farmer. 'I was allowed to wait in reception. The custody sergeant let me sit on the bench. I came back here for a pee and someone closed the door.'

'Told you could come out again, were you?'

'I think it was understood. By the custody sergeant.'

The shutter slammed. This time the wait was long enough for Charles to sit on the bed and open *Jane Eyre* again. The first line was apt: there was indeed no possibility of taking a walk that day. Eventually the keys rattled and the door opened.

'All right, come on.' The new policeman looked as morose as he sounded and there was now a different custody sergeant, taking details of another handcuffed youth while giving loud instructions to someone behind him. The shift must have changed. When eventually he noticed Charles the sergeant jerked his thumb at him and turned to the surly policeman.

'That your prisoner?'

'Nothing to do with me. Says he's allowed out, to sit over there.'

Anxious to maintain his privilege without appearing to assert it, Charles explained as compliantly as he could.

The sergeant cut him short. 'All right, sit on that bench and don't move.'

He read in the intervals between prisoners, glancing at the clock every few minutes. It was a continuing comfort to know the time. When the state deployed its apparatus against you, it owned you and disposed of you as it pleased. The physical freedoms you took for granted, possessions that felt like part of yourself, being able to communicate with whom you chose, everything except life itself, now depended upon decisions in which you had no say. But the state could not own time. It could deprive you of knowledge of it, temporarily, but ultimately time was on your side because the state's powers were limited by time. Simply knowing it, therefore, felt like a sliver of independence, almost of power, something to be cherished.

2

It was midday before the sandy-haired detective reappeared. 'Ready for interview now.'

They took Charles to a small windowless room into which was crammed a table, four chairs and some ancient recording equipment. The other arresting officer, shorter with thinning hair and a brown corduroy suit, was already there. They sat Charles on one side of the table and themselves on the other.

'This is a recording machine,' the policeman in corduroy said with solemn deliberation. 'When I switch it on I shall state time, place and date and then each of us will give his name and I will state that there is no-one else in the room. D'you understand?'

Charles nodded.

'Do you also understand that you don't have to say

anything at all? You can say nothing. Although if you do say nothing your silence may be mentioned in court.'

'Just answer our questions truthfully,' said the one with the sandy hair, 'but don't do any more than answer. That's what your lawyer would tell you if you had one.'

Charles felt he was on stage, which in a sense he was. It was tempting to smile, but they might not like that.

The one in the corduroy suit switched on the machine, gave date, time and place and announced himself as Detective Inspector Steggles. The one with freckles identified himself as Detective Sergeant Westfield. Charles gave his name and confirmed that there was no-one else in the room.

It was clear that they must have been shown his old MI6 file and that his arrest had been planned for some time. They went unhurriedly through his career, asking few questions but seeking confirmation of his work against Russians, against apartheid South Africa, against Chinese and against terrorists until the point at which he had requested early retirement some years before.

'Why did you want to leave MI6?' asked Corduroy. 'Still was MI6 then, wasn't it? Fed up with the way things were going? Disaffected?'

Charles was happy to talk about that. 'It was changing, though nothing like as much as it has since the merger with MI5 and GCHQ. I felt I'd done all the jobs I was going to enjoy. There was nothing else in the service I particularly wanted to do.'

'They didn't offer you anything?'

'They did, I could've gone on, could've had a posting. They were very good to me, very tolerant. They'd allowed me to lead an eccentric career, free of management. But after the death of my mother, I could afford to retire on a half pension. And I wanted to write.'

'Write what – journalism?'

'Biographies – one, anyway. Walsingham. Francis Walsingham. Elizabeth the First's spy master. I'd also planned a novel. Historical novel, sort of.' He added that in case they suspected a revealing novel about MI6. Otherwise, it was beginning to feel like *Desert Island Discs* without the music.

'But you do journalism, don't you?'

'A bit of freelance book reviewing.'

'You know journalists?'

'A few.'

'You know James Wytham?'

He remembered the name from the Sunday paper articles based on leaked documents. 'No.'

'Never met him?'

'No.'

'But your friend Dave in Durham knows him, doesn't he?'

'He may do. They write for the same paper. Although

David's freelance, so he might not. Probably doesn't go to the paper very much.' Their calling him Dave was significant. That was what Rebecca called him and their use of it suggested either that they had talked to her – in which case she would surely have told him – or that his phone was tapped. That again suggested considerable preparation. He had spoken to her only once since arriving in London, when he had rung to thank her for putting him up. She had probably said something about Dave then – she usually did. Otherwise, they had talked about meeting when she came down on business.

'Ever discussed James Wytham with Dave?' continued Corduroy.

'Not that I remember. I don't know David very well. We've met only two or three times.'

The recorder was humming slightly and they were both taking notes. Charles looked at Corduroy's thinning brown hair. He had been in the army with someone called Steggles, but this man was surely too old to be Clifford's son. Perhaps not. It was a discomforting thought, in more ways than one.

Freckles looked up. 'A couple of months ago the SIA got in touch and asked you to rejoin. How did that come about?'

'They rang me. Jeremy Wheeler rang.' It was the truth

but not the whole truth. 'He's head of human resources, as it's called now.' They would know this, and more.

'What did he say?'

They waited, pens poised. Charles couldn't see that this was of any particular relevance, unless to test his frankness and recall. 'Well, there was a bit of gossip and catching up. We joined MI6 together.' He remembered wincing at Jeremy's all too familiar voice with its exaggerated articulation. 'He said they had a job for me, something temporary they wanted help with.'

'Your vetting's been updated,' Jeremy had practically bellowed. 'Start as soon as you can get down here.'

The sea had been a surly battleship grey that day, restless and choppy with countless white horses filling the bay. Charles would have enjoyed puncturing Jeremy's assumption that he'd jump at the chance of returning, but for the conversation he'd had with the old chief, Matthew Abrahams, the day before.

'Did Jeremy Wheeler say anything about the job?' asked Freckles.

'Only that it concerned something I'd been involved in years ago, which I took to be a case. I wouldn't have expected him to say more on the phone.'

'It was a case, wasn't it? A case called Gladiator? But you didn't know that when you spoke to him?'

'It was, yes.' He didn't say whether or not he knew it and was careful not to show surprise that they had been briefed on Gladiator. What he needed to know was how deep that briefing went.

'What else did you and Jeremy Wheeler discuss?'

'Timings, how long it would take me to get down, that sort of thing.' It had pleased him to irritate Jeremy – never difficult – by refusing to fly from Inverness and instead taking a couple of days to drive, staying the night in Durham.

'Does Jeremy Wheeler know about the Gladiator case?'

So it wasn't Jeremy who'd briefed them, unless they were playing games with him. 'No – well, I don't know for sure. He certainly wouldn't have when it was – when I was the case officer, years ago. I don't know what access he's had since. He was never very involved in casework. He's generally done non-operational jobs.'

Charles was certain that Jeremy had not been on the indoctrination list for the case-file, but less certain as to whether that meant anything in the post-paper age. It was displeasing to think of Jeremy having access to it now, even to the less restricted volumes. He pictured Jeremy's fleshy features, puffed with the self-importance of secret knowledge. Jeremy always gave the impression of hurrying on to something more important, yet he had never been known to do anything very much – no significant recruitments or cases well run, no headship of important stations, no productive cultivations of a liaison service, no key Action desk in Head Office, no eye for analysis or reflection. He had risen on relish for administrative detail, enthusiasm for process, an instinctive response to the magnetism of power and unabashed, unpremeditated flattery of those who had it. A lifelong talent for offending his peers and inferiors had done nothing to inhibit his career. None except those above him had ever taken him seriously. Alternately assertive, clumsy and contrite, he had been known as Mr Toad on the training course he and Charles had shared. Yet there he was, senior now. He would have access to Charles's file and would know about his arrest, which was another displeasing thought.

'You're sure you didn't discuss anything else about the job?' asked Corduroy.

Charles genuinely struggled to recall. Jeremy had complained that it was difficult to get hold of Charles, taking it almost as a personal affront that there was no mobile phone signal in that part of Scotland. What made it worse was that the computer system introduced with the merger had created an electronic black hole into which many of the records of former staff had disappeared.

'Inevitable when you get amateurs meddling with IT,' Jeremy had said. 'Last twitch of the old office. We're much more up to date now – management, IT, everything.'

'Spying?'

Jeremy sighed. 'You mustn't take it amiss if I call you a Cold Warrior. I know you did other things as well but you'll find it very different now – if I may say so, somewhat improved. In fact, beyond recognition from what you're used to, all that endless diplomatic pussyfooting and faffing about with natural cover cases. You know we've got Nigel Measures in charge now, don't you?'

'I thought he was deputy chief.'

'CEO, deputy CEO. We've got rid of all that chief nonsense. He'll take over when Matthew Abrahams goes, which won't be long now. He's not been well. You know him of old, of course. D'you know NM?'

'We go back a long way. I haven't seen him for years.'

'Moderniser to his fingertips. He'll make big changes. Has done everywhere he's been. Brilliant career, you have to admit, whichever side you're on: Foreign Office, European Parliament. Wouldn't surprise me if he went back to politics one day. How d'you know him? Didn't serve with him when he was in the Foreign Office, did you?'

'We knew each other at Oxford.'

Jeremy had always disliked hearing that people had been to Oxford or Cambridge. 'Might have guessed. Would he remember you?'

'Yes.'

'Come to the front door at eight on Thursday morning. We start earlier than in your day. Got to keep up with the modern world. None of the old gentlemanly ten-till-six stuff that you're used to.'

'Ten o'clock. I'll be there at ten.'

'Too old office, Charles. You're going to have to change.'

The head of a seal had broken through the ruffled waters around the headland. It was still tempting to say he wouldn't be there at all, that they could come to him if they wanted; but he knew he would go. 'Ten o'clock,' he repeated firmly. 'Ten o'clock Friday. Not a minute before.'

Charles realised he had been silent for a while and that the policemen were waiting. 'No, I don't think we discussed anything else about the job. We talked arrangements, he warned that I'd find much changed. He mentioned the change in leadership.'

'Which hasn't happened yet, has it? The old one hasn't resigned, has he – Sir Matthew Abrahams? But he's still unwell. He doesn't come into the office now?'

Charles smiled. 'You're well briefed.'

They smiled back without comment. Freckles put down his pen and leaned back. 'When did you first know that Gladiator going missing was the reason for your recall?'

'I was briefed when I got down here by Nigel Measures.'

Again, it was true but not the whole truth, and thus a lie by omission. He recalled his late father's dictum: the essence of a lie is the intent to deceive. There was no more to be said about that.

'You're well in with the SIA leadership, aren't you, despite having left MI6 some years ago? You used to work for Sir Matthew?'

'He was my boss, more than once.'

'When you were running the Gladiator case.'

It was a statement, not a question. 'Yes.'

'And you also used to know Nigel Measures?'

'Yes, though we've not been in regular contact since he went to Washington. After that he left the Foreign Office for Brussels. We've come across each other a few times since.'

DS Westfield frowned. 'But you knew him before that, didn't you? At Oxford University, through his wife?'

'I knew him and his wife, yes.'

Corduroy nodded. 'What about coffee before we get on to your visit to Durham?'

After recording that they were having a break, they switched off the apparatus, stood and stretched. Freckles went for the coffees.

'Lucky to get you in here, in Belgravia,' said Corduroy. 'Much better than the bloody pandemonium in somewhere like Wandsworth where we could have gone.'

'I'm glad you did. There are a lot of formalities, aren't there? As well as recording who comes and goes, all this sort of thing. '

'We have to. PACE – Police and Criminal Evidence Act – lays it all down. If we don't follow it to the letter it doesn't count, gets thrown out.'

Charles kept him going with questions but his mind was on the one they had asked – asked as if merely in confirmation – about his having known Nigel Measures at Oxford through Nigel's wife. It was slightly but tellingly inaccurate. He knew Nigel because they had been in the same college, not through Sarah, whom they had each met independently. But ever since he had married Sarah, Nigel had given the impression to others that he had introduced Charles to her; that they had been rivals and that Charles had been worsted. Charles's guilt in relation to Sarah meant that he rarely corrected the impression.

'So did Mr Measures show signs of future greatness when you first knew him?' continued Corduroy. 'Was he destined for the top?'

Charles shrugged. 'Not obviously. But then nobody was.'

If Nigel had briefed the police on him and Gladiator, there was certainly more to his arrest than its ostensible reason. And if the real reason was what Charles thought it must be, it was equally certain Nigel would not have briefed the police on it.

Freckles returned with three plastic cups of coffee on a tin tray. 'Okay with milk? Had to add it, couldn't bring it. There's sugar here, though.'

'Milk's fine, thanks.'

'Not that it is milk. Continental muck, never been near a cow.'

Charles stood to stretch his legs while drinking.

'Sit down, please,' said Corduroy, more tersely than before.

Charles sat. Corduroy leaned forward, elbows on the table, hands clasped. He had small, hard brown eyes. 'You knew Rebecca Ashdown, with whom you stayed the night in Durham, from your time together in the old MI6, where she was a secretary? And she is married to or partner of the journalist, David Michael Horam, with whom she has a son?'

'I don't think they're married. Her son is by her former husband, whom I never knew.'

'When you knew her in MI6 she was single?' Corduroy waited for Charles to answer in the affirmative, then spoke with obvious deliberation. 'Would that relationship have been one that you would have described as having been, at any time, close?'

Charles had noticed before that questions they thought important or delicate were more convoluted and were often phrased in the passive voice, as if it conferred greater precision. 'She was secretary to the instructors on my training course,' he said. 'We all got to know her well. She and I were then involved in a case together, which brought us personally close.' Clandestinity breeds intimacy, he was tempted to add to spare them the trouble of asking, but he was curious to see how they would do it.

Freckles took over, looking as if he were reluctantly intruding upon private grief. 'Would it be true to say that it would not be incorrect to describe your relationship, at that moment in time, as an affair?'

What constitutes an affair? he wanted to ask, but it was important to appear helpful, not to play clever-clogs, as Rebecca herself might have put it. 'Yes, at one period it was an affair. It began in Southwold, in Suffolk.' An unnecessary detail, which he thought they would like. 'Then it evolved into a friendship, which has continued ever since.'

'Are you intimate with her now?'

'No. We have been occasionally. The last time was three or four years ago, after her marriage broke up and before she was involved with David Horam. Before she was living with him, anyway.'

'Has she any other contacts within the SIA?'

'I don't think so. Most of the people she and I knew left before the merger. She works for a local radio station.'

They wanted every detail of his visit to Durham – how it came about, why, how he got there, times of arrival and departure, who said what. They treated it as a crime scene – which, in their eyes, perhaps it was. He spared them a lyrical description of powering the old Bristol through the fast bends and swooping hills of the A832 highland road. Telling them he had reached Durham at about eight conveyed nothing of the wet and fretful rush-hour around Glasgow, worsened by inadequate wipers, a misted windscreen and a smell of petrol, which reinforced his prejudice that things got worse as you went south. A southerner by birth and upbringing, he now preferred the bigger country, farther horizons and fewer people of the north; so long as he could have his regular shot of London.

'So you arrived, chatted over a drink or two, had dinner, chatted and drank a bit more, went to bed,' said Corduroy. 'What did you chat about? How did they greet you?'

If they want detail, they can have it, he thought, as much as they want. It was still raining when he reached Durham and it was hard to find a parking space on the steep terraced street. Two of the street lights weren't working and Rebecca had taken a long time to answer his knock.

'God, you look young, you rat,' she'd said. They kissed on the cheeks.

'Not as young as you. Sorry I'm late.'

'You're not. We all are. Dave's only just got in and I was worried I wouldn't be back in time. Bloody meetings.' She closed the door and squeezed his hand. 'A wet rat, too. Bet you've been up and down to Sctoland a dozen times without dropping in.'

'No, I've been in Scotland a while, reading and writing.'

'With some handy highland lass within reach?'

'Not at all. A silent, sedentary, solitary, private life, as someone else put it.'

'Tell that to the marines.' She pointed upstairs. 'You're in John's room. He's at Winchester. Final year, would you believe. I can't. Take your things up and come and have a drink. And stop staring at me. I know I'm coming out of my jeans. You haven't put on an ounce, have you? Rats don't, I s'pose.'

Her dyed brown hair was cut short, making her face rounder, but despite what she said she had kept her figure, more or less. Unlike David, whom Charles found on the sofa with a laptop and a good deal more fat and less hair than when they last met. Formerly a thick-set, energetic man, he now struggled to get up.

Charles held up a hand to stop him. 'Don't.'

29

'I need another drink. Anyway, we've got to hang around Rebecca in the kitchen and get in her way and irritate her, otherwise I'll be in trouble for having blokes' talk with you and leaving her out.'

Corduroy picked up his pen again. 'So you're all three in the kitchen with drinks and talking. What about?'

'About the book I'm writing – supposedly finishing – and about Rebecca's job, people we'd known, why I was going back to the office—'

'What did you say about that?'

'That I didn't know yet; but that it was temporary; and involved looking at some old case files.'

'What did Dave Horam say about that?'

'Nothing. But it was at that point that he asked me about the cinema bomb in Birmingham, which had happened that day. I didn't know about it. I'd turned the car radio off because the rain gets into the aerial connection and it becomes very crackly. So he told me about it.'

'What did he say?'

'He just described what was on the news. He assumed it was someone in al-Qaeda wanting revenge for the death of Usama bin Laden. He also assumed that I'd know all about al-Qaeda, which I don't. He was angry about the bomb.'

'It's still an open question, the AQ angle,' said DS Westfield. 'Could be a self-starter, an autonomous AQ sympathiser who's taken it upon himself to put the world to rights, or a lone fruitcake. Still no identification of the body.'

'But definitely a suicide bomber?'

'Not necessarily,' said Corduroy. 'Crude device, unstable. Could've gone off accidentally.' He held his pen upright. 'So your friend Mr Horam was angry about it, was he?'

'He's not my friend, he's Rebecca's. But yes, he was. Anger fuelled by alcohol.'

He described how David kept returning to the television in the sitting-room, channel-hopping for more of the story, demanding to know why the bombers couldn't be stopped. 'Why aren't they under surveillance, these al-Qaeda fruit-cakes? Enough bloody cameras everywhere.'

'It may not be them at all,' Charles remembered saying.

'Fat lot of difference if you're blown to pieces,' David shot back.

What most interested the two policemen was whether Charles had said anything about how many people it took to keep someone under twenty-four-hour surveillance. He remembered David asking but couldn't remember what he'd answered; the figure in David's article of thirty to forty, including foot followers, mobile followers, interception and transcribing, was familiar. It could have come from him, or it could have been put to him by David, or it could have been a figure he'd seen in the newspapers. If he had suggested it, he told them, it would have been based on guesswork rather than knowledge. He had spent most of his operational career as one of the hunted, not a hunter, apart from a couple of periods with an MI5 surveillance team in London and a week with the FBI on a joint operation in Hawaii.

'Anyway, it's not a secret figure, is it?' he concluded. 'Not a breach of the OSA?'

'It's very authoritative, the way it's put. The article says it's from a spokesman.'

'Does it? I don't remember. I only skimmed it when it came out.'

They looked surprised. Freckles produced a photocopy from a blue folder. 'Take your time, don't hurry.'

Charles re-read the article. The sentences about surveillance were underlined in red. They were nothing exceptional. He had read them, or similar sentences, dozens of times. He took his time over reading. The police were treating him decently, but they had arrested him, they were the enemy, he owed them no favours despite the mutual civility of their exchanges. They could wait. Time, he thought again, was on his side.

'Do you recognise any of these words or figures as yours?' asked Corduroy eventually.

'As I said, they're familiar, but I don't remember whether

or not I said them. Either way, they don't amount to much.'
Certainly not enough to have someone arrested, he thought.
There was a pause.

'You appreciate we have to follow things up in the current climate, with all these Whitehall leaks,' said Freckles.
'Especially as they quote the SIA assessments, Cabinet
Office papers, that sort of thing. Lot of pressure on us at the
moment.'

Charles nodded. Whatever his feelings, it was important
to appear sympathetic. 'You have to do what you're asked.'

Freckles produced more photocopies. 'This sort of thing,
you see. Have a look through.'

They were more cuttings from David's paper under the
James Wytham byline, going back nine or ten months. The
earlier ones quoted mainly from Cabinet Office papers, the
later from SIA threat assessments. Some passages were
marked in red. There were no quotes from raw intelligence
reports, but there were extracts from what were described as
intelligence assessments prepared for ministers. Although he
hadn't seen the original assessments – they dated mostly from
before his return – Charles could see they were genuine. The
phrasing was typical, the judgements plausible. The source
must be a serial leaker, and a clever one, because what was
leaked was not seriously damaging. The extracts were chosen
with care. Whoever had done it had made sure it was the fact

of the leaks rather than their content that was dangerous. They discredited the SIA without revealing its secrets.

'You've got your hands full,' Charles said.

'Do you recognise any of the documents on which these articles are based?'

'Not as far as I know.' He flicked through the cuttings again. 'No, I don't recognise them.'

'Could you have seen them if you wanted? Do you have access to them?'

'Probably. I guess they're on screen. But the only documents I've read since starting with the SIA are old MI6 ones, paper files related to Gladiator. Plus some more recent emails.'

There was another pause. He resumed reading, again taking his time. Trying not to make it obvious, he lingered over a short unmarked paragraph near the end of one article. It quoted the CIA as saying they had no assets in core AQ. He read and re-read it. He knew where it must have come from, where it could only have come from, and it made up his mind for him. No longer would he wait for his innocence to be accepted in the absence of evidence to the contrary. He would engage; he would take the battle to the enemy, certain now that there was one.

He handed back the papers. 'I think I would like legal representation after all.'

3

They switched off the recorder and Freckles left to fetch the list of legal aid lawyers. He also returned with the name of a partner in a City firm recommended by the SIA.

'He's the one they use in cases like yours, the one I mentioned earlier,' he said. 'He's specially cleared and briefed to represent you, not them; but they pay for him.'

'Are there many cases like mine?'

Freckles shook his head and smiled.

Charles asked them instead to look up the number of another City firm. 'I think I know someone there,' he said. 'I'll try her first.'

He had to make his call from the phone on the wall in reception. It was busier and noisier now, with more prisoners being processed. A policeman leading a young man by the arm brushed his shoulder as he asked the firm's switchboard for her, giving both her maiden and married names. 'We don't have a Sarah Measures,' said the soft-spoken switchboard girl, 'but we do have the other one, Sarah Bourne.'

'That's the one. They're the same person.'

A prisoner started shouting and a woman sitting alone on the bench began to weep. Doors banged, voices were raised, more people came and went but no-one paid the woman any attention. Charles put his hand over one ear.

'Sorry, I didn't catch that,' said the girl.

'Sarah Bourne – that's the one.'

'Sorry, could you speak up, please?'

He repeated it twice more, then had to do the same with his own name. The prisoner who was shouting was the pale young man he had seen brought in that morning. Still handcuffed, he was undergoing more processing and tried to kick one of the officers holding him. A policeman shouted at him to pack it in, and he shut up. The silence that followed was broken only by the woman snuffling, until Charles was put through.

'Charles?'

She had always had a slight catch in her voice when she began to speak on the phone. It was so intimately reminiscent that it was a moment before he replied.

'Yes, I'm here. It's me. Sorry to surprise you.'

'That's all right. No need to be.'

'I was wondering if I could use your professional services.' He explained as briefly as he could. The woman stopped snuffling and listened. He wished the pale young prisoner would resume his protests.

When he finished she said: 'I'd no idea you were in the SIA. Nigel hasn't mentioned it. Does he know?'

'Yes. Can you come?'

'Of course, of course I'll come.' She hesitated. 'I don't do criminal work any more, so I'll have to clear my lines here with the people who do. But I will come, Charles, I promise. As soon as I can.'

Back in his cell, sitting on the green plastic mattress with *Jane Eyre* again open and unread before him, he was filled with the sense of approaching completion, of a circle about to be made whole. It seemed irresponsible to be pleased with this fusion of the public and private, but it felt like a summation.

Decades before, when they were undergraduates together, Sarah had said: 'I know what you should do, you should join MI6. You should be a spy.'

He was kneeling before the gas fire in his room, trying to toast a slice of bread on the end of his father's old army jack-knife and changing hands because of the heat. 'Why?'

'You'd enjoy it. It would be fun, all that subterfuge, secret inks and following people. You don't want a proper job. You don't want to work. You want fun.'

'I have fun. I have you.'

She knelt and put her arms round him, causing the bread to drop off the knife. 'I'm not your bit of fun, Charles Thoroughgood. I'm much more serious than that. You may not realise it, but you've got me for life.'

She proved prescient, though not in the way either might have thought. By the time they'd left Oxford they were already estranged and he had joined the army, not MI6. The army offered a decisive break, a dramatic gesture, albeit one addressed more to himself than to her, because she was no longer around to witness it. It was on leaving the army that he found he knew someone who knew someone and was offered an introduction to MI6. He remembered her words when he accepted; but by then she had married Nigel Measures, and he thought he would never see her again.

He and Nigel had lived on different staircases in the same college. Their subjects overlapped and they'd shared tutorials for two or three terms. Nigel was short and assertive, with black hair, restless dark eyes, a quick intelligence and a fondness for innuendo. He invented apt, sometimes cruel, nicknames for people. He and Charles had never been close but there was sufficient mutual respect and wariness for each to take care to get on with the other. Only once had they approached hostility and only once greater intimacy, both occasioned by Sarah.

It was true that Nigel had met her first but Charles had got to know her himself, without knowing that. A collision in the door of the Pusey Library while she struggled with books and folders led to apologies, embarrassed smiles and the explosion of an enormous Yes. Charles made frequent needless visits to the library, which in turn had led to further sightings, brief acknowledgements and then, at the second time of asking, a morning coffee in George Street, when the five minutes she said she had became fifty, and later – made possible only by Charles's having a car – dinner in the Studley Priory hotel outside Oxford. Then all that followed.

One day, in the early weeks of the affair, he'd suggested tea in his room. She hesitated. 'D'you mind coming to mine again?'

'Okay.'

'It's just that – to be honest, I'm uneasy in your college because there's someone there who's been pursuing me. It's embarrassing, because I haven't told him about you, and every day I don't it becomes more difficult. It's stupid of me, I know. I'll have to find a way.'

'Who?'

She told him, explaining that she had met Nigel at a birthday breakfast party, punting on the Cherwell. She had found him charming, saw that people were a little in awe of him and was flattered by his attention. But the aggression of his pursuit had put her off, conducted as it was in public without regard for how she might feel in front of others. By the time she'd begun to see Charles, Nigel's invitations – usually notes he dropped in her pigeonhole or delivered by college messengers – were arriving daily. She accepted some of the more neutral and social ones, avoiding the personal, but his campaign intensified. Now he had invited her to the Merton ball.

'I've got to tell him, I must. I can't let him take me without him knowing. But it'll be awful, because it'll be perfectly obvious I should've told him before but chickened out.'

'Can't you just say no?'

'Of course I could, but it's difficult without a reason. And I don't want to lie. Anyway, I'd love to go to a ball.'

'Tell him you can't because you're going with me.'

'Am I?'

'Looks like it.'

Neither he nor Nigel mentioned it and their relationship continued outwardly as before. The frequency and urgency of Nigel's invitations to Sarah diminished but he still asked her to social events, and sometimes she went. She was always in demand but Charles didn't mind. It flattered him that other men were keen to show off the woman who filled his waking moments. Nor did he doubt her; the at first barely credible fact that he really was preferred to all others made him more generous than jealous. In retrospect it seemed a golden age, a time with no beginning and no end; but the reality had been no more than a few weeks.

Early one morning, after a forbidden night spent in her all-female college, Charles left as usual over the garden wall before anyone was about and walked across the university parks back to breakfast in his own college. He loved those cool summer mornings after hot near-sleepless nights and this time detoured into the fields on the other side of the Cherwell. Returning, he saw Nigel standing on the high arched bridge, elbows on the railings, looking down into the slow water. He must have been aware that someone was approaching but did not look up. His dark eyes seemed more bulbous than usual and his expression was remote and self-absorbed. He would have made no acknowledgement if Charles had not stopped.

'Don't do it, it's not worth it,' Charles said, regretting it immediately.

Nigel straightened and turned. 'I wasn't going to,' he said quietly. 'Where – you've been—'

Charles nodded. Neither of them wanted it said. 'How about some breakfast?'

'No, thanks.'

Detachment, remoteness and introspection were uncommon in Nigel. He normally seemed fully engaged, whatever he was doing. He clearly wanted to be alone now but Charles didn't know how to leave. It felt too abrupt to walk on without saying more, but he wasn't sure what note to strike.

'I really love her, you know,' said Nigel, suddenly. 'I hope you do.'

'I do.' Charles walked on, wondering why he had never told her.

Although neither he nor Nigel ever referred to the encounter, they began to see more of each other and became friendlier, though still without quite being friends. Nigel lingered to talk after the tutorials they shared, sometimes sat on the bench next to Charles at meals in hall; Charles reciprocated in the JCR bar or in the White Horse, the narrow pub on Broad Street. There was no awkwardness; Nigel was a stimulating companion who normally made no demands on his audience other than that they should share his humour, which was sharp and playful. He neither offered nor sought intimacy. They never discussed Sarah, but Charles would mention her in passing, trying to show that she wasn't an issue between them. In fact, just hearing himself say her name was a constant and secret pleasure.

Once, Nigel came to his room late at night, grinning, his eyes shining. 'Sorry, bloody rude of me, bloody late. I'm a bit pissed, boozing in the JCR since dinner. Got an essay crisis, too. Have to be up all night; but got to sober up first. Couldn't give me a coffee, could you?'

He sat heavily in Charles's armchair, an ancient sliding wooden structure that creaked loudly. 'Hume and causation. Or Hume and something. You've done that one, haven't you?'

'I've written it. Haven't had my tutorial yet.' The essay was on his desk. 'Here.'

Nigel took it. 'They want me to run for president of the JCR. Nicholson, Richards and the others. They hate the thought of Miles getting it.'

'Do you want to?'

'Don't know.' He watched Charles plug in the kettle and spoon the instant coffee. 'Surprised you don't make real coffee. You seem the sort of person who would.'

'Do I? Perhaps I should then. But it takes longer.'

'Thing is, Miles is such an egregious shit. One of those people whose face is always in front of you, you can't get away from him. There'll be even more of him if he's running the JCR.'

'Do it, then. I'll vote for you.'

'But is it really me, Charles?'

'I don't know. Never seen you look so solemn about anything.' Except for that morning by the Cherwell, he thought.

'I mean, this could be the start of my political career. It's truly a life-changing decision. Don't you think?'

'I'd never thought of the JCR like that.'

'It is, though. It's a question of whether to enter the public arena, to wield the broadsword, or whether to exercise power from behind the scenes, as I imagine you would.'

'Do you?' Charles had never thought of himself like that. 'Do you seek power?'

'Not yet. But if I do it changes everything. I become a different person. My life will be completely different. Who I marry, what I do, everything.'

'Milk?'

'No, thanks.'

Nigel talked about himself for an hour. At the end, when he stood to go, his eyes were duller and he looked tired. 'Thanks for the coffee. Doesn't mean I wouldn't marry Sarah, if she wanted me, even if I did seek power. I'd still marry her.' He spoke as if reassuring Charles. 'I would. I wouldn't abandon her.'

'I don't blame you.'

'Thanks for the coffee.'

'Good luck with the essay.'

'I'll drop it back when I've finished.'

He did, but afterwards, reading it aloud in his own tutorial, Charles discovered that Nigel had done the same and passed it off as his own, without telling him. His tutor all but accused him of plagiarising. It was a minor dishonesty but indicative, he later concluded. He was going to tax Nigel with it, but by then so much else had happened that it seemed of no account.

In retrospect there were early signs of his and Sarah's shipwreck, but at the time he was aware only of an unspoken tension, something unacknowledged, an edginess, a wariness, as if each were expecting to resist some unreasonable demand from the other, though none was made. It was by then the term before Schools – their final examinations – and she worried more about hers than he did about his. She was keen to do well and worked harder than he, but his attempts to reassure her counted for nothing, and her worry increased. He attributed the tension to this, but later suspected it was also because their affair had, without their realising it – or perhaps without only him realising it – reached a point of decision. The harbinger of what was to come was, as usual, something fairly trivial, a sudden lurch, a single, unseen, sickening sea-swell that came from nowhere and passed as suddenly, leaving them becalmed for a while.

Her birthday was approaching and he had booked dinner – not on the day but near enough – at the Restaurant Elizabeth, allegedly the best and certainly the most expensive in Oxford. It would cost about a quarter of that term's grant but he had money saved from his holiday job as a dustman and would make it up in the summer.

Sarah was still seeing Nigel, who had meanwhile won the JCR election and embarked upon what he called 'the political trajectory'. This had led him towards the Oxford Union which offered, he said, a bigger stage and the prospect of office. With a general election approaching, an Oxford Union debate featuring a Treasury minister and his opposition shadow attracted national press attention. Nigel had invited Sarah to the debate, in which he was to speak. She told Charles she had accepted.

'But that's the night I've booked dinner at the Elizabeth.'

'You didn't tell me.'

'I said I was going to.'

'But you didn't say when.'

'I'm sure I did.' He wasn't, but he thought he probably had. 'Sorry if I didn't.' He knew he sounded insincere.

'Can't you change it?'

'It's difficult. They get very booked up. Probably not for ages.' He wasn't sure of that either, but he was irritated. What he had meant as a celebration to ease things had already made them worse. They parted with the issue unresolved.

Back in his college, checking for mail in the porter's lodge, Charles ran into Nigel doing the same. Had he not met him at that moment he might never have said anything, or might have said it differently. But he was still irritated when he said: 'Your debate date with Sarah. I'm afraid she can't make it. We're going to the Elizabeth. She didn't realise I'd booked it.'

Hostility showed briefly in Nigel's eyes, like the flank of a fish turning beneath the surface. 'Fine,' he said.

Charles immediately felt guilty. 'Sorry, but I didn't realise she'd said she'd go to the debate.'

'That's fine, Charles, just fine.' Nigel walked away.

Charles sent a note to Sarah saying that Nigel was fine about it. They had arranged to go for a walk after her tutorial the following afternoon. In the morning he looked fearfully for a cancelling note but when he called on her that afternoon her door was locked. They met in the quad as he was leaving.

'Dr Philpot overran,' she said. 'Then she brought out the sherry. She always does.'

'You got my note about Nigel?'

'Yes, I did.' She turned towards her room. 'You might have asked me before refusing on my behalf. I don't like letting people down.'

'I thought you'd decided not to go.'

'You assumed it, you mean.'

The walk was short, because she was cold, but it eased things. She told him she would rather have dinner with him than go to a debate with Nigel, though she didn't want him in her room that night, pleading tiredness and work. After dining in her college he walked back to his own in a penetrating wind and a few erratic, unseasonal snowflakes.

It snowed much more on the day of the debate, provoking national wonderment. Charles rose early, partly because of the unaccustomed brightness and partly to enjoy the pristine quads and backstreets before boots and tyres turned them to slush. At breakfast in hall someone said the debate had been cancelled; more snow was forecast and both main speakers had seized upon the excuse to pull out. Later, when he ran into Nigel, residual guilt made him want to be generous.

'Sorry to hear about the debate. You must have put a lot of work into it.'

'You could say that.'

'What will you do?'

'Don't know. JCR. Have an early night.'

'Come to the Elizabeth with Sarah and me.'

Nigel, who had wealthy parents and a reputation for expensive living, looked at him. 'You can't mean that.'

'I do, I mean it.' Charles knew he didn't as he was saying it. It was stupid, a gesture was all he had intended, but he felt obliged to go on. 'No, come with us. We'd both like it.'

Nigel hesitated. 'Okay, if you're sure. What time?'

Sarah was sitting at her desk brushing her hair, a mirror propped before her, when Charles broke the news. He sat on her bed with his back against the wall, much as he would later in his cell, watching her face in the mirror. When he said it she was holding her hair with one hand and brushing it with the other. She stopped in mid-stroke and their eyes met in the mirror. Her expression betrayed a brief struggle for self-control, swiftly achieved, then settled resolution. She resumed brushing.

'Oh, right, it'll be nice to see Nigel. At least he won't feel rejected now.'

'Sorry, it was clumsy of me. It was an impulse, I didn't mean him to accept it. I've been clumsy throughout all this. Sorry.'

'No need to apologise.'

'There is. I'm sorry.'

'Don't be.'

Soon he was apologising for apologising and by the time

they reached the Elizabeth they were not speaking. Nigel was there already and they fell upon him with relief at not having to confront each other. The meal was presumably good – Nigel said it was – and certainly expensive. Charles paid. Afterwards he remembered nothing of what he'd eaten, but knew she'd had only a first course and toyed with a trifle. Nigel was at his most entertaining, blooming under their dual attention and failing to notice that neither addressed a word to the other.

It was snowing again when they left. Charles drove slowly through the quiet, whitened streets, dropping the still loquacious Nigel at their college before continuing north to Sarah's. They said nothing. The squeaking windscreen wipers appeared to brush the same flakes away at each sweep. He drew up at the back of her college, by the usual nocturnal entrance for forbidden male visitors. Snow covered the parked cars and hung heavily on the tree branches; the street lamps showed it already obliterating his tyre tracks.

'Rotten evening,' he said. 'Except for Nigel. He enjoyed himself. All my fault. Sorry.' He switched off the engine.

She got out and shut the door without looking back, picking her way through the snow to the black wooden door in the college wall. At least she hadn't told him not to follow. He watched as she carefully brushed the snow off the latch with her rolled umbrella before touching it with her suede gloves. She left the door half open behind her.

He followed. When he reached the door he saw she had paused on the garden path leading to her hall and was doing something in the snow with the tip of her umbrella. Still not looking back, she moved on without waiting for him. When he reached the spot he saw that she had written 'I love you' in the snow. It was that night, he believed ever after, that she became pregnant.

4

Now, waiting in his cell for her, he tried to remember how many years had passed before he ceased to think daily about it all. Ten at least, years in which he confided in no-one and pored over every detail until it was as familiar to him as his face in the shaving mirror. Yet he knew all the time there was nothing new to be thought.

He was excited by the prospect of seeing her again, though not because he anticipated any resurrection of the past. It was an unquantifiable prospect; he could not anticipate what he would feel, still less she. It was not, after all, as if there had been nothing since Oxford to complicate things between them.

For now, it was less the personal significance of events than their sequence that he had to get right. Yet where the facts were feelings, personal significance could not be ignored, however distant. Never blessed with the equivocal gift of prophecy, he had been sure that night in her college that she was – or would be – pregnant. It had dropped upon him like a great weight as he lay beside her in the narrow bed, propped on his elbow, gazing on her dreaming face.

'When is your period?' he asked, waking her.

She blinked. 'About a fortnight.'

He had been certain from that moment but she refused to accept it for almost another two months. Normally practical and pragmatic, a woman who faced and said things as they were, she would not even discuss it, reacting with dismissive irritation when he tried. She was focussed on Schools, she said, the eight exam papers she was revising for, and had no time to worry about anything else. Whereas he thought about nothing but, and worried not at all about his own exams. Meanwhile, stupidly – amazingly now – they had simply carried on, while there grew between them the unspoken assumption that she would do nothing and that they would not marry.

But he had asked her, he remembered, almost saying so aloud to himself now as if in self-justification. It was one day when the exams had started, as they walked back across the parks to her college. They had both had papers morning and afternoon, and she felt – wrongly, it turned out – that she had done badly. She would never be a lawyer now, she said, because a poor degree in law never got anyone into any decent firm. She would have to do something else; she had no idea what, she had made a mess of everything. He tried to reassure her, but she did not respond.

'Not to mention—' she said eventually, and didn't.

They walked in silence, he a pace or two behind. The university was playing cricket against a minor county. He tried to remember which, as he stared now at the cell wall. It used to come unbidden to his mind as one of those insistent, unwanted, irrelevant details, but now it was gone. God alone knew what else might have gone with it. He remembered the batsman hitting a four, then the slow ripple of applause, while asking himself whether he really meant what he was about to say.

The way it came out wasn't much of a proposal, he acknowledged to her years later, yet he felt he had never given himself more to anyone than when he said, 'Whatever happens, I would marry you anyway.' She walked on without answering.

When he caught up with her he saw tears in her eyes. He wished he hadn't said it. It was a self-centred irrelevance that solved nothing. She would still be pregnant, her future was still a mess. That was what mattered to her, he thought. The batsman was out next ball, caught in the slips.

As the baby grew inside her, they grew apart. He felt he

was caught in the undertow of a great tide while she, increasingly self-absorbed, seemed content to float with it, except when his attempts to discuss it irritated her. At the end of their final term she returned to her family in Northumberland, not yet visibly pregnant and determined that the baby should be adopted. Neither he nor she had told anyone.

'He'd have a better life if he was adopted,' she had said one night, over a miserable Chinese meal. She seemed to take it for granted that it would be a boy.

Charles was secretly, and guiltily, relieved. 'If that's what you really want?'

'It's better he has a proper home with a couple who want him, don't you think?'

'I suppose it would be.'

She toyed with her rice, not looking at him. 'I mean, we don't, do we?'

'I guess not.' It felt wrong to say it, despite its truth.

She glanced at him, then looked down again and placed her chopsticks neatly on their rest, side by side. 'Can we go?'

They spent some time together in the summer, intense, uneasy days of compromised passion that were to prove their last. When they were apart they wrote several times a week and, decades later, he still had all her letters in his flat.

They would now make unproductive reading for the search team, he thought. Telephoning in those days meant having the right coins and finding call-boxes; he couldn't use his parents' phone without being overheard. There had been few calls and fewer visits, either way. These were difficult from the first and became more so. 'I want to see you, but when I see you I want to hurt you,' she wrote after one, with an honesty that made her growing hostility easier to take than the polite indifference that followed it.

Another prisoner began banging on his cell door and shouting – presumably the disruptive young man – as Charles tried to recall how he had known that she was seeing more of Nigel, who would drive down from his parents' home in Edinburgh. She must have told him by letter because he remembered her writing that Nigel was being 'very sweet'. Judging by her next letter, Charles must have replied intemperately – if again prophetically – since she crossly accused him of being 'silly'.

The baby – the boy she had expected, whom she named James – was born on a spring morning of sun and showers. He was duly fostered and adopted, despite her parents' offer to bring him up. Sarah permitted Charles to pay the foster fees, a fairly small sum that was nonetheless gratifyingly hard to find. To his parents' growing worry, he did nothing about a career but spent the year following Oxford in a series of labouring jobs, as if physical work might somehow assuage his guilt. It did not, but he still felt that a sentence of nine months' hard labour might have been about right.

After that he had joined the army and Sarah went to law school, equipped with a better degree than she had predicted. Their letters became fewer and shorter. Nigel had already joined the Foreign Office. Three years later, on the very day he had started with MI6, came the letter from Sarah telling him that she and Nigel were to marry. He sent a reply which it still shamed him to recall – to the effect that he hoped they would both be as happy as they deserved – and went off to MI6 feeling that his old life had dropped away entirely.

All this, and much more, was known to his former mentor, Matthew Abrahams. It was known, too, to Sonia, Matthew's sometime secretary and later Charles's confidente; but to no-one else still serving apart – now – from Nigel himself. When Matthew had rung Charles in Scotland the day before Jeremy Wheeler's call, he had come characteristically to the point, with no preliminaries.

'This is to warn you, Charles, that you'll get a call from Jeremy Wheeler asking you to come back for a while to help out with an old case. The case is Gladiator, who has disappeared. In seeking your help, they won't know what they're asking. That is, they don't know the full story. They know only that you were his first and most influential case officer. They do not know the real reason I have instructed them to ask you. I'll explain when we meet. If we meet.'

The voice was lighter than Charles remembered, but it was still the same precise, slightly daunting, slightly playful Matthew Abrahams he had revered and loved. Tall and stooping, with mordant humour and ruthless integrity, he had more than once been Charles's boss and latterly, his protector, as Charles had chosen an increasingly eccentric career. Liked and respected by those who worked for him, but treated warily by peers and superiors, he was the most complete intelligence officer Charles had known. He treated Charles with an assumption of equality that Charles never believed he merited.

'I'm warning you to give you time to think before Jeremy rings,' Matthew had said. 'You may not wish to reopen that particular can of worms. I hope you will, of course – not least because I have my own agenda, as ever.' His chuckle had become a cough. 'But if you do come back you'll find the office much changed and you'll hate it. Not only because of the merger. The old office you and I knew has succumbed to management blight: meetings, mission statements, jargon, targets, obsession with process, the mania for measurement. Everything that can be counted, is; which, almost by definition, is what doesn't matter. Nothing of value can be measured, so it's not valued.'

'But you're still there. You're running it, aren't you?'

'I'm here, just. I'm still in charge, I'm responsible for the SIA but I don't run it. Nobody runs it. It's become a self-regarding, self-perpetuating bureaucracy, like all the others. If I insist on something – such as asking you back – it happens. Everything else is being delayed pending my imminent departure, for which they can barely wait.'

'So the amalgamations haven't worked?'

'They have. That was their point, to make it as it is.'

'Why did you stay on?'

'Because I could see the awfulness coming and hoped to ameliorate it. I failed. Now it's too late. We'll discuss that when you come. If you come.'

'Meanwhile I read that Nigel Measures has forsaken Europe to return to the bureaucracy and take over from you?'

'That is why you are needed, Charles,' Matthew had said.

The door-banger was banging less frequently now. Presumably it hurt your hands after a while. And, presumably, if you did too much of it in prison you would be silenced by the other prisoners. It was the prospect of living with them that worried Charles more than the law, or the system, or even the plot that had put him where he was.

He continued trying to reconstruct all that had happened

in the few weeks since his return. When he reported to the new Head Office on Victoria Street he found a renovated 1960s building guarded by two armed policemen, who were drinking tea from plastic mugs and did not see him enter. In Visitor Reception there were red plastic seats and notices forbidding smoking or proclaiming the SIA an equal opportunities employer. Half a dozen people were waiting, four men and two women, all, like Charles, in suits. A man and a woman were negotiating with another woman behind a plate glass window, repeating their names and business into a microphone. Eventually Charles was summoned. The woman behind the glass had a round face and listened open-mouthed as he gave her his and Jeremy Wheeler's names.

'Photo ID, driving licence, passport, other government office pass or similar,' she said.

'Sorry, I didn't know.'

'You should've been told.'

'Perhaps you could ring Jeremy Wheeler and tell him I'm here.' If she would only close her mouth now and again, he thought, she could look like a goldfish.

'Extension?'

'Sorry.'

She sighed and turned to her screen. 'Name?' she asked again, then turned off the microphone and picked up the phone. When she'd finished she turned back and said something inaudible. He pointed at his ears and she switched on the microphone. 'Take a seat.'

After a few minutes he was summoned back to the window to see an overweight, balding, florid man wearing jeans, a wide brown belt with a silver buckle and a pink shirt. He realised, rather than recognised, that it was Jeremy. Jeremy nodded to the woman and turned away, looking cross.

Charles was directed into a corridor, where his jacket and the book he was carrying were put through a machine by two men in white shirts and black ties. They put his mobile phone in a cage on the wall and gave him a ticket for it.

Jeremy's handshake was limp, which seemed out of keeping with his manner. They probably had not shaken hands since the day they had reported for their training course, decades before. Jeremy led the way to the lifts. 'We'll have to get you a pass and all that, assuming you feel up to the job.'

They waited with two unshaven men in T-shirts and trainers and a similarly dressed but cleaner-looking woman escorting one of the other suited visitors. 'Dress down Friday,' Jeremy murmured.

'Compulsory?'

'Of course not, but everyone does, except for a few fuddy-duddies.'

In the lift were notices about a talk on emerging terrorist

technologies and a lunchtime meeting of the gay and disability rights group.

'It's not just Fridays, as you'll see,' said Jeremy when the others had left the lift. 'We're much less formal than the old office. Quite rightly, have to move with the times, be more egalitarian. No time now for all that stuffiness and poncing about of your day.'

Jeremy's talent for gratuitous offence had evidently not been discarded with his pin-stripes. It hadn't mattered with his peers, who had never taken him seriously, but it might have with inferiors, Charles thought; and would have with agents, if he had ever run any.

'We've changed operationally, too,' Jeremy continued. 'Much more coal-face work, direct approaches, take-it-or-leave-it. We get our hands and knees dirty now. All that faffing about pretending to be diplomats chatting up other diplomats, all those endless cultivations and natural cover operations leading nowhere – sort of thing you used to get involved in – all that's gone. We just get on with the job now.'

They headed along a corridor decorated with child-like paintings of bushy-topped trees and crooked houses until they came to a large open-plan office crowded with desks, screens and printers. Televisions lined the walls, mostly showing football repeats with the sound turned down. It was busy and noisy and everyone was young.

Jeremy waved his arm. 'The heart of Prevail. Our counter-terrorist – CT – strategy. Valerie's very keen on CT.'

'Valerie?'

'Valerie Hubbard, our new security minister. We have our own now instead of messing about with the foreign secretary and home secretary. You must have read about her. Nigel – Nigel Measures – is very close to her. They go back a long way, politically. How he got the top job, I s'pose. Useful to have a CEO who's politically well plugged-in.'

There was another corridor, then another open-plan office. Jeremy waved his arm again. 'My empire. HR.'

'Don't you find it distracting, working like this?'

'Encourages activity and communication.'

'Need to know? Supposing you have to discuss something sensitive?'

Jeremy pointed to a round table and chairs in a corner. 'Break-out area. You talk there. But all that need-to-know stuff you and I were brought up on just got in the way, really. As I said, we get on with the job now.' He led Charles into a private office at the end of the room and closed the door.

'You still have your own, then?'

'Have to. Everything I do is confidential. I only deal with what's important. If it's not important it doesn't reach me. Personally, I'd sooner be out there on the factory floor, but there we are. Can't be forever discussing people's futures in front of other people. Or telling them they haven't got one, which happens more often now. Much better at getting rid of dead wood than we used to be.' He chuckled. 'Coffee? We make our own. No more secretaries waiting on us hand and foot like you're used to. We'll get it in a minute.' He sat, his plump features briefly clouded by reflection. 'Used to have some nice secretaries in the old SIS, though, didn't we? Smart girls, capable, bright, attractive.'

'We did.'

'Many with naval connections. Or Scots. Very good people here now, though.'

'I'm sure.'

Jeremy was lost in reflection for a few more seconds, then abruptly resumed, as if having to bring Charles back to the business in hand. 'No, but the point is, this job. Reason you're here. Gladiator. Why you? You may well ask. Recruited him, didn't you? You were his first case officer, back when he used to report on the IRA? Then Afghanistan and the Taliban and all that. Well, he's still in business, reporting on international terrorism. Or was.'

'Which international terrorists?'

'Islamists. We're not supposed to call them that – religious stigmatisation. Anyway, he's gone missing and they want you to go back through the file – it's such an old case, there's still a paper one – to see if it offers any clues as to motive or contacts. Not my idea, frankly. Came from the chief himself, the old chief, about to be ex-chief. Apparently he knows the case – you were working for him when it started, something like that. Not often he intervenes now.' He paused and became solemn. 'You know he's very ill?'

'You mentioned it when you rang.'

'Hardly comes to the office now. Not that he'd have lasted much longer, anyway. Can't cope with change. Frankly, the sooner Nigel's formally in the chair, the better. He's effectively CEO as it is. CEO Dep is his title. As I said on the phone, no more of this old chief or C or CSS nonsense that you're accustomed to. Time for a new broom. He wants to see you, though.'

'Who?'

'Both of them, actually.' Jeremy's solemnity, which Charles now remembered came over him whenever there was any mention of illness, had been replaced by irritation. 'You might know why. I don't. But then I'm only HR. We'll go to Nigel's office first. Matthew Abrahams wants to see you in his flat this afternoon.'

Nigel Measures's office was on the top floor, with a view of Parliament Square and the roofscape of Westminster Abbey and school. It was quieter than the other floors; the carpets newer, the staff better dressed, the men shaved. From the outer office, marked CEO, they could see Nigel though the open door of his inner sanctum, talking on the phone. He was suited but tie-less, another new convention. Watching the still sharp and energetic figure as he spoke rapidly into the phone, gesticulating with his free hand, Charles recalled their last meeting. Nigel would do the same, he was sure. Unsatisfactory from both points of view, it had been a meeting that could have no successor; unless they both pretended to forget it, as they doubtless would now.

It had not been a dramatic meeting, they had had no great falling out, but its context had given it venom. They had seen nothing of each other following Oxford until after Charles had joined MI6. In his first post there he had had occasional dealings with Nigel's Foreign Office department. There was no outward awkwardness; they simply resumed at the point they had left off as if nothing – including Nigel's marriage to Sarah – had happened in the interval. Nigel had a slightly patronising attitude towards the Friends, as MI6 was known in the Foreign Office, but was on the whole more inclined to be helpful than not. During the next few years they lunched a few times in Westminster pubs, compared experiences, gossiped about mutual acquaintances, speculated about their respective futures. They were both, Charles concluded later, natural compartmentalisers, capable of sustaining a relationship in which everything important was sidelined. Although he was doing well in the Foreign Office, Nigel was still considering a political career.

'One disadvantage of your service – which I briefly considered joining – is that it's a very narrow pyramid,' he said during one of their early lunches. 'Very few top jobs compared with the Foreign Office. Fun for the first few years, no doubt, but thereafter narrow in scope, limited horizons and, frankly, rather a limited contribution to policy. If you want to influence things, particularly if you want to change them, you're much better off where I am. Better off still in politics, of course. Especially if you're in government.'

He would refer to Sarah occasionally and in passing, just as Charles had used to do with him. She was training with a City law firm and teaching part time at the law school she had attended. As soon as she was qualified, they would start a family, he said, making it sound like booking a holiday. The baby was never mentioned.

'You must come to dinner sometime,' he always said on parting. Charles always replied that he would love to and they would leave it at that. But one day – it would have been in the mid-eighties, Charles thought – Nigel surprised him by ringing him in his office. 'Sarah and I are giving a small dinner party. We don't do it very often. Just a couple of friends.'

The address was an Edwardian house in Clapham.

Charles hesitated at the garden gate. The last time he had seen Sarah was the day after the birth. Surrounded by banks of flowers in a nursing home in Northumbria, she looked relaxed and radiant. In his hurried drive north, having pretended to his mother that he was going to a last-minute party at Nigel's, he had spurned the about-to-rot cellophaned flowers at motorway service stations. By the time he reached Hexham there were no florists open, only a single off-licence. He considered champagne, but doubted its aptness, given the circumstances; also, whether it would be acceptable in a nursing home. He ended up with a sham-ing box of Black Magic chocolates which she received with humiliatingly good grace, tucking them behind a bunch of Interflora roses on the bedside table. He saw from the card that they were from Nigel. He could not imagine why it had not occurred to him to do the same. He had never felt more useless, nor more grubby.

Now, he could remember nothing of what he and Sarah had said to each other that evening. He did remember that she was friendlier, no doubt because more indifferent, than when they had last met a month before the birth, over tea and a slow walk around Bamburgh Castle. Her hostility then had at least been a positive reaction, an indication that he mattered; but this distancing politeness could have been deployed with anybody, which meant he had become nobody. Neither more nor less than he deserved, he remembered thinking.

He'd been directed to Baby Bourne on the way out. There was a room to the side of the ward filled with babies in cots, watched over by a nurse who smiled brightly.

'Baby Bourne? This one here.'

There was a name tag tied to his wrist. He had wisps of dark hair and his eyes were closed. To Charles, all babies resembled each other or Winston Churchill. He didn't expect to see himself reflected, and didn't know what to look for, anyway. Nor could he see whether there was anything of Sarah. The nurse stood watch as he lingered by the cot, trying to imagine the unimaginable life to come. He laid the tip of his middle finger on the baby's forehead and silently, as if in prayer, wished him well.

Lacking any immediate instinct for the paternal and conscious of no dynastic urge, Charles soon persuaded himself that life without family was probably more enjoyable, certainly freer, than life with. During the ten years in which he thought more or less daily of Baby Bourne it was not with longing, nor with any sense of progression; he merely registered the child's existence, every day, finding nothing to think beyond the fact of it and no point in speculation that was limitless. He thought more particularly of Sarah, his heart crammed with the unsaid, with questions, memories, debates and imagined arguments, a decades-long interior dialogue that would never, he thought, be had. So he had put his heart aside.

Certainly, it would not be had across the dining table in Clapham that night. But seeing her again would be enough to be going on with.

He arrived to find two couples and a plump, pretty woman called Liz who was an economist with the Bank of England. She laughed easily and was quick and bright. Bank employees could have Bank of England accounts, she said, and over drinks recounted the problems she had convincing traders her cheques weren't toy-town. Charles liked her and wished he could relax. He hadn't yet seen Sarah because the door had been answered by Nigel. When eventually she came in from the kitchen they were all laughing at something Nigel had said.

'Charles, how nice to see you again.'

She presented herself for cheek-kissing. She looked as he remembered, though in both dress and manner she was now the middle-class London hostess. He wondered how he seemed to her.

'Charles and I met at Oxford through Sarah,' Nigel explained. 'Now it's the Foreign Office that brings us together.' Like most diplomats, he took seriously the obligation to maintain cover for the Friends.

Charles felt no more relaxed as the evening went on. He suspected no-one else did, either. There was a brittle tension that kept everyone talking as if in competition, with a lot of laughter but no humour. Liz played her part valiantly and he helped as best he could, thinking she would make someone a good and capable wife. Sarah seemed edgy and assertive, as if conversation needed sprinkling with the salt of contrariness. It was a tendency he remembered in her from before, but it had been less marked then. Nigel drew paradoxes and made verbal sallies which everyone laughed at. Charles did not see them address a word to each other, except once, when they were both in the kitchen between courses and he passed the door on the way to the loo. Nigel was standing holding the pile of dirty plates and she was on one knee before the open oven, wearing oven gloves, heedless of how far her skirt had ridden up her thigh.

'Where shall I put them?' Nigel asked.

'Anywhere.' She spoke shortly, without looking at him.

It meant nothing, of course; it was how people were under pressure, it was marriage. He didn't like to hear her speak like that, but he wasn't displeased.

There was another exchange, not involving her, that much later bubbled to the surface of his memory, under the pressure of a very different circumstance. It began over coffee, when Liz asked Nigel something technical about the

Single Market negotiations which, as a junior member of the Foreign Office European Community team, he was helping to conclude in London and Brussels. As often, when asked a specific question, Nigel made a joke of it.

'The first time I ever heard of the Single European Act I thought it was about legalising brothels. Long overdue.' He laughed. 'But I really can't say, Liz, because it's one of the areas we're still grappling with, thanks to that old nanny goat in Downing Street. If it weren't for that niggling bitch we'd have had it all wrapped up months ago.'

Liz would not be put off. 'But it was partly Mrs Thatcher's initiative, wasn't it? We – the British – helped start the process.'

'Only because she was persuaded it would be easier for British bankers and insurers and builders and whatever to get into Europe. Not through any enthusiasm for the European project itself. There's not a shred of idealism in her.'

'I'm not sure I blame her. They're all out for themselves as far as I can see, from where we sit.'

'I blame her. I blame her absolutely. She's a brake on the whole thing. Anything – *anything* – I can do to expedite the European project, I'll do. She's got no feeling for it, no feeling at all – probably no feeling for anything, if truth be known. But luckily, she's also got no idea of the political difference the act is going to make. She's such a bloody Philistine, she sees it only in economic terms. Doesn't realise it's a huge step towards integration. That's why we want it, not just so that your filthy rich bankers can get even richer and filthier.'

Liz smiled. 'Hence the photo?' She nodded at the mantelpiece on which stood a photograph of Nigel and the newly-appointed EC Commission president, Jacques Delors. They were smiling at the camera and shaking hands.

Nigel shook his head. 'You won't find any of those in the witch's den in Number Ten.'

It was Nigel's tone, as much as what he said, that struck Charles at the time. He spoke with an almost personal bitterness rather than with his usual raillery and mocking detachment. It was unusual, too, for him to show such enthusiasm for ideas and ideals. He normally scoffed at enthusiasm.

When Charles was leaving, he and Sarah repeated the cheek-kissing ritual. 'So lovely to see you,' she said. Those, and his response, were the only words they exchanged all evening. He wished she had not said 'so' with such distancing emphasis.

5

The door-banger eventually gave up. Charles became aware of the silence without realising when it had started. He was again picturing Nigel in his SIA office, hand raised to show that he had seen Charles and Jeremy waiting. Nigel had not hurried his call, leaving them to stare at the Westminster clock through the wide window while his secretary sorted papers.

'Not quite the paperless office, then?' Charles said.

Jeremy ignored the remark. 'Has the ear of ministers, Nigel,' he murmured. 'Not only Valerie's. Well thought of in Brussels, too. People think being an MEP is a backwater, but Nigel proved them wrong. He wasn't just influential in the parliament; he was a regular channel between parliament and the Commission and between ministers here and the Commission. Gave up a lot to come to us, but I doubt his political career is finished. Probably go on to bigger things, once he's sorted this place out. You could do worse than hitch your star to him. Especially as you knew him when he was in the Foreign Office.'

'How did he get this job?'

Jeremy was spared an answer by Nigel ringing off and striding out to greet them. He took Charles's hand in both of his. 'Charles, Charles, it's so good to see you. You haven't changed a bit. Must be God knows how many years. Not since before I went to Brussels, is it? That's about a century ago. Very good of you to come back and help out. Thanks, Jeremy.' He nodded at Jeremy, who was about to follow them, and shut the door.

He had put on weight, not unduly, and had lost hair, not dramatically, but was otherwise tanned and looked fit. His suit was well cut, though fashionably un-vented. He wore a wedding ring, a Breitling watch and gold cuf-flinks. He smiled all the time. The walls of his office, which in the old MI6 would have displayed portrait photos of previous chiefs, were adorned with photos of Nigel with various dignitaries and well-known politicians, though not the one with Jacques Delors from his mantelpiece at home.

They sat. 'So, tell me about your life, Charles. What's it been? When did you leave the old office? What are you doing? Why did you leave? Sarah's very well and sends love, or would if she knew I was seeing you.' He laughed. 'She's back at work full time now with Kent & Kent, where she was before we went to Washington. Extended career break, though she did some work for them in Brussels. Good of them to take her back. Senior partner's an old friend. Great fun, she's enjoying it hugely. Doing very well, too. You've never married.'

It was a statement rather than a question. From that and what followed, it was clear that Nigel must have read Charles's file. He asked only questions to which he would have known the answers.

'Now, Gladiator, the missing Gladiator.' Nigel leaned forward, elbows on the desk, hands clasped. His brown eyes bulged at Charles. 'Must admit, I can't always get my head round these nicknames or codenames you – we – use. But at least Gladiator's memorable. Are they really necessary, d'you think?'

'So long as you want to protect agent identities, they are. Nicknames or numbers.' It was an unnecessary question, designed to ingratiate. He wondered inconsequentially whether Nigel wore reading glasses now, or whether he had contact lenses. The way his eyes bulged and glistened gave the impression of someone struggling against worsening sight.

'Sounds a bit Cold War-ish nowadays. This one was later than that, wasn't he? In his origins?'

'Yes, he was. The IRA – the Provisionals – first, then Afghanistan.'

'Versatile fellow. He's the one Sarah introduced you to, isn't he, years ago? The one she told me about first?'

It was lightly put, and impossible to tell how much Nigel knew of the context of that introduction. 'That's right.'

'Quite a coincidence.'

'Huge.'

'Anyway, he's gone missing.' Nigel sat back, his hands palms down on the desk. 'What seems to have happened is that he went on one of his occasional trips back to Pakistan – for which read Afghanistan, clandestinely – then came back and reported as usual. This was when UBL was still alive. Then, after UBL was killed, they suddenly summoned him back again. He wasn't going to go. Then he disappeared. He changed his mind, he did go back – we know that because we checked the flight manifest. Hasn't been heard from since.'

'What would he report on now?'

'Al-Qaeda remnants, Taliban general extremism, usual thing. You know he's a convert?'

That was hard to imagine. 'He was Catholic when I knew him, in so far as he was anything.'

'Quite a high proportion of converts are – were – Catholics. It never stopped him reporting to us, surprisingly. You'd think it would've, given how keen converts of all kinds usually are. Hates extremism, apparently. He's against violence.'

'He's seen enough.'

'What worries me is that they might have turned him and be running him back at us in order to do something dastardly. They did it with that Jordanian, who blew up all those CIA handlers when they were debriefing him.'

'What's his product like?'

'Excellent, I'm told.'

'Have you read his file?'

Nigel nodded. 'That's why we've got you back, Charles. To go through everything and see if there's any insecurity on our part or his that could have given him away. Or any indication that he might be a double – double agent, that's the term, isn't it? In other words, we want you to do a security review.'

It was a politician's answer. A nod could mean either that he had read the file or that he was acknowledging that Charles had hit the nail on the head, that it was necessary for someone to read it. If Nigel had read it himself – in full – he clearly wasn't giving anything away.

'It was Matthew Abrahams's idea to get you back, as you

probably know from Jeremy. With my enthusiastic support. Brilliant idea, of course. Brilliant man, Matthew. You knew him well, didn't you? Highly regarded in Whitehall, in his day. Very sad about his cancer. You know about that?'

'I knew he was ill.'

'Not much longer for this world, I fear. Still, there we are, comes to us all. Jeremy's sorting out with the A desk – action desk, I've got that right, haven't I? – for you to get briefed and have access to the files. Must get a grip on this new terminology. Like a foreign language. Any problems, come to me. Don't hesitate.' He stood and held out his hand, smiling. 'Welcome again, Charles. Great to have you on board.'

They shook hands again. By unspoken agreement it was as if their last conversation, years before over a hurried lunch in the National Theatre, had never happened.

Matthew Abrahams's flat was in a 1930s art deco block in Westminster. He had been CSS – Chief of the Secret Service – when Charles had left, and it was hard to reconcile memories of the austere and authoritative figure of the later Cold War with the culture of the new SIA. Still less with the title, CEO.

The walls of the flat were lined with books, mostly in

English but some Classics and some in Chinese and Russian. In gaps between shelves and windows, above doors and fireplaces, were pictures of birds. Matthew was an ornithologist and a chronicler of the Chinese gulag. He smiled as they shook hands.

'Don't be shocked. I am dying. But there is enough life left, I hope, to enjoy working with you again. And for us to conspire together one last time. Come in.'

Charles was shocked. The tall figure he had known was shrunken and skeletal, like a relic of one of the secret labour camps he meticulously catalogued. His skin was blotched parchment, his cheeks sunken, his hand a chicken's claw. Charles knew Matthew would eschew consolation. 'What is it?'

'Prostate. The one that gets us all eventually, if nothing else does first. Spread to the liver. I accept some alleviation in the hope of delaying it until this business is sorted out. I am not in pain. Do you prefer any particular tea?'

The flat was suffocatingly warm and the winged arm-chair too soft. 'How is Jenny?'

'In Cambridge, coping. I'm there most of the time now. Our sons find it harder because there is nothing for them to do. She wants me to stop work, of course. Biscuits are in the tin.'

Refusing help, Matthew lowered the tea tray onto a

lacquered Chinese table and then himself onto the sofa, where he leaned back, rubbing his thighs. His bespectacled grey-blue eyes rested on Charles like the gaze of a judge weighing sentence.

'I did not, of course, ask you to tear yourself away from your researches, and to confront something you may not wish to be reminded of, simply to investigate the disappearance of Gladiator. Anyone could do that, or no-one. How is your book?'

'Becalmed. Either it's been said before, or it isn't known and can't be said. It's a good time to have a break and take stock.'

'Is Walsingham hero or villain, d'you think?'

'Something of each.'

'We at least have a simpler task. Our man is only one.'

Charles poured the tea.

'The reason I asked you to return is that we have an insider problem. We get one about every ten years, as you know. But this particular problem has been around a long time, as you also know. In fact, you and I are two of only three still serving who are aware of it. The other is Sonia, you'll be pleased to hear. It was very tightly held at the time, since when people have retired, moved on or died. There is only one record: the secret annex to the paper file which you were once familiar with. No-one conducting an electronic search would discover it, unless they already knew where else to look. We have become an intelligence service which no longer knows what it knows, and has no way of recovering what once it knew, which is a slow suicide. But the urgency now is that our insider has become nastier. We might even call him malignant, a word I've heard quite often recently.' He smiled and sipped his tea. 'You're ignoring the biscuits.'

Charles had not lunched. He helped himself to two shortbreads.

'Too many things have gone wrong,' Matthew continued. 'You may have seen leaks of SIA assessments in the press. They amount to a pattern, an agenda. But there's more than that, though it wouldn't be visible to any other security reviewer but you. There's something internal, relating to Gladiator.'

'Nigel Measures thinks he might have been turned.'

Matthew's eyes rested on Charles's. 'Is that what he said?' He looked down at his withered hands, nodding. 'He was very anxious not to have you back, although he didn't want to say so outright. Instead, he argued that you might be indiscreet, now that you are a writer. That is of a piece with his saying that Gladiator might have been turned. Neither is what he really thinks, or knows. You'll have to be careful.'

'Of what?'

'Nothing in particular, therefore everything. Measures wants you to fail. He does not want Gladiator found.'

'So Nigel is the problem – again?'

'Not only because of what happened in the past. Or could be happening now – we don't know. But he's a problem because of what he's prepared to do to cover that up. The cover up, you see, it's always the cover up that gets people.' He nodded to himself.

'I was very surprised when I heard he was to get your job.'

'A political fix, over my dead body. But not quite, not yet.' He smiled again. 'If they'd left it a little longer, it would have been. And he'd have got away with it. He could still, if you can't help.'

'I came back because it was you that asked. I wouldn't have done it for anyone else. I'll do everything I can.' Charles was glad of the chance to say it, while there was still time. He and Matthew had rarely discussed personal subjects, still less feelings. The unsaid was understood, and Charles always felt that their communication was better – subtler and more honest – for it.

Matthew inclined his head. 'So, Gladiator,' he resumed after a pause. 'He did a lot for us in Afghanistan before 9/11, and for a while afterwards. But, foolishly, the office let him drift away, until a couple of years ago when they re-contacted him and he agreed to become re-involved. He did a few trips to Pakistan, for which he has genuine business reasons, but during which he was able to re-establish contacts among the AQ external operations people. After UBL was killed he went on another and hasn't been heard of since. His AQ and Taliban contacts are arranged via cut-outs and couriers and he doesn't always meet face-to-face. It takes weeks to set up each trip and he travels incognito into Waziristan and Afghanistan. If they do meet, it's a big deal; usually he returns with intelligence on their tasking and plenty of leadership gossip. Very risky for him, of course, not only because of the threat of discovery but because he might be killed in a US drone strike.'

'The Americans don't know about him?'

'Too dangerous. Either it would leak, or they'd be unable to resist killing any AQ figure he was with, and him too. During his last visit, he met no senior leaders, but a number of second-rankers. They speak freely before him – they've known him for years, regard him as tried and tested, the blue-eyed emir they're always seeking who can come and go freely in the West. He gives them good stuff. At least, what they think is good stuff. They once suggested he might like to martyr himself over here as a suicide bomber, but he said his faith wasn't strong enough and they've not mentioned it again. Anyway, this last meeting was reasonably productive, but nothing sensational. Then, about three weeks after he returned, he got a message to go back. This was unprecedented. The message came via a contact on the fringes of al-Jazeera, the television station, from a man who has family connections with AQ. Not the usual route, but the reason given was that this was urgent. They wanted his advice in connection with a forthcoming wedding – you know that they sometimes refer to attacks as weddings.'

'Nigel Measures told me this morning he wasn't going to go back, then abruptly did.'

Matthew nodded again. 'True, so far as it goes. We advised – through his case officers – that he shouldn't go. It sounded too fishy, too pat, and why should he have to go there to give his advice? He agreed, and sent a message back via the not-really al-Jazeera man saying a backlog of court cases wouldn't permit another absence so soon – he's set up his own law firm, by the way, handles a lot of Pakistani marriage and inheritance cases – but he'd send any advice he could via the same route. Then – suddenly, unexpectedly, without a word to his case officers – he went. Since when nothing has been heard.'

'That's what Nigel said.'

Matthew sipped his tea, swallowed slowly and conspicuously, then carefully lowered his cup and sat back with his hands fingertip to fingertip. 'Except that something has been heard, the full significance of which is apparent only to me. A while after he went back we intercepted a call between one of the people he saw on his last trip and a colleague in Yemen. They were speaking Arabic, but the caller repeated and translated two sentences into English because, he said, it was important to get it right. Those sentences were: 'The CIA say they have no agents in Core AQ. Their cupboard is bare.'

Charles put down his own cup. 'How do they know that?'

'That, of course, is the question. But there's a hidden significance in those two sentences, beyond the obvious one. The real significance is that they were mine. They were my sentences. I wrote them in a record I made following my last trip to Washington. I was ill shortly afterwards; I never circulated a formal record of the trip. I still haven't. But I did show my notes to Nigel Measures, who had by then arrived to take over from me.

'So how did my words reach AQ? The intercepted speaker was very careful to repeat them exactly, which suggests someone must have given them word for word, not just the gist. It wasn't anyone from Washington or Langley, or anyone else the Americans might have told, because they were not CIA's words, they were mine. CIA's words to me were: "We have no assets in AQ Central. The shelf is empty, our cupboard is bare. But if the drone strategy continues to work, we won't need them." If AQ's source had given them all that, they would have quoted it all. Note, too, that the CIA typically referred to "assets" where I say "agents"; and their use of AQ Central compared with our Core AQ or AQ Core. It could have come only from my notes, which means Measures, the only person to have seen them. And the only way I can think those sentences might have reached AQ from Measures is via someone who might have had contact with both, which is Gladiator. I have no evidence that he did, but I'm suspicious. The question is, did Measures meet Gladiator before he went back, and did he offer him those sentences as a titbit?'

Charles was sceptical. It was intrinsically unlikely. 'They wouldn't have met, would they? An agent wouldn't meet anyone in Nigel's position. The only people who'd have contact with Gladiator would be his case officers. And that's much more than a titbit, anyway. It would be hugely important to AQ. No-one would give intelligence like that away, surely? Not if it were true. And Nigel hardly knows Gladiator. They met only once – you know, years ago, in the early days, not long before the Paris trip. At dinner at Nigel's house, I think.'

'Of course Measures wouldn't have, shouldn't have seen

him, or have had any other contact with him. Normally. But Measures's situation is not normal. If what we know about him came out he would be sunk, holed beneath the water-line, even though it happened long ago. Remember who's still around and knows about it. There's Sarah, his wife – have you had contact with her?'

'No.'

'She is still—' Matthew broke off and smiled thinly, nodding. 'And there's me, but I'm on my way out and dying, so that's all right. There's Sonia, buried deep in some bit of the SIA that Measures has never heard of and longing for early retirement. He never knew her, never knew she knew, so probably she's safe. Then there's Gladiator, or was until he disappeared. Measures knows that he witnessed the incident, with you. Some idiot in Foreign Office security let it slip a few years later, when Measures was clamouring for another Europe job and wanted to know why he wasn't getting one. So it must have been very disagreeable for him to find when he came here that we were still running Gladiator. And finally, there's you, of course. You know the whole story, but you were out of sight, out of mind, until I brought you back, much against his will. He did all he could to delay it or sidetrack it, short of being seen to do so. That's why you must take care, Charles.' He smiled again.

'But, given all that, why should he want to risk returning

89

and taking your job? He was doing well as an MEP, very comfortable, well paid, highly thought of. Why not just continue to keep well away, keep quiet, as he has for so long? There was no risk of anyone saying anything until he came here.'

Matthew raised his eyebrows and parted his fingers, as in supplication. 'Ambition? Revenge? Who knows what bitterness stirs in all our murky depths. And what better way to revenge yourself on MI6 than by taking charge of it? He's off to a pretty good start. The SIA and its legions of lawyers and mud-slides of management will castrate and suffocate the old office. He's keen on all that.'

Charles remained sceptical. Everything Matthew said was plausible, given Nigel's personality and what they both knew of his past, but it was unlikely in practice. 'I still don't see how Nigel could have contrived contact with Gladiator without anyone knowing. He couldn't just go and look up the contact details himself. It would be too extraordinary. He'd have to ask someone for them.'

'Maybe someone does know.'

'You haven't investigated?'

'I can't, in my position, without others knowing and therefore probably without Measures knowing. All eyes are always on the monarch, there's no privacy for a chief without gross and elaborate deceit. But you can make inquiries, you can mount discreet investigations. You're below the radar.' A bus pulled up outside. Matthew closed his eyes and rested his head against the sofa until the bus pulled away. 'Measures mounted a massive behind-the-scenes campaign to get this job, a very political campaign. I'm as certain as I can be, without actual evidence, that he is behind all these press leaks. If you look at the coverage in its entirety, especially the Sunday pieces by James Wytham, there's a pattern. It begins with opinion pieces about the SIA being a new body in need of a new head, a new way of thinking. Then there are leaks from documents, accusations of insecurity and poor morale, signs that things are going wrong, calls for an outsider to take over, someone who understands the new world and its challenges. But when Measures arrived it all changed. Coverage since then has become more favourable; there are no more leaks, criticism is muted and there are calls for more resources. Soon, I predict, there will be a few more leaks, but they'll be of triumphs under the new regime. You don't know anything about James Wytham? Pity.'

Matthew sat back and closed his eyes. He looked drained, and shook his head at Charles's suggestion of more tea. Charles wanted to go on but could see his friend ebbing before him. 'I will do all I can,' he said. 'Everything, I promise you. And I'll keep you informed.' He stood.

Matthew struggled to his feet, despite Charles's protests, steadying himself by clutching Charles's arm. 'This time we must nail him for good. Did he have contact with Gladiator? That's what you have to find out. But he'll want you out of the way. Remember that. I'll give you all the help, all the access I can, but if I'm no longer available, recruit Sonia. Go and see her anyway. Tell her everything. You'll need help.'

They shook hands at the door. 'Good luck,' said Matthew.

Charles held on to his hand. 'Goodbye.'

Matthew, smiling, patted Charles's arm. 'Farewell, dear friend.'

6

The surly policeman swung open the cell door. 'Your lawyer's here.'

Charles followed him through reception to the cramped interview room, expecting to find his two interviewers and Sarah. But there was only Sarah, standing by the desk.

'Call when you're ready,' said the policeman, closing the door on them.

They stood looking at each other. It had happened too quickly. There should have been time to prepare. After a moment, they both smiled and shook hands. As if the years had made us strangers, he thought. As they should have, as was only natural. As if we really were the grown-ups we pretend to be.

'Thank you for coming,' he said. She said something but

he didn't take it in. 'I'm sorry that we should meet like this, after all this time. Funny, in a way.'

'I'm sure it will come to seem so.'

Her hair was shorter and tinted, her face more drawn, her figure thinner. But the shape of her features, her voice, her mouth, her eyes, were immediately familiar. His own mouth felt dry, which surprised him, because he had thought he was beyond all that.

She looked businesslike in a tailored black skirt and a matching jacket, over a crisp white blouse.

'How long have we got?' he asked. A professional question, one you asked your agent at the start of a meeting.

'As long as we want. You're allowed to confer privately with your legal representative.'

They sat on the chairs at the near side of the desk, facing each other. She took a black Moleskine notebook from her handbag. In trying not to look at her legs as she crossed them, his eyes were caught by her wedding and engagement rings. She took a Mont Blanc pen from her handbag and eased the elastic strap aside to open her notebook.

'Tell me everything.'

He kept back only his conversation with Matthew Abrahams and, for the time being, the identity of Gladiator.

'I'm just so surprised he hasn't told me you were back,' she said, interrupting his account of his meeting with Nigel.

'I'm sure he will.' Just as soon as he hears who the defendant's solicitor is, he thought.

When he had finished she said, 'The police will want to go over the same ground again, now that I'm here. Answer their questions clearly and simply but don't do more than that, don't say any more than they ask of you. If you do start saying too much, I'll interrupt. Otherwise, if I'm not saying anything, it's all right.'

Charles nodded, thinking about the next step, his real purpose. 'There is something else. It doesn't affect what's happening here, now, but it is important context. Are you free for dinner, assuming they release me?'

She looked at him.

'It is important,' he repeated. 'It is business.'

'Well, I could be. Nigel's out this evening, as it happens.' She hesitated again. 'I suppose there's no impropriety, personally or professionally. It could put Nigel in a difficult position if there were proceedings. Not that I think there'll be any.'

'It shouldn't, surely, as long as you really are my lawyer. And it's not as if he doesn't know we know each other.'

'No. All right. So long as it's early.'

She got up and opened the door. Freckles and Corduroy must have been waiting outside because they entered before she sat down again.

As she predicted, the questioning went over much of the ground already covered, albeit more formally. She intervened only once, leaning nearer the microphone.

'I think we should make it quite clear, for the record, that there is no allegation that Mr Thoroughgood has any connection with the journalist James Wytham, author of the leaks that are the principal concern of this enquiry, nor that he is suspected of being the source of any of those leaks.'

'Correct,' said Corduroy.

During the pause that followed, the unasked questions – then what are we here for? Surely not for the harmless David Horam piece? – were palpable. Both policemen looked awkward.

Freckles broke the pause. 'All right, you came down to London, you were briefed on the missing Gladiator, you got your pass, you were given an office—'

'A desk.'

'—given a desk and you set to work on reviewing the Gladiator case. Could you describe what that involved?'

Corduroy held up his hand, looking from Freckles to Sarah. 'I don't want to throw a spanner in the works. But this is a sensitive case, on which we were specially briefed.' He looked again to Charles. 'As was Mr Thoroughgood, of course, but his legal representative—'

Charles abandoned his plan not to tell her until later. 'She knows the case,' he said.

They all stared. 'Mrs Measures – her married name – was involved in the case from the start, many years ago. It was she who introduced Gladiator to me.' He saw understanding growing in her eyes, and with it questions. He turned back to the police. 'You can ask what you like about Gladiator.'

'Well, it's not the case itself; it's what you did, establishing what you were doing, that concerns us,' said Corduroy. 'So, you started reviewing it. What does that mean exactly?'

'I began reading the files. Because it's an old case it still has paper files. Seven volumes. Only the most recent papers – if you can call them that – are electronic.'

And nothing like as detailed and revealing, unless by omission, he forbore to add. The change in record-keeping was striking. The old paper system, rigid, cumbersome, labour-intensive and tedious, had been enforced by middle-aged women in registries who mercilessly pursued careless young officers for failing to sign off minutes, complete contact notes or file telegrams. Often needlessly duplicated, it had at least the advantage that it always told the story. Everything that happened, all the intelligence produced, what motivated the agent, what he thought of his marriage or of his job, what he was paid, how his case officer felt about him, what decisions were taken and by whom, the identities of everyone who had access to the file – all of it was recorded in wearisome detail.

But narrative disappeared when files went electronic. The intelligence reports were still there and significant case developments still recorded, but there was no sense of a controlling influence, and little record of how, why or by whom decisions were taken. Above all, there was no sense of history, no awareness of what had already been said and done. No-one, it was clear, read files any more. Gladiator's recent young case officers were keen and competent but they could not appreciate their agent's hinterland, what he had been at their age, where he came from, nor how much more he knew about spying than they did.

Charles could not resist the self-indulgent lure of the early volumes, most of which he had written. It was something of a shock to find that, even in the short space of one career, papers he had drafted as a young man were now redolent of another age, of assumptions, attitudes, ways of seeing and doing that seemed as obvious and up to date then as the latest practices did now. And as permanent.

But these files were also uniquely resonant of four people – Gladiator, Sarah, himself and Nigel, though Nigel was in most volumes an off-stage presence whose significance became apparent only later. For Charles, the interpenetration of their characters infused the notes, minutes, telegrams and letters he had written, even those that were not about them. Despite his intimacy with the story, he was surprised by how much he had forgotten, and by how each recovered detail released clouds of others, like dust from old books.

He described none of this to the police. There was no point, they could read the files for themselves if they wanted. If they did they would see that the very first papers were not his. A pink memo from the mid-nineties recorded how Nigel Measures, a desk officer in the Foreign Office, had told someone on the MI6 European liaison desk that his wife knew someone who might be of interest to 'your people' in the Irish context. Measures, whom the memo described as not always very helpful to MI6, had said that his wife taught law part time in London and Dublin. One of her Dublin students had connections with the Provisional movement and struck her, she reported, as the kind of person someone should talk to, especially now that the Provisionals had broken the ceasefire. Measures himself knew no more than that and – frankly, he said – didn't want to. Anyone interested should talk directly to his wife, though he doubted there was anything in it – 'But you people must be used to chasing hares.'

The next memo recorded that a desk officer from the terrorist section had rung Sarah and had got the student's
name – Martin Worth – along with a summary of remarks
he had made, suggesting inside knowledge of the recent
Docklands bombing in London and his own disapproval of
it. The desk officer had arranged to visit her in London and
to trace Worth but she'd rung back to change the meeting
because she would be in Dublin. The desk officer was sent
abroad on another case and someone noted that Charles,
who had just joined the section, was on a familiarisation
visit to the embassy in Dublin; he could see her while she
was there. The name Martin Worth came back No Trace.

Next was a telegram sent to Charles in Dublin, giving the
background and suggesting he call on Mrs Measures, using
an alias. A short reply from Charles explained that he knew
her from Oxford, so would have to use his own name. Head
Office agreed, reluctantly.

Of course, this brief exchange conveyed only what had
happened but nothing of what mattered. That was the
problem with files, even the best-kept. He remembered that
when London's telegram had come through he was reading
in the embassy's communications centre – the comcen –
supposedly the most protected part of the building. The
comcen was not yet computerised and the floor was littered
with encoded ticker-tape from the cipher machines which

the Foreign Office cipher clerk, who was deep in his newspaper, had allowed to accumulate. When one of the machines resumed its mechanical chatter he got up with a sigh, pressed a few buttons, shrugged and walked away.

'Something from your lot. You'll have to get Angie from chancery if you don't know how to unwrap it.'

Charles had been trained on that machine, once, and had forgotten. MI6 traffic was double-enciphered and Angie was out to lunch. Charles approached the machine. His fingers hovered over the buttons, then he thought better of it and looked back at the clerk.

'Press that red one first,' said the clerk, pointing. 'That's what Angie does. Then hold the bar, press green and wait till they ask who you are. Then tell them.' He lit a cigarette.

Charles watched the telegram come chattering through, gathering the punched tape and tearing it into little pieces before dropping it into the empty Secret Waste bag, where the tangled mess on the floor should have been.

Sarah's name and his designation were the first words he read. He had not seen her since the dinner party and had seen little of Nigel. They had no children, he knew from when he had last looked up Nigel in the Diplomatic List, the form book of Foreign Office pedigree and postings. Charles was in the embassy in Bangkok then, awaiting a briefing from the head of station before making a cold approach to a Chinese diplomat, which hadn't worked. Nigel and Sarah were in Geneva, he read. Nigel was first secretary political, which was early promotion. Charles suspected that, like most busy and successful people, they lived as if the past had never been.

He did not. When he had seen her name that morning in Dublin, coughed out in staccato by the cipher machine, it was a shock that felt immediately apt. Of course it had to be her; the past lived in the present, there was a pattern in the carpet, and perhaps it mattered after all.

He went up to Angie's empty office to make the call. Sarah answered, he remembered, with the characteristic slight catch in her voice he had noticed again when he'd rung her from the police station. 'Sarah, it's Charles Thoroughgood.'

'Hallo, Charles.'

She sounded as matter-of-fact as he imagined he did. They asked each other how they were, agreed they hadn't spoken for ages, that life had flown by since the dinner party in Clapham. 'I've been asked to ring you about the person you mentioned to Nigel,' he said.

'Oh, yes.'

'Might we meet today? I'm in Dublin.'

'If you like.'

He suggested the bar of Jury's hotel, which he had heard

had an international clientele and was safe, the sort of place where British officials and business people could meet.

Waiting for her in reception, pretending to read a paper, he was surprised by his own nervousness; an indication of how little one knew oneself.

She was punctual, carrying a raincoat and wearing sensible grey trousers and a dark roll-necked jersey. She held out her hand, smiling. 'Hallo, Charles.'

'Hallo, Sarah.'

His file note recorded that they talked in the bar for an hour and a quarter. She started with orange juice, then acquiesced to white wine. They discussed mutual acquaintances and her and her husband's careers. His note explained that they had known each other as undergraduates.

Martin Worth, the note explained, was a student on the law degree course she taught. Only half Irish, he had been brought up in Newcastle, where his English father had been a barrister. Following his father's early death from cancer, his Irish mother had moved the family – Sarah thought there were a couple of sisters – back to Dublin. Martin was active in student politics, but Sarah had known nothing of his republican connections until she'd run into him one day as he was leaving the Provisional Sinn Fein office.

'I said something stupid,' she said. 'You know, it was one

of those moments when you can't think what to say but feel you have to say something. I said, "What are you doing here? I didn't know you were mixed up with that lot." It must have riled him, because he immediately attacked me for being a British diplomat's wife and supporting the army of occupation in the North. I'd never heard him speak like that, he'd always been very polite and pleasant, and his Irish accent was more pronounced than usual. Normally he has just a bit of one, though I've since noticed it fluctuates according to whom he's with. Also, I was surprised he knew what Nigel did. As you can imagine, I don't broadcast that here.'

'Have you asked how he found out?'

'No, I haven't. I should, I suppose. Anyway, after that I didn't see him for a couple of weeks. I teach part time here, you see, popping across for a few days a month for three seminars, so anyone who misses a class I don't see for a while. When he did reappear, he seemed back to his normal self and I thought, well, that's fine, neither of us will say anything about it. But he hung around afterwards and I thought, oh dear, trouble. Instead, he said he wanted to apologise for the way he'd spoken to me and asked if I'd have coffee with him. I said okay, assuming we'd go to the students' union or somewhere, but he suggested we met half an hour later in a little tea shop just off O'Connell Street.

'It was all very amicable – he's a nice boy – but he seemed

nervous. Eventually, he said, "Look, about that afternoon, what I said to you, I had to speak like that, you see, because we were right outside the PSF office where I'd just been. I work for them a bit, I'm involved in the Republican cause. Which doesn't mean I approve of everything they do. I mean, I believe in a united Ireland and think the British should get out and that someone should have murdered that Thatcher woman for what she did to the hunger strikers. But that doesn't mean I agree with everything that's going on, all the bombs and that. I'm half English myself; I can't really hate the British like many do here." At least, that was the gist of it.'

Charles nodded. He was concentrating rather than taking notes. The hatred she had referred to was still palpable to him, from his time in Belfast in the seventies.

She took up her wine. 'Then he told me some rambling story about a friend from school in England – sorry, Scotland, a boarding school, can't remember which – whom he'd run into at an army checkpoint in Belfast before the ceasefire. His friend was a bit older than him and had become a British Army officer; he was standing there watching his soldiers search the cars. Martin said they didn't recognise each other until he and his republican friends – all good Provos, he said – were made to get out and be searched. They recognised each other then, but neither said anything. They couldn't, not in front of Martin's Provo friends. It would have been the death of him, he said, to be pally with a British Army officer – a Para, I think he was, which was even worse. Fortunately, his friend must have realised that just as he did, and it was all right.

'But he thought about it a lot afterwards, he said. You know – what kind of world are we in where we have to do that, where's it leading us, and so on. Then he read in the papers that his army friend had both legs blown off by a bomb. His republican friends were making jokes about Paras getting legless and all that, but Martin just had to keep quiet. Then he read that his army friend had died. He wanted to go to the funeral – he'd stayed with the family once or twice in school holidays – but felt it would be dangerous for him, and maybe for his mother, if word got back. Eventually, he wrote to them, without giving his address.

'Finally, he said to me, "All that made me realise it's no good going on as we were, it's not how you get anywhere you want to be. And now the ceasefire's ended I've decided it's time I did something to help, to increase understanding, to bridge the divide. We can't always be killing, it gets no-one anywhere. Could you please tell your husband that."'

'He actually asked you to tell Nigel? It wasn't that you offered?'

'No, he asked. I'm sure of that. I was surprised. I didn't

see how Nigel could help anyone really, but I promised I'd pass it on. When I did, Nigel didn't seem to think much of it at the time, but one day he said he'd mentioned it to your people – the Friends, he called them – and that someone would get in touch with me.'

That much Charles had summarised in his file note. It was there for the police to read if they wanted. He had not, however, recorded that she added, 'He never said it would be you, Charles.'

'He didn't know, he really didn't. I didn't know myself till this afternoon.'

She raised her eyebrows. 'Are you seriously saying you didn't fix this? That it's just a mighty coincidence? I mean, I know spies have to be professional liars, but this one's just a wee bit implausible, don't you think?'

'Spies are the midwives of truth.' He smiled. 'This is coincidence, I promise you.'

She pursed her lips.

'More wine,' he said, standing and picking up their glasses.

'I haven't finished this one. I ought to be getting back. I've got work to do.'

'Such a mighty coincidence shouldn't be just a one-glass occasion.'

'All right, but just a spritzer.'

'I'll tell you another coincidence,' she said when he

returned. 'The evening I was about to tell Nigel what Martin had said, he started talking about changing his job. He finds the Foreign Office frustrating, can't get anything done, no real power, narrow horizons, narrow pyramid. He said he was thinking of applying to the UN, or maybe going into politics. He still is, as a matter of fact. Anyway, quite suddenly he said, almost in the very words Martin had used, "I want to help create greater understanding, to do something for the world, build bridges between peoples." Just the same sort of thing. It made me laugh. I said he wasn't the only one, which didn't please him very much. Thought I wasn't taking him seriously.'

'I thought he was doing well in the Foreign Office. He's well suited, isn't he? Good at it.'

'He is, he's doing very well. But he thinks it's insufficiently internationalist.' She shrugged. 'That's how he sees it, anyway.'

'Its detractors are always saying the opposite.'

'Nigel's a citizen of the world now. He's broadened his horizons. Unthinking loyalty to a narrow interpretation of the national interest doesn't do any good for this country, nor for anyone else. He says.' She picked up her glass. 'Anyway, Charles, how are you? How is life? Do you like what you do? Why aren't you married?'

'How d'you know I'm not?'

'You can tell with some men. Everything about you is obvious. You must be a useless spy.'

He talked about his job for a while, without saying much. When she asked why he had joined the army after Oxford he said, 'Various reasons. No doubt something to do with my father having been in the war. Also, I wanted a new start, I guess.'

Their eyes met for a moment.

It was not until she had got up to go and he was helping her on with her coat that he asked what he had wanted to ask all evening. 'Have you ever heard anything from or of James – Baby Bourne? He'd be old enough to get in touch now, if he wants.'

She picked up her handbag. 'No. Nor do I expect to. Where are you staying?'

Afterwards, he pondered the crow's feet around her eyes and the faint vertical lines either side of her mouth. They had been etched into her since that dinner in Clapham. Her hands were changed, too. The girl's hands he had known, soft, expressive, darting like swift birds, had become a woman's, still quick and deft but more used and worn now, more noticeably veined. He thought of such changes with a tenderness that surprised him.

7

Corduroy was not interested in the origins of the case. 'So the early volumes cover the years when Gladiator was working against the Provisional IRA. And the latest volume, or electronic record, covers the most recent period, including his trips to Pakistan.'

'Yes. All recent case records are electronic, but older cases with paper origins are supposed to be maintained in that state with print-outs.'

'Is this one?'

'No. At least, it wasn't. I doubt many of them are. If the case officer doesn't bother, there's no longer anyone to remind him, or her. But I've now printed out all the emails I could find and put them on it.'

'Are you normally such a stickler for procedure?'

'No, rather the opposite. But it's quicker and easier to read a paper file, and I find I remember it better.'

Corduroy leaned forward, his elbows on the desk. 'Would you say, then, that otherwise you're a bit cavalier with procedures?'

Charles smiled. 'Well, perhaps with administrative procedures I don't see the point of. I imagine there might be comments to that effect on my own file.'

'And with security procedures?'

'I hope not. But, again, my file is probably a better record than my memory.' He knew he had no major security breaches, though he also knew that, like almost anyone with an operational career, he had cut corners.

'Does the file say why Gladiator went back to Pakistan this last time, the trip from which he never returned?'

'No. It refers briefly to the debate as to whether he should go and the conclusion that he should not. It also records the excuse he gave for not going. But it says nothing about his change of mind, only that he had gone. It gives his flight number and shows that they checked he boarded it.' He didn't see where this tack would lead them. Whatever had happened to Gladiator had nothing to do with his own alleged leaks to the press, unless, like him, they suspected a hidden connection. But that was unlikely. They were probably just fishing because there was nothing left to ask about the leaks.

'Why do you think he went back?' continued Corduroy. 'What is your opinion?'

'I don't know why. As I said, there's nothing on file about it.'

That was true, so far as it went. The emails between London and the SIA station in Pakistan described a series of telephone messages through various cut-outs, including the man who wasn't quite al-Jazeera, all purportedly concerned with Gladiator's legal practice, just as Matthew had told Charles in his flat. They simply recorded that Gladiator, against all advice, appeared to have suddenly changed his mind and gone.

Charles had talked to the two case officers, Adrian and Katharine. Both in their twenties, both from Yorkshire, they made an attractive pair. She was open-faced and lively, with an infectious laugh; he was tall and sallow with black hair, hazel eyes, a sensitive face, two or three days of stubble and a quiet ironic manner. Charles at first assumed they were a couple, then that they weren't, then that they might be after all, then had given up trying. They had both been to Cambridge.

'City of spies,' said Katharine, 'but we never met there. He joined first so he's my mentor and I'm his mentee, though it doesn't feel like that.' She laughed. 'I bet they didn't have a mentoring system in MI6, did they? Probably much nastier to each other.'

Questions bubbled out of her. They knew he had worked with Matthew Abrahams and wanted to know about him. Already the old MI6 and MI5 were becoming mythologised; he realised they must see him as part of history. They were talking over coffee in the basement staff restaurant. Adrian had an unopened packet of Mayfair cigarettes on the table before him, which he spun slowly with the tips of his fingers.

He saw Charles looking at them. 'Sorry, I'll put them away. Just something to play with till I get outside. Distraction therapy.'

'Don't. Dare to be different.'

'Gladiator was such an awful chain-smoker, wasn't he?' said Katharine. 'Is, I mean. I used to come away from meetings in the safe flat in a complete fug and my hair and clothes would smell for days. It just made Adrian worse, of course, the pair of them puffing away like steam-trains. I suppose that's what it was like all the time in your day?'

Charles had forgotten that Gladiator smoked. He remembered overflowing ashtrays in Dublin bars and Gladiator lighting up in hire cars. Charles smoked during those meetings, too, to keep him company. 'Conversion to Islam didn't stop him, then?'

'More the opposite,' said Adrian.

'Stress?'

'Or he just likes smoking.'

'You're the one he mentions most out of all his old case officers,' said Katharine. 'He was disappointed that we didn't know you, and he occasionally asked if we heard anything of you. We pretended we did, gave him your best wishes, that sort of thing. Such a pity former case officers aren't allowed to keep in touch. Though I see it could cause problems.'

They had no idea why Gladiator had changed his mind about going. They hadn't been his case officers for long and were a little in awe of him. When Charles asked why Gladiator continued to spy following his conversion, they couldn't say. They hadn't known him before he had converted, and he brushed away any attempt to discuss his beliefs.

'I'm not sure how sincere he is,' said Adrian. 'He once said something like, "I could believe in Islam but not in Islamism".'

Charles recalled the young law student he had met in Dublin fifteen years before, whose initial bravado and moderate dissipation only partially hid his seriousness. 'I believe in a united Ireland,' he said once, 'but not in violent republicanism.'

'I think he enjoys spying,' said Katharine.

Charles nodded. 'People do. Hard to give up, once you've got the habit.'

Adrian spun his cigarette packet round one more time, then put it in his pocket. 'Maybe you should ask CEO Dep – Nigel Measures – if he has any idea about why Gladiator went back. I think he went to see him.'

Katharine put her hand to her head. 'Of course, yes. I was completely forgetting. We got this call from CEO Dep last thing on the Friday before Gladiator went. He wanted his number and address from the file, which we held then. He said he used to know him but hadn't seen him for ages and thought it might be a good time to get in touch. Did he know him? There's nothing on file about it.'

'He met him socially, years ago.' Charles tried not to show too much interest. 'Did he go to see him?'

They looked at each other. 'Presumably not,' said Adrian. 'At least, if he did, there's nothing on file about it. Maybe he didn't ring until it was too late.'

Charles nodded again. 'Maybe.'

The interview continued until the police really had run out of questions. Charles solemnly agreed that they might never know why Gladiator went back, unless he returned to tell them. Corduroy declared the interview over and switched off the machine.

Sarah said: 'I take it Mr Thoroughgood is to be bailed?'

'Police bail. Soon as we fill in the forms.'

She stood and handed Charles her card. 'I'll go back to my office. Ring me when you're home.'

Freckles showed her out and a uniformed policeman escorted Charles to his cell. Again, he failed to get beyond the first page of *Jane Eyre*, distracted this time by worry about what people would think of him, particularly Katharine and Adrian. They were so young, so enthusiastic, and he felt that, merely by being arrested, he had somehow let them down. They would surely think it possible he was guilty, even if they wanted to believe him innocent. And they had no reason to believe him innocent.

Jeremy Wheeler, of course, would assume he was guilty, with relish. Charles imagined him shaking his head and lowering his voice over lunch, saying that between you and me, within these four walls, on a strictly need-to-know basis, not for onward transmission, it had come as no surprise to anyone who knew Charles well. There'd always been question marks and, frankly, he wouldn't be surprised if there were more to come. Not outright treachery, of course – Charles probably wasn't up to that – just a series of grubby, small-change indiscretions. It wasn't even certain that money had changed hands – at least there was no evidence as yet – but it was yet another example of an Old Office old stager who couldn't accept modernisation, didn't know how to cope with the modern world. All very sad.

It was dark by the time the release and bail formalities were complete. They returned his possessions, minus mobile, diary, SIA pass and address book, and offered to drive him back to his flat, since it was coming on to rain. Conversation during the short journey was freer than in the morning.

'It'll be a while before you get your computers and phone,' said Corduroy. 'There's a backlog in the section that goes through them. All these terrorist cases. That's why your bail date is set for six months.'

Charles nodded. His own case didn't concern him any more. They were beyond that. He needed to do a little fishing of his own. 'Trouble is, it doesn't take you any farther forward on the James Wytham leaks.'

'No, that's the big thing, of course. Your case was referred to us as part of that, you see, which was why we had to investigate.'

'I suppose the SIA lawyers felt obliged to bring you in.'

'Came from higher than that.'

Charles feigned surprise. 'Not CEO level, surely?'

Freckles glanced at Corduroy, who nodded. 'Almost,' he said. 'Mr Measures himself, no less. Quite a coincidence, your lawyer being his wife. Could that be a problem for him?'

'Not really.'

'Give her something to talk about over dinner when she gets home, I suppose.'

They drew up next to the Bristol. 'Never seen one of these before,' said Corduroy. 'Seen photos, but never in the metal.'

Charles offered the keys. 'Take it round the block.'

Corduroy wrestled with temptation. 'Better not. All hell to pay if I crash it when I'm on duty.' The three of them spent a further five minutes discussing the car before shaking hands.

'So where will you look now for Mr Wytham?' asked Charles.

'You tell us. Any ideas?' said Freckles.

You could start with Nigel Measures himself, Charles wanted to say. But that door opened onto issues he wanted to resolve himself.

'I'll let you know if I have.'

The flat was as he'd left it, except that his laptop was missing and some of his research papers on Francis Walsingham had been moved. If Walsingham's searchers had done the job he'd never have seen his papers again. Nor, perhaps, would anyone have seen him, save for his gaolers in the Tower; a fate different in quality, but not kind, from what Nigel Measures intended.

He made a mug of tea and opened the french windows

onto the balcony. The rain fell steadily now, spattering on the metal table and sounding like rushing water on the leaves of the plane trees dominating the garden at the rear of the flats. His balcony looked straight into their tops, worlds of their own, unnoticed by groundlings. He leaned with his tea against the door-jamb, forcing himself to slow down, to think, not to ring immediately.

When he did he got straight through.

'Are you all right?' she asked.

'A free man, and hungry. When and where?'

They settled on an Italian restaurant in Pimlico. That gave him time for a quick shower and to consider, yet again, what to say and what to hold back. He might need to tell all to get her cooperation; he wanted to, anyway, always had, but it might have the opposite effect. In which case, not only would Gladiator's case remain unresolved but he would be left for the rest of his life with the sense of something incomplete, an unfinished conversation. There would never be a better time or better reason to tell her everything, but there was also the rest of her life, and he had done enough to that already. By the time he set off he was late, and feeling as if he were taking a loaded gun to the meeting.

8

Until that afternoon in the custody suite, the last time he had seen Sarah had been in Dublin. The file recorded the meeting but not, once again, the whole story. The essence of that was recorded but elsewhere.

The clue was a handwritten list inside the front cover of the first volume. It gave the numbers of related files, some of them general subject or policy files; others the personal files of terrorists on whom Gladiator reported. Among them was a file numbered in a series of general files on operational techniques, but which was in fact an RS annex. RS – refer to security – meant that any request to see it would go to the head of security, who would reply blandly that it referred to old operational techniques or equipment developed specifically for that case and no longer applicable. The annex itself was further protected by an access card saying that only the Chief, the head of security, Sonia and Charles could have or grant access to it.

Charles, going through the list, recognised the number. He knew what it contained, having written most of it, and decided to send for it only later, as a memory check. He intended a painstaking excavation of the past, careful neither to destroy nor rudely awaken. But his arrest changed that.

Sarah had arranged Charles's first meeting with the student, Martin Worth, for early one evening in her Dublin teaching room. She was to tell Martin – not yet honoured with his codename – that her husband had suggested he should talk to someone who worked on terrorism. Charles was to rehearse the meeting with Sarah in her room beforehand, then leave and reappear after Martin arrived.

She answered his knock almost too promptly and was standing by her desk when he entered.

'Sorry if I'm early.'

'I was only marking papers.'

Both smiled because they had spoken at once. She made tea while he sat and took a pristine A4 pad from his briefcase. She had to ask whether he took milk or sugar. He couldn't recall whether she did, either.

'I'll use another name with Martin,' he said.

'Why?'

'In case he changes his mind and goes and tells the IRA.'

'Well, he knows mine and I'm as deeply implicated as you. I have a job here. They could knock me off anytime.'

'I know. I didn't want to but my office is insisting.'

'It's too late. I've already told him your name.'

'That's fine, then. We're in it together.'

She paused, holding the kettle. 'Sorry, I should've thought. Is it really all right? I don't want to be responsible for your murder. Would your office want you not to meet him, if they knew?'

'They might. They're incurably cautious. If they knew.'

Over tea he went through with her what he would say to Martin – the need for understanding and knowledge, for mutual confidentiality, insistence that this could not be any sort of exchange or negotiation, arrangements for future contacts not involving Sarah.

'It would be ideal if you could leave us alone for five minutes while I arrange to see him again. It would help distance you from me.'

'Wouldn't that look contrived?'

'Not if we don't contrive it. I'll simply ask.'

'I hadn't really thought about danger until you mentioned it. Could it be dangerous for Nigel, too?'

'Not if Martin's as you described. Swinging back the other way would mean repudiating the death of his army friend.' Assuming that were true. There was still no answer from the Ministry of Defence on the background of the dead officer; also, tracing of Martin himself was incomplete. There was still no proof that he was who he said he was.

'He might change his mind if the army killed one of his IRA friends.'

'True.'

'How are your parents and your sister?' she asked after a pause.

'My parents died, my father first. But my sister thrives. Married, three children.'

'I'm sorry about your father. I was rather fond of him.'

'And he of you. I think he fancied you. You raised my status in his eyes.'

He was about to ask after her parents when she said, 'Did you ever tell them – your parents?'

He was surprised she mentioned it, having decided he wouldn't this time, that he would keep to business. 'No, nor my sister.'

He did not add that they had clearly hoped that you were it, that you were the one, that we would marry. Their reticence had been eloquent when he told them it was all over. He remembered his mother was sitting by the fire and had just put on her reading glasses when he announced it, as if merely in passing, while looking for his copy of *Exchange & Mart*.

His mother took off her glasses and stared at him. 'Oh dear, Charles. That's very sad.'

He didn't trust himself to continue. 'I'm sure I was reading it in the kitchen, but it's not there.'

'It's very sad, it really is. She's such a lovely girl. I thought she was very fond of you.'

'Maybe I left it in the bathroom.'

She saw through his affected casualness, of course, and for weeks afterwards he could feel her silently longing for him to talk about it, but he never said any more. He had always been good at not talking. Too good, perhaps.

'Your parents were very understanding about it, weren't they?' he said to Sarah. 'More than. Are they still alive?'

She nodded. 'Just about. Dad's beginning to get a bit doddery. It's only as I've got older that I've appreciated how understanding they were. Of course, attitudes have changed and things are much easier now, but then it was different. I'm sure their religion helped. They believed – believe – in forgiveness and in helping others. I'd quite forgotten – it was probably seeing you the other week that reminded me – that they offered to bring him up. That was a big thing then.'

'Big thing to forget, too.' There was another pause. 'Theirs has been a good marriage, hasn't it?'

Her eyes widened, as if surprised at the thought, or surprised that he should say it. 'Yes, it has, I think it has,' she said. 'They're very gentle, very devoted.'

He felt he ought to get the conversation back to the professional. 'You're sure you're okay about Martin, happy with it all?'

She sipped her tea. 'Happy if you are. Hadn't you better be going soon? He's due in fifteen minutes.'

For half an hour he walked the streets of Dublin, noting brush contact sites, meeting places, anti-surveillance routes, while trying to decide what he thought about the city. It had been a forbidden city when he had been in Belfast with the army, and therefore an alluring imagined playground of Georgian squares, dark elaborate Victorian bars, foaming black and cream pints of Guinness, wonderful talk from *Ulysses* and, somewhere, somehow, a beautiful, exciting and magically attainable actress from the Abbey Theatre.

That was then. The real Dublin, the contemporary Dublin, seemed to be a place of tourists, chain stores and sturdy beggars. Many of the Georgian squares had been vandalised by developers and there were estates as uninviting as any in London. He forgot to imagine the actress.

As he knocked on Sarah's door Charles was filled with the familiar reluctance to re-engage, the desire to prolong floating and dreaming that always, with him, preceded action. It no longer bothered him; he knew it would evaporate as soon as he opened the door.

Martin Worth was taller than Charles, with thick hair the colour of rust, grey-green eyes and freckles. He wore the usual student uniform of jeans, a jumper and a drab shapeless jacket. He stood to shake hands, his grip firm and brief.

Charles went through the introductory remarks he had planned, then the warning London insisted upon about the need for confidentiality because of how their contact could be construed.

Martin cut him short. 'You mean my friends would think I was spying for the British.'

Charles had not mentioned spying. Some agents thrilled to the word, others would never confront it. He looked Martin in the eye. 'That's exactly what they'd think. And if they thought it was true they'd torture and murder you.'

'And how would you describe what I was doing?'

It was an unusual question, so early on. Sarah sat motionless, side-on to her desk. They should not really be talking like this before her but he noticed Martin glancing at her once or twice, as if to make sure of her witness. 'That depends on what we do. If our meetings are secret and you tell me secrets then you are my agent or spy and I am your case officer.'

'And who are you exactly – James Bond and M and MI5 and George Smiley all rolled up together?' Martin smiled as if to soften his mockery, but not very much.

Declaring yourself as MI6 in your own name, without approval, in an allied country in which you were operating without the knowledge of the government, to a virtually unknown putative agent whose loyalty was not established, was forbidden. Anything which might embarrass Her Majesty's Government required Foreign Office approval and being caught operating in Dublin would certainly be construed as embarrassing. It had happened some years before and the MI6 officer was released only after prime ministerial intervention. Charles knew very well what his response should be: confirm nothing and refer back for advice.

'MI6,' said Charles.

'Not sure I know the difference.'

Later, Charles dutifully recorded all this for the file. Since all went well and HMG was not embarrassed, no-one scolded him. What the file did not record was the impression Martin made of someone more mature, more decided, less impulsive than the young man Sarah had described. At one point her questioning eyes indicated the door. Charles shook his head. If Martin was prepared to be so frank before her, he probably wanted her there. Unless it was a set-up and he was secretly recording them both. But it was too late to worry about that.

'Why do you want to spy for the British?' Charles asked.

Martin shook his head and pushed his hair back. 'I don't *want* to spy for the bloody British. I don't even like them. Well, institutionally, if you know what I mean. Individually, I've no problem. I'm half British myself. But it's the Brits in Ireland I don't like.'

'So why spy for them?'

'You trying to persuade me not to?' He glanced again at Sarah. 'There was an incident a while ago which made me think a bit. You may have heard about it.'

'In outline. Tell me.'

He described meeting his school-friend at the checkpoint, then the reactions of his colleagues to his friend's death. He spoke without dramatisation, indicating rather than dwelling on his own feelings. 'Jokes about legless Brit stiffs in two-foot coffins and all that. Then the breaking of the ceasefire. Got me thinking.' He concluded with a statement that sounded prepared: 'I do not approve of British occupation of or control over any part of the island of Ireland, but nor do I believe violence is the way to end it. I therefore want to do what I çan to increase mutual understanding, so that the republican movement and the British government can talk to each other and sort something out.'

'I can't engage in any sort of negotiation.'

'And I can't promise to answer all your questions. There are things and people I'm not prepared to talk about.'

'So long as you tell me, that's fine. If you don't know something, or don't want to talk about it, just say. Don't mislead.'

They stared at each other.

Sarah stood. 'Sorry, must go to the loo.'

While she was out Charles took Martin's contact details, gave him a London number and suggested they meet the following week in the bar of Jury's, where he'd met Sarah. 'I take it we're not likely to run into any of your friends? So long as you can think of a plausible reason for being there.'

'No problem.'

'What reason? What would it be?'

'You're very thorough, Mr Thoroughgood.'

'It's your life.'

'Yours too. I'd say I was meeting my British uncle who's over here on business.'

'Okay. We'll agree on what my business is when we meet.'

This much the file recorded. There was a good deal of minuting between Charles's account of their first meeting and his account of their second a week later. The A desk queried the extent of Martin's access, his genuineness and the security of running him in Dublin. There were unanswered questions about his background, as full tracing details were still awaited. His offer of service was suspiciously complete, the security officer commented, but willing agents with access to the republican leadership in Dublin were not two-a-penny. The case could go ahead.

After that first meeting, Charles rang Sarah's study from his hotel but there was no answer, and he did not have the number of the friend with whom she stayed. The phone rang when he was in his bath. He jumped out to get it, dripping, assuming it was the office.

She sounded nervous. 'I'm sorry. You don't mind me ringing you? Only you gave me this name and number. It's all right, is it? It's okay?'

'Of course, of course it's okay.'

'I thought you'd want to hear how he was after you left. He thought you were a typical British army officer type. His words. He asked whether you'd been in the army and I said I didn't know. Was that right?'

'Am I typical?'

'Well.' She laughed. 'I doubt he's very familiar with them, despite his friend.'

'I've never thought of myself as typical.'

'Don't lose sleep over it. You're the same as you always were, even before you joined the army.'

'I guess that's all right, then.'

'Not necessarily.'

Martin seemed content with the meeting. He had said nothing about his arrangement with Charles for the following week, which was good. 'But he did say one slightly surprising thing,' she continued. 'He asked how long we'd known each other. I was evasive and just said we'd met at Nigel's request. That was right, wasn't it? But I'm not sure he believed me.'

'Why not?'

'Because then he said, "Funny, I had the impression you already knew each other." I don't know what made him think that.'

The thought pleased Charles. 'Intuition.'

'Yes, but – anyway, it's not a problem, is it?'

'Not at all.' His answer hung in the air. He felt that neither of them knew how to end the conversation. 'How about dinner?'

'Sorry. Work. Papers to mark.'

She sounded decided. He took her friend's number, needlessly adding 'for future reference', which made him feel that the conversation ended on an unwelcome official note. He dined alone in the hotel.

9

Walking briskly towards Pimlico after his release that evening, Charles tried not to think any more about what he would say to Sarah. Successful meetings – even those that were purely social, which this was not – usually went the way of those who knew what they wanted, who planned and rehearsed, who prepared their spontaneity. He didn't want to do that with her, yet he knew that what he wanted to tell her, and what he wanted of her, meant using her, meant calculation. It made him uncomfortable.

He had chosen to walk because walking was better for thinking, but his thoughts were about the past, about everything that led up to what he was about to do. It was a form of preparation, but at least it was not planning.

He had certainly planned his first solo meeting in Dublin with Martin. It was to begin in Jury's and then move on. He had recce'd several restaurants and bars, seeking good table separation and, in terms of Martin being entertained by his notional businessman uncle, plausibility. Martin arrived wearing clean black jeans and a new-looking blue jersey. Charles asked if he'd like to move on straightaway or have a drink first.

'Always drink when you can. You never know how long till the next one,' he said. 'So my father used to say and he wasn't even Irish.'

'Tell me about your parents. Is your father dead, then?'

'Dead and doubtless very thirsty. He was a lawyer. A cursed breed which I guess I'm destined to continue.'

After a while Charles realised that Martin was enjoying the novelty of Jury's, and guessed he was hungry. Table separation in the restaurant was good, so they stayed.

They chose steak and claret. While they waited Martin lit another cigarette. 'So what do you want to know?' he asked quietly.

Reading it in the file recently, Charles found that those words still had the power to make his skin tingle. It was an unusual question at the start of an agent relationship; often you had to work for such directness. But when you did hear it, you went for it: no generalities, no hypotheticals, no holding anything back for later. There might not be a later. He remembered looking into Martin's grey-green eyes and thinking it was like dealing with a fellow professional, or at least a natural.

'Operational detail, names, addresses, telephone numbers, plans, who said what to whom, when, where, who else was there, who told you, who told him, everything you can think of. Nothing is too small.'

'I don't know any of that, I'm not in the IRA, Sarah should have told you that. I'm on the political side. What I know about is structures, policies, politics, that sort of thing.'

'Identities? Personalities?'

'Some.'

They paused while the waitress brought their first courses. Martin stubbed out his half-smoked cigarette. With one bob of his Adam's apple, he finished the Guinness he had brought in from the bar and picked up his claret. 'And what in return?'

Surprised, Charles misunderstood. 'What do you want?'

'Nothing. I told you, I'm not going to be a spy. I thought I'd made that plain. I want to help bring about some sort of reconciliation, and I want to see how whatever I tell you will do that. I'm not going to feed the Brits information just so that their occupying army can lift more people, or kill them. I want to see how what I'm doing contributes to progress.'

He spoke quietly but with energy. The normal response would have been reassurance – of course he wasn't a spy. He was a sympathetic but objective observer who could give confidential advice to help Charles nudge his government in the right direction and increase understanding, a different thing altogether. That was the off-the-shelf explanation, stocked by intelligence services world-wide.

But it wouldn't do with Martin. He had put his cards on the table and deserved equal frankness, even if it meant an upturned table and cards in the air. Better that than risk both their lives on an unsatisfactory case.

'And I thought I'd made it plain you would be spying,' said Charles. 'If you tell me what your friends wouldn't want the British government to know, you'd be spying. That's what they'd call it, regardless of your motives. And I'm interested only in what they wouldn't want me to know. Secrets, telling secrets, that's what spying is.'

They stared at each other.

In for a penny, in for a pound, Charles was thinking. This had to be sorted out. 'I can't promise you'd get anything out of it,' he continued, 'beyond the satisfaction of doing it. If you get that. If you want money we'd pay you, but you say you don't. If you want to revenge yourself on your republican friends, well, you'd be doing just that. But I don't get the impression that's what motivates you.'

Martin's features were unreadable. 'What do you think motivates me, then?'

'I don't know. I know what you said about your school-friend and about the end of the ceasefire but they both sound more like triggers than the full account. Principle seems important to you. You are republican because of principle rather than family tradition or social conformity. If you were to spy I suspect you'd be doing that through principle, too. And if I had to guess I'd say your principle was that terrorist violence can't be justified in a democracy.'

'You're calling the Six Counties a democracy?'

'If a majority of the electorate voted for unification with the Republic, that's what they'd have.'

'So I'd be a principled spy? Spying for principle?'

'Maybe you'd get a kick out of it, too. Maybe you'd enjoy it.'

Martin stared at Charles, his elbows on the table and the fingertips of both hands lightly cradling his claret. 'Is that why you do it?'

'Partly. I do enjoy it. It's exciting, sometimes. And the people are interesting. As are the circumstances in which you meet them.'

'Is that it, then? No principle?'

'Patriotism, I guess.'

Martin grinned. 'Is that enough?'

'Enough for me.'

Back in the bar afterwards Martin drew with his fore-finger on the table the new power structures within Provisional Sinn Fein and the IRA. These were well known to Charles, but he was appreciative and encouraging. They moved on to policies and personalities, which were more interesting. Charles asked if he could take notes.

Martin lit another cigarette. 'Write a bloody book if you want.'

There was enough for two reports: CX reports as they were known, for historical reasons only dimly apprehended by most of those who wrote them. Enough to help silence the doubters in Head Office, Charles hoped.

Over the next few months Martin involved himself more deeply in the republican cause and reported with disciplined enthusiasm. He never joined the IRA itself but he was politically useful to it, particularly in helping to spread propaganda and support among overseas student organisations. One or two of the IRA leadership confided in him following his suggestions for fundraising, usefully enhancing his knowledge of Provisional strategy. Some of his reports went to Downing Street.

Once he reported on a London bombing team. He did not know their names, but was told by one of their trainers that there was a group of eight from whom four would be chosen; then, separately by someone else, that the favoured four would be informed of their selection in a bar in Drogheda, north of Dublin.

He reported this to Charles late one night in a noisy pub. He had learned it earlier in the evening and the team was to meet the following lunchtime. 'I could go up there myself,' he said. 'Sit in the bar, see who comes and goes. I won't get names, unless I recognise them, but I'll have descriptions. Only I don't have a car and don't know how far it is from the station. Look odd if I took a taxi or hired a car. I never do that. Could you lend me one? Any old Aston Martin will do.'

'The Astons are all out but even if they weren't you mustn't go. If anyone recognises you or if either of your sources gets to hear about it they'll put two and two together.'

'Disappointingly risk-averse, Mr Bond.'

'We'll work something else out.'

'Tell that to the marines. I bet you do nothing.' He held up his empty glass.

Charles had to wait at the bar for their drinks. The recent Manchester bombing meant that the identities of the next cell would be top of the requirements list. He wanted very much to be the dog that brought home the bone but doubted that anything could be done in time, despite his optimism with Martin. The clearance hoops the A desk would have to go through in London would be formidable. No-one liked a hastily-scrambled operation with toxic political fall-out if it went wrong, not to mention the obvious physical risks. But the prospect of more blood and broken glass on English streets would argue strongly for it. If the office wouldn't go for it, he would do it himself.

It was late when he returned to his hotel. His only secure communication was via telegram from the embassy but it would attract attention if he called out the comcen staff late at night. Anyway, no-one in Head Office was going to take that kind of decision in the early hours; it would need ministerial clearance. But he had reason to visit the embassy during working hours, as part of his cover, and so he broke the rules by drafting his telegram in his room and hiding it while he slept. He called on the embassy as soon as it opened, typed his telegram straight onto the cipher machine and sent it at second highest precedence.

Head Office came back promptly. The answer was polite, considered, clear and firm, a competent piece of work by the senior A desk officer. They thanked Charles for his proposal, which they were naturally keen to follow up, but there were insurmountable problems. In the time available it would be impossible to deploy a surveillance team with a reasonable chance of success and assurance of their safety;

there would be no time for a recce and no time for political clearance, which would be essential. If the Drogheda bar was a regular meeting point then a recce could be conducted in slower time – perhaps by Charles himself during one of his visits – but on this occasion, regretfully, the risks were too great. A failed operation or one that went off at half-cock would be worse than no operation at all. And it should not be forgotten that the news of this meeting was from a single source only, and a new one on trial at that.

It was the response Charles expected, one he could have written himself – probably would have, he conceded, if he had been the desk officer. But it was not how things got done, and he wanted to do things.

He ran upstairs to chancery. Angie, the secretary, was on the phone and everyone else was conveniently in the ambassador's weekly meeting. Charles went to the open cupboard and found the Pentax he knew they kept there, with several rolls of film. He mimed asking permission to take it, then left the room before Angie could finish her call. In town he found the nearest car-hire firm, chose a small Ford van and set off north to Drogheda.

His report was factual and precise. The bar faced the road with a single main entrance and a car park to the front and side. Opposite, on a raised bank above the road, was the car park for the local hospital. Charles drove in there and backed the van into a space from which its rear windows looked directly down to the bar entrance. It was far from ideal – the distance was too great and the windows would blur the film – but anything on the next bombing team was better than nothing. There was a reasonable chance he'd be sacked for this, he remembered thinking. Would he mind, he had asked himself? Yes, very much. Better an honourable dismissal than a career of unblemished bureaucratic caution. But he would mind.

For two hours he photographed everyone who entered or left until he ran out of film. Twice he heard voices near the van and stretched out, feigning sleep. Once he froze when two men came out of the bar and stood talking, seemingly looking directly at him across the road. If he'd been spotted and others were coming round the back to seize him, that would be it. He lay on his back, eyes half-closed, his heart thumping. Nothing happened. It was the only time he worried more about being caught than being sacked.

Recently he had found the black and white prints and negatives in an envelope in the file. Some were too blurred, all were distant and grainy, but most were just good enough to confirm an identity already suspected. The file showed that they had been passed to Special Branch in London, who had dismissed them. He remembered his disappointment. Later in the file there were blow-ups of some, allied with possible names from other sources, then, eventually, brief references to the identification and capture of the ASU, the active service unit. Finally, briefest of all, there was a cursory acknowledgement from Special Branch that Gladiator's information and Charles's photos had led directly to the identification of two of the bombers, with the other two identified subsequently through association.

But that was later, after Gladiator had left Ireland. At the time no-one doubted that Charles's initiative had failed. There was minuting accusing him of irresponsible opportunism, with someone from security suggesting he was out of control and should be reprimanded and withdrawn from operations. He had assumed that that was his fate when he was summoned one day by the controller for operations in Europe. It was the first time he had met Matthew Abrahams.

Matthew stared severely over his reading glasses, without inviting Charles to sit. 'You disobeyed your orders, you deceived the office, you put the government, the service, your agent and yourself at grave risk. All that can be said in your favour is that you have not attempted to excuse yourself.'

'I'm sorry it didn't work.'

'That's irrelevant.' Matthew's grey-blue eyes held his unwaveringly. 'Personnel are expecting me to recommend a formal reprimand. In most circumstances I would. But I am reminded of Churchill's dictum to the effect that mistakes made in carrying the battle to the enemy are forgivable.'

Charles began to relax.

'Though not forgettable.' There was a hint of something else in Matthew's eyes. 'If you sin again, sin in company. Responsibility is shared. Bureaucracies find that easier to deal with. Discuss it with someone, make sure someone knows where you are. Even a phone call.'

'Thank you.'

Matthew gave him the briefest of wintry smiles. 'Pity it didn't work.'

Nothing more was said or written about it. Because it had failed, Charles allowed Martin to assume that nothing had been done. 'You're all cloak and no dagger, you lot,' said Martin at their next meeting. When Charles told him later that it had worked after all, he formally thanked him on Matthew Abrahams's orders. Charles himself was never thanked.

The file also showed that Head Office remained uneasy about Martin's motivation. He seemed almost too perfect an agent, someone wrote: punctual, reliable, security conscious, distinguishing in his reports between what he knew and what he assessed or assumed, and usually naming his sub-sources. Yet there was a sense of something un-explained in his motivation, of boxes not ticked, unsettling to the bureaucratic mind. Had Martin been venal, disaffected or ideologically opposed to his cause, Head Office would have been happier. But he accepted no money other than reimbursed expenses, disliked relatively few of his republican colleagues and continued to believe in a united Ireland. Security thought it suspiciously like running another intelligence officer and speculated as to whether he could be a double agent.

Charles had to defend the case while trying to appear objective, since case officers were notorious for siding with their agents. With the exception of the Drogheda ASU, Martin's intelligence had proved reliable and his account of the death of his British Army school-friend was confirmed, as was the time and place of the checkpoint at which they recognised each other. Martin's presence in the car had been logged. At the same time, Charles had to play down how much he liked Martin, liked him for his conscientiousness, his irony, his intellectual poise, his disciplined adherence to unparaded principles. He liked him too for his occasional refusals, for being honest where most would have been evasive.

Once, when asked to name a fellow-student who had just joined the movement, Martin said: 'I'm not telling you that. I don't think he's serious, I think he's just being led on by a bit of heroic talk and glamour. He's not a natural hater and I think he'll drop out pretty soon. I don't want his name on your list for evermore, especially if he's no longer involved.'

'Just tell me if he does get seriously involved.'

Security argued this as evidence of Gladiator's lack of commitment; Charles that it showed reassuring honesty.

He liked Martin too for his reserve. As with Matthew Abrahams, personal matters were conveyed via elliptical shorthand.

'Women?' asked Charles, one evening after they had finished business.

'As and when. Depending. Yourself?'

'The same.'

'Sarah?'

It was not the first time Martin had teased him about her. 'She's her husband's, not mine.'

'But you'd like her to be.'

Charles smiled despite himself. 'What makes you think that?'

'Intuition, genius.'

They usually met in hotel rooms; occasionally in bars or restaurants where Charles played the part of visiting uncle. He always stayed in a hotel other than that in which they met, walking the streets facing traffic so that it would be harder for a car to pull up and bundle him in. They communicated as little as possible outside meetings and when they did, it was by phone under cover of family arrangements. Few documents came Martin's way and those that did were not urgent, so there was usually no need for dead letter boxes. For a heady few weeks, however, Martin was asked to drive various senior republicans in the evenings, which gave him the chance of prolonged chats and the possibility of intelligence that would not wait for the next meeting.

'Can't you give me a concealed mike?' he asked. 'Then I could leave cassettes for you to pick up in secret places, like real spies.'

Charles promised him one, only to find that the technical department was unaccountably lacking in portable concealed devices, whether cameras or recorders. Affronted by Charles's obvious dismay, they offered to wire up the car, which would be much more effective. But Martin drove vehicles borrowed for the night without knowing in advance which he would get. Eventually all Charles had to offer him was a bulky cassette recorder disguised as a fat diary which could just be squeezed into the wallet pocket of a jacket.

'I'd be better off with a house-brick,' said Martin.

'Weighs the same, and I'm more likely to have one of those in my hand than wear a Harris tweed jacket to carry it in, for Christ's sake. They must think I'm like you.'

He took it, however, and recorded half a dozen conversations over the next few weeks. For transferring cassettes Charles chose lavatory cisterns in bars or hotels used by students, with the cassette taped to the underside of the lid. Each time he cleared one he paused before lifting it, his fingertips hooked over the sides, lightly feeling the weight. Each time he rehearsed once again the unlikelihood of Martin betraying him, or of having the location beaten out of him. In that case, they might wire it up so that lifting the lid would be the last thing he did. And each time he failed to think any profound last thoughts, because each time there was no intense white flash, no oblivion, only the neat little package, securely taped.

Heady days, he had thought as he leafed through the file, years later. But not only for that reason.

10

He cut through to the King's Road on his way to Pimlico that night. The pubs and food shops were thronged, traffic was at a standstill and there was a fine drizzle, just enough to wet the pavements. He imagined his Scottish house; dusk would be more advanced there, with a leaden sea silvered by a strip of light on the horizon and wavelets lapping the rocks. That would be all. There was a time when, in the midst of city life, he longed to be there. Now he was not so sure. The early evening bustle was cheering, he was rediscovering his liking for crowds and he was stepping out to see someone. You could do that in a city. He imagined Sarah at that moment, putting on her coat, hurrying from the office, dashing back to check something, hurrying away again. He slowed his pace. He was in good time for Pimlico, time to take another deep breath and submerge himself in the past.

Whenever he recalled that bright morning when he had made the discovery, he was struck by the limited part played by facts in the sense of an individual past. Facts were like longitude on a map, measurements of temporal relativity, evoking but not containing the myriad associations, tones, colours, remarks, incidents, feelings that formed the patchwork brocade of a life. It was they that drenched and infused the memory that was the person. Also, there were always gaps among facts, missing longitudinal lines whose absence was invisible to the reader, crucial to the participant.

That morning, the blinds in his eleventh-floor office in Century House, the old MI6 head office in Lambeth, were lowered against the sun. He shared the office with two others, one of whom was ringing his girlfriend while the other was trying to persuade Alison, their Scottish secretary, to bring him coffee from the secretaries' room.

'What's it worth?' she kept asking in joshing Glaswegian. She had untidy dark hair and laughing eyes. 'Come on, Paul, cough up, put your money where your mouth is.'

Negotiations continued, but Charles was no longer listening. Among the sheaf of papers Alison had just dumped in his in-tray was a copy of Martin Worth's birth certificate. Attached to it was a note from Vetting explaining that tracing had been delayed because the subject had been adopted and his current name was not his birth name. Charles was asked to send the certificate on to Registry for filing.

He remembered holding it and noticing that it was quite still in his hand. He stared at the name, James Bourne, at the name of the mother, Sarah Bourne, at the line struck through where the father's name should have been. The blinds rattled in the breeze, Alison told Paul to come off it, somebody laughed in the corridor, and Charles went on staring. The coincidence was too great, almost too great to be credible; yet there it was, a sliver of bureaucracy, a pink form completed in black ink in a clear round hand.

His first, self-centred, reaction was a quiver of resentment at his exclusion. Perhaps she had meant to protect his identity, though he would not have minded about that; he was not ashamed. More likely she had wanted to deny him.

He remembered the blinds dappling sun and shade across the back of Paul's white shirt, the triumphant twirl of Alison's skirt as she left the room with a promise of cakes. He tried to think what might be the consequences for the case, whether to tell the office, how it would react, whether to tell Sarah, whether to tell Martin, how he would feel meeting him again. Was it possible that Martin already knew about Sarah? He had every right to see his own birth certificate. But he wouldn't have known his mother's married name without further enquiry, and if he had discovered it he would surely have said something by now.

Footsteps and voices in the corridor heralded the weekly section meeting. Charles's phone rang and he ignored it, knowing that by convention the caller would ring off after three rings. He remembered thinking, as the others left for the meeting, how busy people were with things of temporary consequence and ultimate futility, how there would come a time when nothing of what this piece of paper said would matter to anyone. And how if this didn't matter, nothing mattered. That was worse. His thoughts returned to Sarah, to whether he would tell her. It was she, more than Martin, he thought of then.

They saw a little of each other during his Dublin visits, but only enough – apart from one occasion – to be useful as cover activity and as a check on Martin. Each time they parted she said he must come to dinner again in London. He realised she did not share his attitude to the past. For her it was water under the bridge, something of no contemporary consequence, not something to be siphoned and examined. A supremely practical attitude, he conceded, but one he was incapable of achieving. For him the past informed and enabled the present, it was the only way it could be understood. He remembered his relief at finding, as he began to see more of her in Dublin, that what he had liked in her in the past, he liked still. It had not all been wasted.

In fact, it was a period in which he saw more of Nigel than of her. They both attended Current Intelligence Group meetings in the Cabinet Office. Charles's interests did not overlap with Nigel's European Commission work, but there were occasions when they coincided.

One CIG was held in the Treasury Board Room, a domed, ornate eighteenth century masterpiece with a throne last used by George III and a large circular oak table within a table. Nigel came over to Charles as soon as he entered.

'Hoped you'd be here. Something I want to ask you.'

'You've got a bit of custard cream on your lower lip.'

'Thanks. Always trust you for a correction, Thoroughgood.' He wiped his mouth with a red handkerchief that matched his braces and socks. 'Completely over the top, this room, isn't it? Perpetuates delusions of imperial grandeur.'

'Probably why I like it.'

'You don't change, do you? Still driving around in ancient British cars in honour of the ancient British motor industry? Just as it's all going down the tube, whatever our leaders like to think.' He rested his elbow on one of the Georgian chairs and drew closer, lowering his voice. 'No, but what I wanted to ask you about is this business of spying on friends. The principle of it, whether we should be doing it at all.'

Charles hesitated. 'All the people I've spied on have been enemies.'

'Of course, on the Russian or terrorist side it's straight-forward. But even there it's not entirely straightforward, is it? I guess – well, I know from Sarah – that one at least of your operations is in the Republic of Ireland, a European Community partner. I know you're spying on the IRA, not the Irish government, but our Irish partners wouldn't be too pleased if they caught you at it, would they? Trespassing on their patch, fishing in their waters. Lot of embarrassment potential.'

'They wouldn't, no.'

'What I wanted to ask was, do we spy on other EC part-ners? France, for example. I'm talking to the French at the moment, you see, about these amendments to the Maastricht Treaty. They're being straight with us. What worries me is, are we doing the same? I mean, if knowledge of what you're doing in Ireland came out they'd assume we might do it in France too, mightn't they? Maybe even doing it *to* them, against them, whether we are or not. D'you follow me? Of course, we'd brazen it out in the usual way but we'd have to choose our words very carefully, if we were doing it. D'you follow me?'

Charles followed him in one sense, while physically trying to back away. Nigel lacked any understanding of the distance people normally keep from one another, and must never have noticed that his interlocutors were forever in retreat. Charles wondered whether Sarah had told him about it. 'I don't know what the European controllerate gets up to,' he said. 'I've never worked in it. So far as I know, it's only liaison.'

'No operations at all?'

'Doubt it. Though they may do joint operations with European partners against third parties. But I don't know. It's not my area.'

Nigel drew closer, forcing Charles back against the long-case clock. The room was not warm, but there were tiny beads of perspiration on his upper lip. 'Could you find out? I mean, it's a clear case of need-to-know. The negotiating team needs to know if there's a potential Pooh-trap ahead of us, come the day when we're caught spying on one of our closest allies.'

'Ask your head of department. He'd know, because he'd see the product if there were any.'

Nigel's bulbous dark eyes were fixed on his. 'You mean there could be intelligence product that we in the third room don't see?'

'I've no idea. But it can happen with need-to-know stuff. Sometimes not even the head of department sees it.'

Charles was spared further interrogation by the start of the meeting. He did not think much about the episode afterwards, putting it down to Nigel's ambition to be in on everything.

When Charles discovered Martin's paternity he said nothing to anyone at first. Instead of sending it off for filing, he kept the birth certificate in his in-tray. He was waiting to feel. Each day he looked again at the certificate, buried beneath other papers, each day waiting for some lurch of feeling, some revelation, something. But each day passed and work went on, just as before he had known about it. Normality was like gravity, forever pulling everything back into itself, so pervasive as to be imperceptible. Martin must know he was adopted – it was a condition of adoption – and his having never mentioned it perhaps meant that it was not an issue. He referred to his parents only occasionally but always quite naturally, like anyone else. Unless he didn't talk about it because it was too big an issue, too personal or even shameful.

With regard to Sarah, Charles was clearer: unless she indicated otherwise, he would not trouble her by bringing back into her life something she had successfully put behind her.

His new knowledge sharpened his eagerness for the next meeting with Martin. It should be routine, business as usual, though he knew he would study Martin's physiognomy and demeanour, searching for signs, marks, mannerisms, would perhaps tangentially probe his family background. In the event there was no time.

Martin entered the hotel room with a broad smile but no words. He helped himself to a can of beer, flopped into an armchair and put his feet on the coffee-table. He was wearing new trainers. Charles raised his eyebrows, surreptitiously searching for likenesses. Martin had Sarah's eyes, he could see that now. Maybe his hair was a thicker version of Charles's when he was younger. Martin emptied most of the can.

'You should be proud of me. I've been a good student, done just what teacher wanted. You'll never guess.'

Charles helped himself to a beer.

'You know you're always telling me to watch to see if I'm being followed, all that James Bond anti-surveillance stuff? Except that Bond would never do it on buses. It may surprise you that sometimes I do.'

Charles felt his stomach contract even as he smiled. He guessed what was coming.

'I did today, and definitely I was being followed. There was a couple, a man and a woman, at the end of my road when I came out, just hanging about, you know, not obviously doing anything. They'd been dropped off by a car round the corner – I have the attic bedroom with a view into the next street and was looking out to see if it was going to rain. I saw them get out of it. Some sort of Ford, blue. Later, when I was out and walking towards them for the bus, they turned and walked ahead of me, crossing the road before I got to them. I stopped at the bus-stop and they carried on walking. Then they crossed back again, both looking round, and carried on walking out of sight round the bend. I got the bus and they got on at the next stop. I was tempted to go and ask for their tickets. They got off where I did, at the bottom of O'Connell Street, so then I did what you've been saying – you know, open spaces, crowded places, open spaces, crowded places, to see if they kept hurrying forward and dropping back. They did, both of them. They must be Garda Special Branch. So guess how I lost them.'

'You're sure you did?'

'Sure as sure. Chuck another beer and I'll tell you.'

Charles threw a can across the bed, silently planning what to say if the Garda burst through the door. Any cover would be thin to the point of transparency, but any cover was better than none. So long as you stuck to it. 'Why are you so sure they're Garda? Why should they be following you?'

'For the company I keep. They're hotter on the Provos down here now, I keep telling you. And the heavies I keep company with – on your behalf – some get followed, some get lifted. Maybe they wanted to see if I was meeting someone interesting today, someone they're looking for.'

It was possible that Martin was imagining it, but he wasn't usually fanciful or fearful. In which case either it was coincidence that he had been on the Garda surveillance list that day or they must have been tapping his phone and knew he was going to meet someone. They wouldn't know who or where, because the place had been agreed at the last meeting and neither Martin nor Charles used names on the phone. So surveillance was the only way to find out.

'How did you lose them?' Charles asked.

Martin grinned again. 'I walked straight into the Garda headquarters with a fake query and then left by another door, but not before I'd seen them being asked for their passes. Embarrassing, having to search their own headquarters for their quarry. My heart bleeds.'

There were voices and footsteps in the corridor. Charles was about to speak but stopped, waiting for the knock. 'If they burst in here now and lift us both,' he said as the voices faded, 'we stick to the cover we agreed. The family cover. Okay? You've broken no law, they can't keep you. Nor me. Not for long, anyway. They might have all the suspicions in the world, but unless we confess to something there's nothing that will stand up in court. We've done nothing that breaks Irish state law. Remember that.'

'Getting lifted would be good for me. Masses of street cred.'

'Not if the Garda let it be known to your Provo friends that you were with me, it wouldn't.'

They got on with the business, but this time Charles took no notes, in case he was arrested afterwards. Waiting for room service, he made Martin repeat the episode in detail. Plenty of people imagined they were being followed; not only agents who had been warned they might be, but the innocently anxious, the egotistical and the credulous. Once you thought surveillance possible you began to see it everywhere. But Martin's account was persuasive.

Before they parted Charles arranged time and place of the next meeting, so there would be no need for contact. But he wasn't sure there would be one. It would depend on the A desk.

Later, in his room in the Chesham, Charles had leisure to probe once more his feelings about his own flesh and blood, and again found little to probe. The only connection between the man before him and the baby on whom he had once laid his finger was an intellectual construct: the knowledge that the one had become the other. The thought that this man was flesh of his flesh, bone of his bone, was simply that: a thought. It could lead to wonder, to incredulity, to curiosity, but carried with it no particular emotion. They might have passed their lives in daily contact and never guessed. It was knowing that made the difference, though it was still not clear what the difference might be.

After he returned to London the A desk forbade any more meetings until Martin could travel to the UK. Charles argued that their next meeting should be safe, since no further contacts were needed to arrange it; and anyway, it was necessary to agree future, changed, contacts. The file showed him winning the argument, until Special Branch had got in touch to say they had been asked by the Garda SB to help trace an Englishman who had some sort of clandestine relationship with a target of theirs, Martin Worth. The Garda were interested in Worth because he was close to leading Provisionals, and they suspected this unknown Englishman might have some undisclosed role. They had tried to follow Worth to a meeting recently but he had given them the slip. Could the Met help identify this visitor? Special Branch had come to MI6 in case it was one of theirs.

That clinched it for the A desk: absolutely no more meetings in Dublin. Charles fought on without much hope, adding that police interest in Martin would enhance his standing with his IRA friends, but the A desk insisted that Martin's days as an agent were over. On the Irish terrorist target, anyway.

The case was referred to Matthew Abrahams, now director of operations worldwide. The contesting parties met in Matthew's spacious tenth floor office. Serious, pin-striped, bespectacled, Matthew was Charles's idea of a judge in chambers, as he sat with his elbows on his invariably clear desk, his long hands poised fingertip to fingertip. He listened to the arguments and when they were finished spoke with quiet precision, as if from a script he had learned by heart.

'The Garda have small surveillance resources. They will not have Gladiator under round-the-clock coverage, and may not cover him at all while waiting to hear back from the Met. If Charles does not appear on any flight manifests, but simply travels to Belfast and takes the train to Dublin, they won't know anything about it. This last meeting may therefore go ahead.'

Charles suppressed any sign of gratification. It was short-lived anyway.

'At that meeting, Gladiator should be told that we shall either discontinue the case or continue but declare it to the Garda, sharing the product with them.' Matthew paused to watch the effect of his words. Everyone, including Charles, was too surprised to react. 'Given what he fears about PIRA penetration of some parts of the Garda, he probably won't want to continue. Since his Legal Practice course finishes at the end of the term, Charles should give him the money to fly to London to discuss his future in more relaxed circumstances. We may have other work for him if he wants it.

'Meanwhile, following Charles's safe return we shall contact the Garda and start giving them the product from the case, suitably disguised. We shall not identify the source and will make it look as if there's more than one. They may work it out, but I think their Special Branch is secure, at present. We'll tell them we're sharing it as an earnest of our intention to share all future product with them and not to run any future sources in the Republic without their cooperation.' He paused again, looking at each in the continuing silence. 'The PIRA can be contained, but they cannot be defeated without the full cooperation of the Irish government. A small step towards building that cooperation is to be open with the Irish authorities about what we're doing and sharing what we know. Their cooperation is worth more than the gain from any independent operation south of the border, especially since it now looks as if Sinn Fein and the IRA are moving towards a lasting truce. You should know – but not repeat – that this is part of a wider political initiative launched by the prime minister, and that there's a serious possibility of disarmament. Any questions?'

There were questions about the mechanics of disclosure but none about the principle. When the meeting ended, Matthew asked Charles to remain. He closed the door to his outer office and they moved to armchairs by the coffee table. 'Are you happy with that?'

'I think so.'

'Only think?'

'I'm surprised. I didn't expect to be allowed to see him again. Are you sure the Garda won't leak if they work out who he is from his reports?'

'Sure enough for it to be worth the risk. We'll give them a compendium, anyway, so they couldn't work back from individual reports. But Gladiator won't be in Dublin for much longer, will he? His mother's moving back to Newcastle, according to one of your contact notes. And he's not planning to stay on, so far as we know?'

'We've never discussed his future in detail. I should've, I suppose. I know he intends to qualify as a lawyer, but whether here or there I don't think he's decided. I'll find out.'

'Do. We need to know. He hasn't discussed it with Mrs Measures?'

'Not as far as I know.'

'You know her husband, of course.'

It was not a question. Charles nodded. There was a pause, which Matthew Abrahams seemed in no hurry to end. His grey-blue eyes, enlarged by his glasses, rested on Charles. 'Would Gladiator be willing to go on working for us in another area, if it could be made to fit in with his plans?'

'It would depend on what he was working against. He turned against the PIRA because he was revolted by their methods. I think he'd need to feel the same sort of commitment. He's not a gun for hire. But he's got the taste for espionage, he enjoys it. He also enjoys making fun of it.'

'Do you like him?'

It was not an easy question. At first he had neither liked nor disliked Martin. You tried not to worry about whether you liked agents; your job was to recruit and run them securely and productively. If you liked them, so much the better; if not, you tried to make them think you did.

Charles's response, when it came, was unpremeditated; he surprised himself.

'It's hard to say. It's got rather beyond that.' Again he hesitated. He hardly knew Matthew but he trusted him. And, quite suddenly, he wanted to talk. 'I've discovered he's my son.'

Matthew's expression did not change. 'Go on.'

Charles told him all. It was a relief to talk, like being lifted off rocks by a great helpful wave. Matthew was reputedly ambitious and formidable, but there was something in his manner, in his calm listening detachment, that encouraged confidence, in both senses. He conveyed a strong impression of intellectual clarity and judgement. Although the clarity was somewhat forbidding, it was necessary to the judgement Charles sought. He did not want sympathy or offers of emotional support, but practical advice.

They were interrupted by Matthew's secretary, Sonia, announcing that the Chief's weekly board meeting was about to start. Charles got up to leave, but Matthew waved him down. 'Send my apologies,' he said. 'Ask Ian to go in my place.'

Telling all meant, of course, that Charles had to tell all about himself, Sarah and Nigel. When he had finished, there was another pause.

'I've met Nigel Measures,' said Matthew. 'I don't get the impression he's a natural ally of ours.'

'I'm not sure he is of anyone's. But he's sincere. He's an idealist, of sorts.'

'They don't always go together.' Matthew stood. 'Thank you for telling me. It was the right thing to do. We must consider what else – if anything – should be done. Will you join me for lunch? Not here, we'll go to the Athenaeum. If you can put up with the food.'

During lunch Matthew asked Charles about himself, his background, his army service, his time in the office, his current job. It felt like an interview for something, and he couldn't tell whether he was passing or failing. Over coffee in the library upstairs, Matthew summed up.

'There are two issues: whether you tell Gladiator and whether you tell Mrs Measures. The office has a right to be informed in terms of the case, but not a determining interest. Gladiator may or may not continue as an agent, you may or may not continue as his case officer; there would be no pressure on you either way. But you must inform the office of what you intend before you do it. Which is to say, you should tell me and me only and it will be recorded in a secret annex to the Gladiator file accessible only to you, me, Sonia, the head of security and the Chief. No-one else in the section will know it exists and your personal file will contain only a cross-reference, which will reveal nothing.'

Charles nodded. The decision was being handed back to him, not taken away. Perhaps that was how it should be.

'You are therefore free to decide what, if anything, to do. My only counsel is that it would be illusory to think you can tell either Gladiator or Mrs Measures without telling both, given that they know each other. You could not trust either not to tell and you need to weigh, so far as you can, the effect that that knowledge might have on them. Think of them rather than yourself, of how they might feel rather than how you feel.' He smiled. 'That may sound hard. But I'm saying it because it would almost certainly affect them more than you. It will affect you, of course, more than you may yet appreciate, but for them it could be seismic. Tread carefully, Charles, and keep me informed.'

Charles nodded. 'Just stop me if I bore you too much.'

Matthew smiled again. 'I shall, don't worry.'

The Gladiator file, as Charles had seen during his recent reading, still gave no hint of a secret annex beyond the single cross-reference Matthew had promised. No-one – Gladiator's later case-officers, the A desk, the security officer – would know it existed. Charles had delayed calling for it because he wanted to familiarise himself with the main file first, to see what had happened in the case since his day. When eventually he did send for the annex there was at first no response. He rang IC – Information Control, the section that had replaced Registry – and spoke to a helpful woman who became rapidly less helpful when she realised it was a paper annex he sought rather than an electronic one.

'It takes ages to find them,' she said.

'Presumably they're all filed by number? It should be straightforward.'

'Yes, but only the computer can find them now, and the systems have changed, which means that the new system can't do it very well. And it can't be done by hand because they're all stacked by bar code, not number.'

'So if we have a complete systems failure we can't find anything?'

'No. I mean yes.'

Eventually she agreed to put in a request for it to be done over the weekend, when the computers would be less busy, but he had to email it because an oral request couldn't be entered on her response target figures. When, after the weekend, he rang again she said she'd have to reply by email because that counted towards her delivery target.

'Can't you just tell me?'

'I'm not supposed to do that.'

'Couldn't you tell me what your email will say?'

'I'll have to ask my line manager.'

'Just the gist of it, so I know what to expect.'

She hesitated. 'Well, it's hard to give the gist of it because there's not much to say. Your requested search object—'

'My what?'

'The file you want, that's what we call it. It's a very restricted annex available only to the CEO, what used to be called the chief, his deputy, what used to be called director of operations and his secretary and the head of security. And one other person called OPS/A/4. That's all the email will say.'

'But we know that. That's what I told you in my email. I was OPS/A/4. That was my designation. I can prove it if you like.'

'I think I'd better discuss this with my line manager.'

Charles tried to moderate his tone. 'Discuss what?'

'This. What you're asking for. It's an unusual procedure, you see. I've never had one like this before.'

'You mean, a file request?'

'This sort, yes.' She paused. He could hear her keyboard clicking. 'Actually – hang on – yes, there has been one other request for this file. I've got it now on my screen. Don't know why it didn't come up before. I didn't deal with it, anyway. Nothing to do with me. CEO Dep asked for it.'

So Nigel Measures had got there first. He wouldn't like what he found, thought Charles. 'Does it say when it went to him? Last request, I promise.'

'Well, I suppose, I don't know whether—'

'It would save us all a lot of time and trouble, you see, because if he's had time to read it I can go and talk to him about it, and then there'd be no need for you to get it for me at all.'

She was relieved. 'Oh yes, I see that, yes. If we've got a delivery date record. It's not on the screen.'

They must have, he assured himself during the next two days. He remembered Matthew Abrahams saying that an intelligence organisation that didn't know what it knew, or what it had done with what it knew, couldn't function. But maybe it could if it didn't even realise that it wasn't functioning.

She rang back, sounding pleased. 'Yes, like I said, it definitely went to CEO Dep, and it's still with him.'

'But when did it go to him?'

'When? D'you mean what date did it go?'

Charles was careful with his tone again. 'Yes, if you've got it. It would be helpful.'

'I've got it, yes, I have got it. At least, I had. It was on the screen, I saw it.' There was another pause. 'I remember now, that's what you wanted, wasn't it? The date.'

'That's right.'

'I've been off, you see. I'm only part time. I do a job share.'

'Do you?'

'I do three days and the other girl does two. So that's a full week between us.'

'Ah, yes.'

Yes, here it is. At least, I think it is. Yes, this must be it, yes. The twenty-fourth.'

'Twenty-fourth of what – last month?'

'Suppose so. Must be, mustn't it? Where are we now? Yes, last month.'

So Nigel had called for the annex three days after Charles had started work with the SIA. He would have known there had to be a record somewhere, and the Gladiator file was the obvious link. Charles didn't need to know any more.

11

The main file recorded Charles's flight to Belfast in a different name and his having to hire a car to get to Dublin because of a bomb on the railway line. Avoiding the airport car-hire desks because he was known to them under yet another name, he went to an off-site firm he had used on more recent Ulster trips. The firm was in a republican area and asked fewer questions than the larger companies, which was perhaps why it was also favoured by the PIRA.

He remembered the day as grey with a drifting soft rain, the sort people said was good for the complexions of Northern Irish girls. The queue at the car-hire firm was impatient and fretful, with no time for complexions. Except Charles. As always when under alias, he was patient and polite, the customer who never made a fuss, never complained, never drew attention to himself.

He queued for the girl he always used. She had a friendly smile and was familiar enough with him to abbreviate the formalities. Contact with any kind of officialdom was dangerous, and he always used a particular pen on operations: his late father's ancient Conway Stewart. Unscrewing the cap compelled a pause long enough for a brief mental rehearsal of alias name, address, telephone number, date of birth, mother's maiden name and nature of business. Also, she had just the complexion everyone said the rain was good for.

This time, however, the file contained a sequel to the bare record of car hire and payment. Special Branch had passed on a warning from the Ulster police that an Englishman of the name Charles was using was going to be kidnapped the next time he visited that car-hire firm. Most of the staff were PIRA sympathisers, and they were suspicious that an English visitor should use a company in a republican area. A girl working on the front desk, who was secretly engaged to a policeman, had overheard them plotting and had told her fiancé. Someone from security minuted that Charles, under one name or another, seemed to be attracting rather too much attention. Charles still regretted that he was never able to thank her, even anonymously.

The drive to Dublin was wet and vexatious, the car-hire queue writ large. He was stopped by police on both sides of the border, and on the way into Dublin took a wrong turn that led into a maze of housing estates whose grim neglect and anarchy resembled those he had known in Belfast with the army years before. Eventually he found the Chesham, checked in, then drove over to Jury's, where he had arranged to meet Martin in the bar. He checked in there, too, under another name. They would use his room for the meeting, but he would spend the night at the Chesham.

Arriving thirty-five minutes early, he sat at the side of the foyer with a copy of the *Irish Times*. This gave him a view of the approach outside, of the doors and of the entrance to the bar; he would watch Gladiator in to see whether he brought surveillance with him, leaving him in the bar for ten minutes before joining him. The foyer was loud with Americans who had just arrived for a conference. The appointed time came and went. It was unusual for Martin to be late.

'You were supposed to meet in the bar. What are you doing here?'

It was Sarah, from behind his chair. He moved as if shot at, which made her laugh. 'I might ask the same of you,' he said.

'I've come to meet you. You weren't trying to spy on Martin coming in, were you? Playing spy games?'

He struggled to control the broadsheet *Irish Times*. 'No, I was just – I thought I'd watch him in, make sure he was okay. Is he?'

She retrieved an errant page. 'You're really not a very good spy, Charles. You're so obvious, I'm always telling you. Martin's fine. But he wasn't sure the Garda weren't following him earlier today – sorry, too many negatives – and didn't want to risk bringing them to you this evening. He went to a callbox and rang the number you gave him in London, but they said you were travelling and they couldn't contact you. So he rang me and asked me to come instead and tell you.'

There were people nearby. He moved her away. 'We were going to eat early,' he said. 'I'll still need to get a message to him about another meeting – through you, if that's all right. But the table's booked, so shall we eat, you and I – assuming you can stay?'

'I've got a better idea.' She was smiling and looking straight at him. 'I've booked a table at a place out of town called Charlie's. I've never been there, but people say it's really good. Appropriate name, I thought.'

Charles had planned the evening, seeking as always when on business to control the agenda. It was still a business evening, but his sense of control was draining like water through his fingers. He stared back at her. She was confident and somehow different, wearing boots, an expensive-looking beige raincoat, a black skirt and a red jersey that suggested her figure without clinging to it. He felt the agenda was hers now.

'Okay,' he said.

'You don't sound very enthusiastic.'

'No – I am, I am. I was just thinking. I've got a room here, you see, where Martin and I were going to talk. I'll keep it on – it would look odd if I check out now – but I'll have to slip upstairs to get my car keys.'

'We'll go in mine.'

'You've got a car?'

'Not mine. One I borrow from my landlady friend once in a blue moon. She's only too pleased to have it used.'

Charles hesitated again. Mixing the professional and the personal troubled him, especially with Sarah, and especially with what he now knew. Porous borders threatened the compartmentalisation of his life.

'We don't have to,' she said, more seriously now. 'You look as if you don't trust me, or something.'

His immediate reaction was to query her and Martin's motives, to suspect some sort of alliance, to ask whether he was being set up. That was a professional reaction. He dismissed it as soon as he thought it, resenting it, but he couldn't help thinking it. Martin – yes, he could just about imagine Martin betraying him because there was something unknown about Martin's motivation, some part of him that remained invisible. But Sarah – that was inconceivable. If Sarah betrayed him, then anyone was capable of anything. Yet he did conceive of it, and for a moment hated himself for it.

He smiled. 'It's not that, I'm just working out the logistics with the hotels, this one and my other one. It's okay, it's not a problem. Even though the place is called Charlie's.'

The file gave the facts of the evening in a single paragraph. The next entry was an account of his subsequent meeting with Martin in London, arranged through Sarah that night. But the facts were incomplete.

They said nothing about the hour-long journey that was supposed have taken half that, nor her unfamiliarity with her friend's Volvo.

'I can't be doing with clutches,' she said after another juddering down-change. 'Our car in London is automatic. Why aren't all cars? It's so much easier.'

'Perhaps they will be one day.'

'You don't have to be so irritatingly self-restrained. You know I'm a rubbish driver. I always was.'

'You probably don't do enough of it.'

'But I am rubbish, aren't I?'

'Pretty much.'

'That's what I always liked about you, Charles. You give a girl such confidence.'

He wondered what it would do to her confidence to know about Martin. After twice retracing their route they arrived in a dark, deserted yard at the rear of a large unlit house. There were no other cars. It was easy, too easy, to imagine his door opening and someone ordering him out.

'We must have come the back way,' she said.

She opened her door, flooding them in light. It would be now if it was at all, he thought.

'Aren't you coming, then?' she asked.

'I'm just folding the map.'

'I'm just this, I'm just that, you haven't changed a bit, you know.'

'Is that good or bad?'

'You decide.'

He overcame the map and got out. His shutting the door was the only sound apart from the rain on roofs. They stood in pitch darkness. 'The house must be that way,' he said.

'I'm told there's a back entrance.' They felt their way to the front of the car and headed towards the looming bulk of the house. After a few steps they brushed against each other. Both parted smartly. When they reached a door their hands touched as they felt for the handle. It was locked.

179

They set off back across the yard to find a way round to the front. Charles had good night vision and soon began to pick out puddles as darker patches. She slipped her gloved hand under his arm, releasing it as soon as they were on the road. At the front of the house were two cars and, reassuringly, lights in curtained windows.

'You're sure this is a restaurant?' he asked.

'It had better be. You know why I insisted on something a bit special, don't you? On this day.'

He knew the date – he had written it three or four times that day – and he knew that was the date of her birthday, but somehow he had failed to connect the two. He put it down to having been in business mode, thinking only of Martin and not expecting to see her.

'Of course I did. But I haven't got you anything, because I didn't know I was going to see you.'

'Liar, you'd plain forgotten. Anyway, this can be your present to me. If it really is the restaurant.'

There was no bell but the wide oak front door opened into a panelled hall, with a panelled dining room off it. There was an open fire and only half a dozen tables. A party of four and another couple were making enough noise to drown out whatever he and Sarah said. He ordered rabbit and pigeon pie, which reminded him of rough shooting with his father in Chiltern beechwoods. She had venison; she had always been a good eater, he remembered, unlike many of the women he'd been out with, and was lucky it didn't show.

'What did Nigel give you?' he asked.

'He rang from Paris just before I came out. That's something, I s'pose. Normally he's in meetings and I get a call at about midnight. I expect he'll bring back something expensive and easy to find. But at least he remembered.'

'He's still keen on his European crusade, isn't he?'

'Very.'

'No sign of defecting to Brussels or the UN yet?'

'No, but the talk goes on. He wouldn't see it as defecting, of course. He'd see us as the defectors, the un-idealists. I told him I was seeing you. He sent his regards.'

'Does he mind?'

She shrugged. 'No idea.'

She asked what was to happen with Martin. 'I hope you do find something else for him,' she said after Charles had explained. 'I doubt he'd find the law exciting enough. I think he's a bit in love.'

'Who with?'

She smiled. 'No need to look so alarmed. We've had tea a couple of times recently. I think it's because I know what he's doing and he feels he can talk about it a bit. Or ask questions, most of which I can't begin to answer. He's in love with spying, MI6 and all that. He reads books about it, knows the names of all the chiefs. Doesn't he ask you about it?'

'Never. If he refers to it at all he's usually ironic or mocking.'

'He strikes me as a boy – man – who needs a cause, something to believe in. A bit like Nigel in that respect. Martin used to have the Cause, of course. Perhaps he still does to an extent, even though he's spying on it. But he certainly has your cause in a big way, too. He likes the fun of it, always refers to you as uncle. He's a nice boy. I like him, don't you?'

It was the perfect moment to tell her, an intimate dinner, rare time alone; there would never be a better. He rehearsed the words, tried to imagine how she would take it, considered whether it might be best done over coffee, all the time feeling sorry for her because she was so unsuspecting and because it was her birthday. But still he hesitated; it could change the rest of her life, hers and Martin's, a change he couldn't quantify.

'Funny how he's taken to spying,' she continued. 'I'd never have thought of him as the sort of person who becomes a spy.'

'There's no such thing. We're all spies. We tell each other's secrets all the time. It's human. It just depends on the context.'

'Very wise, Mr Smiley.'

Over coffee she continued happily, relaxed, talkative, even slightly flirtatious. They paused only once, while their coffee was being refilled. The waitress turned away but they waited until she was out of earshot before resuming. That was the other chance to tell her. He knew it, and let it pass.

The drive back was easier. When she drew up outside Jury's she kept wipers and engine running. The message was clear, but the space between them was suddenly filled with the unspoken, which for him was that earlier birthday dinner at the Elizabeth, on the night of snow.

'Well, happy birthday,' he said. 'No snow this time.'

She smiled. 'Dangerous stuff, snow.'

'And no Nigel and no umbrella.'

'There is an umbrella. In the back.'

'I wonder what you'd write in the snow now.' He had not intended to say it.

'I'd write, "Thank you for a lovely dinner." That would be enough, don't you think?'

'Of course.' He kissed her on the cheek and made to get out, but paused with the door open. He would say something, not all he wanted to say, but something of it. There might never in life be another chance and he wanted her to know. 'No, it's not. It's not enough.'

She looked at him.

'I loved you and I thought I'd stopped loving you, but seeing you again has made me realise I haven't, that I never have.' He said it to the windscreen wipers. There was no response from her. When he turned to look she too was staring at the wet windscreen. She sighed.

'Sorry,' he said. 'I didn't mean to put you on the spot. I'm not going to go on about it. You don't have to say anything.'

She continued staring at the screen. 'Why are you telling me this now?'

'I wanted you to know.'

'But all that time when you—'

'I know. I'm sorry. But it's always been you. It's always and only been you.'

'Is that what you say to all your girlfriends?'

'I've never said it to anyone.'

'You might as well close the door.'

He closed it. They sat in silence. 'Don't worry, this wasn't meant to be a seduction ploy,' he said. 'I didn't plan it.'

She looked at him again. 'Well, it's not a bad start.'

Later that night, in his room in the Chesham, she sat up abruptly in bed. Just enough city light showed through the curtains for him to make out the mole on her right shoulder blade. He had forgotten the mole. Her body had the strangeness and familiarity of home after a long absence. He stroked her back, feeling each rib with his finger-tips. She had lost weight in the decade since he had last done that.

'I thought you were asleep,' he said.

'I was, then I was suddenly awake, hearing myself speaking. Perhaps I was dreaming. I heard myself saying, "I'm the first woman in my family ever to have done this." Adultery, I mean.'

'You can't know that.'

'I do.'

He ran his fingers down her back again.

She turned and leaned over him, her breasts pendulous. 'I can't leave him, you know. Nigel. He's   he needs me. He wants children.' She pushed her hair away from his face. 'No need to look so alarmed, it's not about to happen again. Your timing's better this time.'

When Charles awoke to another grey wet dawn she was already up, sitting on the arm of a chair. She was wearing one of the white hotel dressing gowns and staring through a gap in the curtains at the moving streets of Dublin.

He sat up. 'A perfect morning, a perfect moment. You look beautiful.'

She did not look round but he could see she was smiling. 'It's miserable, awful, wretched. I shall never understand your passion for rain.'

185

'I guarantee an endless supply of umbrellas.'

'D'you think you've always been frightened of your own feelings?'

He hooked his arms around his knees. 'Probably. I don't like emotional incontinence. Either that or I don't have the right feelings. Except that I did with you. Do, with you.'

'We can't go on.' She continued gazing at the traffic. 'Not because I don't want you. I want you too much. It would tear me in half.'

His eyes rested on her still profile. If he insisted, pleaded that he couldn't live without her, urged her to leave Nigel before it was too late, to re-start with him the life they should have had, if he importuned enough, begged enough, she might just be persuadable.

But he didn't want her by conquest or theft. Nor did he want only half of her, an affair burdened by deceit. His role in her life had been destructive enough already. He wanted her to give herself freely, or not at all. Besides, it wouldn't be true to swear he couldn't live without her; he could, he had, people did despite what they said, as she had without him.

Yet something, anything, was better than nothing. He got up and went over to her, kneeling by the chair, his hand on her thigh.

She turned her head away. 'Don't,' she whispered. 'Don't say anything, don't touch me. Please.'

It was years before he made up his mind whether obeying her was the best or worst thing he could have done.

There was no hint of any of this in the file, which simply recorded Martin's transfer to London as an agent and his subsequent reassignment. 'He should become a Z agent,' Matthew Abrahams had minuted, 'if he's willing and has the talent for it. And the time. It will be useful money while he's doing his legal training. His current case officer should remain in touch for the time being. We should not forget that he will still have some residual PIRA contacts, even though he's no longer in Dublin. If the current peace talks break down we should be prepared for him to use them, but with care.'

The Z Organisation was a section named after a 1930s predecessor, in those days a part of MI6 that was supposed to be run under business rather than official cover. The section comprised a group of agents with useful jobs in the outside world, who were trained in clandestine skills and could be deployed in operational support.

Martin was keen to do it but worried about combining it with being a trainee solicitor with a large City firm. 'It sounds like 24/7 there,' he said. 'No more student hours.

Plus I have to go back to Dublin now and again until my mum moves back over here. Presumably I could do a spot more spying there. Not all my Provisional friends will accept a ceasefire.'

'Not in Dublin, not any more. You must be as clean as whistle over there. By all means keep in touch with any of their contacts here, but not there. How is your mum?'

Martin did not often mention his adoptive parents and when he did, it was usually his late father. 'She's fine,' he said. 'Can't make up her mind what she wants to do with her life or where she wants to live, but that's normal with her. Right now she wants to be back in Newcastle near her old friends. Give that a few years and she'll want to be in Dublin near my aunts.'

He never showed any sign of being unhappy with his parents, and never remarked on his background. Presumably a successful adoption, Charles concluded; all the more reason for not interfering.

The Z training ate into Martin's spare time, devouring what would have been his social life. However, it paid well enough for him to rent a flat in Marylebone and run a car. Mostly he was in the hands of his trainers, but Charles kept in touch and helped out with exercises.

He joined the end of one to pick Martin up in an SAS Land Rover in a remote Shropshire lane. Martin had spent three days and nights of precious leave alone in a hide, reporting all movement in and around a barn that was supposedly an arms cache. Exfiltration took place at night at a point where the lane narrowed to a rising double bend, densely hedged, forcing any vehicle to slow right down. The Land Rover never quite stopped but as it slowed, Charles, sitting in the back, lowered the tailgate with a rope. At the mid-point of the bend the hunched figure, encumbered with weapon, radio and rucksack, struggled free of the hawthorn and threw himself aboard, beneath the rear canvas. Charles pulled up the tailgate before they emerged from the bend. Martin lay unmoving on the floor amidst his kit.

'You okay?' asked Charles.

'Do I stink?'

'You do.'

'Did I do all right?'

'Spot on. You clocked everything and you weren't seen. All you missed was the two girls sunbathing.'

Martin hauled himself up onto the bench seat. 'Girls my arse. There wasn't a trace of bloody sun either. Not once. How d'you know I clocked everything, anyway? Don't tell me there was someone else there, watching alongside me?'

'There was. It's called a camera.'

'Jesus.'

As time went on their relationship relaxed and deepened. They developed an understanding, expressed largely through ironic reference and understatement, interspersed with discussions of the ethics of espionage, loyalty, patriotism and the moral and psychological consequences of living a double life. Once, Martin asked, 'Could I join MI6 proper? I mean, be a case officer like you?'

'Provided you got through selection, like everyone else.'

'Would I?'

'I don't see why not. I'll put you up for it if you like. But you'd have to become a bureaucrat. The fun bits, the operational stuff which you do all the time, are only part of it. The rest is officialdom.'

'You mean poncing about pretending to be an embassy diplomat? Or sitting behind a desk in London like you? Not sure I could put up with that.'

'And you want to be a lawyer? But at least that's a meal-ticket for life, unlike spying.'

'Trying to put me off?'

'Just being a good uncle.'

Charles would have put him forward, as he had offered, but was relieved not to be asked. He felt a strong but inchoate desire to protect Martin from something; disillusionment, perhaps. Maybe he had a touch of the paternal after all. Although he never for a moment forgot that Martin was his son, he still could not fully realise it. He watched constantly for mannerisms or reminders, not so much of himself – he was invisible to himself – but more of Sarah. A fleeting expression, a movement of the hand, an intonation, an angle of the head sometimes cut him with a stab of recognition. But still he said nothing, except once, over a pizza in Covent Garden, when Martin himself raised the subject.

'My sisters are just like my mother,' he said, 'despite us all being adopted. You know all about that, I guess? On my file, is it?'

Charles nodded.

'They're all three of them busy, constructive, practical people. Salt of the earth, you know. The world functions because of people like them. But I'm more like my father, bit of a dreamer, bit restless. And a lawyer. He was a successful barrister on the northern circuit. Never left the law, but he was always about to, always wanting to move house, always buying a new car whenever he felt rich, always talking about moving to Colorado or New Zealand or the bloody book he was forever going to write. Christ knows what it would have been about. It would've been another *Tristram Shandy*. He had that sort of mind.'

'Have you ever been tempted to find your natural parents?' Charles hoped he sounded casual.

Martin shook his head, his mouth full of pizza. 'Maybe

one day.' He swallowed. 'Doesn't seem much point. The formative influences on my life were the people who brought me up. The rest is just biology.'

Charles nodded.

The main Gladiator file gave an unnecessarily full account of the Herefordshire exercise and of others that followed, along with occasional progress reports. It was thorough and boring, constructed deliberately, as Charles well knew, in order to conceal a gap. More than a gap, a chasm: one that would be visible now to Nigel Measures.

Part of the concealment was a lengthy account of an operational trip Charles made with Martin to Paris. It was prompted by intelligence that two of Martin's former Provisional contacts, who had joined a splinter group of dissident republicans opposed to the peace process, were to visit Paris in connection with an arms deal. The information had come from the Garda in response to the gift of Martin's intelligence. The A desk proposed that Martin should make contact with the couple. He would fly over for the weekend with his latest girlfriend, a trainee in another firm. She would of course be unaware of – *unconscious to* was the term used – what was going on, and would assume she was being treated to a weekend in Paris. During this idyll, with the discreet help of French surveillance, Martin would bump into his old contacts and try to find out what they were doing. Charles would go as his case officer and act as liaison between him and the French.

The file told the story of an operation organised in haste and crowned with success. The MI6 Paris station made good use of its liaison contacts, the French cooperated enthusiastically and Martin's girlfriend – Martha in Charles's memory, but Mary according to the file – had a wonderful, unsuspecting time. Martin, track-suited and notionally out for a solo run in the Bois de Boulogne, left her to luxuriate in the Hotel St James. He was dropped by a French surveillance car just off the Champs Elysees where the Irish couple had taken a table at a pavement bar. For once, everything had worked as planned. Martin jogged past, they saw and hailed him and he joined them at the table. They drank and talked and arranged dinner as a foursome that night. Charles sat in a side-street with Michel from the DST, the French security service, in a blue Citroën surveillance car, where they were kept informed by the foot surveillants' radio reports. When Martin ran back towards the Bois de Boulogne they picked him up just off the Avenue Foch.

'They say they're here on holiday,' he said. 'Crap. They can't afford a pint in Dublin. Jimmy'll talk later if I get him on his own. Bound to, he can't help it. Always boasting.'

The two couples met that night. It was impossible for

Martin to get away for a debrief afterwards, so late on the Sunday morning Charles waited for him in a corner café off the rue d'Astorg. Martin had left Mary in bed while he went for another run. Charles had taken a table deep in the dark interior, well back from the windows but with a good view of the cobbled junction. It was quiet, apart from a few cars splashing through the puddles and the occasional pedestrian hunched against the rain and trying not to slip on the cobbles. Charles lingered over his coffee, attempting to recover a little more of his French with an old *Le Monde*.

Martin was wet, breathless and exhilarated. He really had run in the Bois de Boulogne, buoyed up by success from the night before. 'Getting me fit, this job,' he said. Then, adopting a stage Irish accent, 'Jenny's not a bad wee girl, I'll say that for Jimmy. We got on fine.'

'Don't go getting ideas. You don't need complications.'

'She's got enough of her own. She's got a boyfriend back in Dublin. Very convenient, this little awayday with Jimmy. Suits them very well. And she's got a weak bladder, which is also very convenient. Went to the loo twice, second time with Mary, so Jimmy and I had a little chat.' He grinned. 'He wanted my advice, bless his dissident soul.'

Charles's telegram, written later that day in the MI6 station, gave the meat of it. Jimmy and his operational girlfriend had what Jimmy called a 'big job' involving the transfer of 'useful tools' for the cause back home. He had to visit a particular site in the woods at Chantilly and could Martin tell him if that part of the woods was within walking distance of the station?

'Never been near the place in my life,' said Martin. 'But I pretended I had, though my memory was a bit hazy, so he gave me a more precise location, based on what he'd been told, and I gave him even more precise and completely imaginary directions. Christ knows where they'll end up if he remembers what I said. But he won't. We had another bottle after that and then some, and he was well away by the time we left.'

It wasn't clear whether they were reconnoitring a new weapons hide or confirming the accessibility of an existing one. Either way, their visit and the site would now be monitored and one day, weeks, months or years hence, the French would make arrests. But that was for others to follow up.

Martin was in no hurry to leave the café, which was beginning to fill with early lunchers, stamping their feet in the doorway and shaking the rain off their umbrellas. Mary would sleep till doomsday, he said, or at least until he'd had his breakfast. They ordered more coffee and croissants, again went over what had been said and watched the downpour spattering like bullets on the cobbles. An elderly couple got up to leave but the woman refused to step outside when she reached the open door, which annoyed the man who had spent some time laboriously putting on his coat and adjusting his cap. It was as they stood bickering in the doorway that Martin, who had been looking past them into the street, said quietly, 'Well, look who it isn't. Your rival in love.'

The first thing Charles noticed was the DST car, the blue Citroën. It had just drawn up across the road, its wipers still going and rain machine-gunning its bonnet and roof. He knew it not only by its number plates but by the discreet additional aerial. There were two men in it, neither of them Michel. So far, so normal; it was probably a DST fleet car used night and day for a variety of jobs, changing numbers and colour every so often. But what Martin had seen was not normal.

Sheltering in the doorway of a tobacconist and struggling to close his umbrella, was Nigel Measures. He was wearing a Loden coat and had a small brown suitcase at his feet. As they watched, the rear passenger door of the Citroën opened and Nigel, having mastered his umbrella, picked up his suitcase and ran across the pavement into the waiting car. The Citroën drove rapidly away.

'Not my rival,' said Charles as they watched the car disappear, conscious that Martin said it only because it always provoked a response. 'I didn't know you knew him.'

'Sarah invited me to dinner a few months ago. I thought I told you. Not my cup of tea, Mr Measures. I can see why he isn't yours, either.'

Charles let that go. They were both still looking at where the car had been.

'That was a pick-up,' said Martin.

'He spends a lot of time in Brussels; has official business here, too.'

'With the DST? On a Sunday morning? In one of their operational cars? That was a pick-up if ever I saw one, the sort we've been practising. Only not a well-chosen place. Three out of ten, you'd have given me for that one.'

Charles nodded. 'Can't think what he could be up to.'

Martin sipped his coffee. 'Obvious, isn't it? He's talking to the French. And not just passing the time of day.'

12

Everything connected with the arms hide was recorded in the main file, but Charles's report of the sighting of Nigel Measures, written for Matthew Abrahams, was in the secret annex now held by Nigel himself.

Matthew had listened to Charles's first oral report without expression, his eyes focussing unrelentingly through his heavy-rimmed spectacles. He said nothing for a while after Charles had finished.

'You are sure, absolutely sure, that it was him?' he asked eventually. 'Despite bowed head, hunched shoulders, intervening rain and glimpsing him for only a few seconds?'

'Absolutely sure. And so was Gladiator.'

One of the three phones on Matthew's desk, the grey one, rang. He waited for it to stop after the conventional three rings. 'Tell me again. And tell me more about the café, the junction, the rue d'Astorg and why you chose it.'

Charles had chosen it because it was close to the Champs Elysees, a part of Paris that any foreigner might visit, but off the main routes, slightly withdrawn; not a tourist magnet, but just busy enough for anyone to have wandered into.

Matthew sighed, put his hands in his pockets and leant back in his chair. 'If this is what it appears you would expect the DGSE – their foreign service – to handle it, not the DST security people. But, who knows, perhaps they swap cars when they're short, or perhaps it's different if the case began on French soil. No matter. There are indications – no more than that – of something going on into which this would fit rather neatly. I shall say no more now and you mustn't mention it to anyone. Write up what you saw and give it to me for the annex. Don't dictate it, a handwritten note will do. Or perhaps not, with your handwriting. Give it to Sonia for typing. Then we must consider how we – you – can find out more.'

Charles was still reluctant to accept the evidence of his eyes. 'But would the French really risk spying on us while liaising so closely? I mean, we have a lot going on with them, they have a lot to lose.'

Matthew shrugged. 'Would we spy on them?'

'I don't know. It would depend.'

'Precisely. If it were easy, relatively risk-free and the rewards were high – say, the French fall-back positions in the current negotiations – would it be surprising if the prime minister permitted us to accept an offer of service?'

'It wouldn't be risk-free. And we'd never get political clearance to recruit a French official, especially not during the negotiations.'

'But if he offered his services? We'd at least get clearance to hear what he had to say, if not from the Foreign Office, then from Downing Street.'

'You think that's what Nigel's doing?'

'I think we need to find out.'

The result was that Charles saw more of Nigel and Sarah. His job by then was to help assess British and allied intelligence reports on the Soviet bloc. The majority were foreign liaison reports, mostly American, but a significant number from the Old Commonwealth and from Europe. He was frequently at meetings in the Cabinet Office and Foreign Office and it was easy to contrive reasons to call on the Western European Department, where Nigel worked.

He did so two days after his conversation with Matthew, deliberately passing Nigel's open door while visiting someone along the corridor. Nigel looked up. Charles waved and paused.

'Spying on us now, Charles?'

'Trying, but it's hard to find anyone in. You're all always in meetings in this place. In fact, I was in Brussels the weekend before last and called your office on the off-chance you were there, but they said you'd gone home.'

Nigel grinned. 'Spying in Brussels, too? We can't have that. No, I came back first thing Sunday morning. We'd worked all Saturday and half the night. Gave me most of Sunday at home and the chance to catch up a bit. You busy?'

'When I can find anyone.' He raised his hand and turned to go. 'Sorry, late for a meeting.'

'Must have lunch sometime.'

'I'll ring.'

Charles did not follow up immediately but instead rang Sarah the next morning at the law firm where she worked part time. Obeying her injunction to the letter, he had not contacted her since their night in Dublin. It had not been easy, but she had been serious, and he wanted to show that he respected that. But he was pleased now to have reason to breach the injunction.

'I'm sorry to bother you,' he began, 'but I know you've seen a bit of Martin, and thought I ought to bring you up to date with what we're doing with him.'

She sounded cool. 'I haven't seen very much of him. He came to dinner a while ago. He seemed happy enough.

He didn't mention you or your office at all, and neither did I.'

'That's good. But I think it would be useful if I let you know how things are going and where we're going with him, in case he wants to confide in you again.'

'Well, he hasn't shown any sign of that. But, okay, if you think it's important.'

'At least it's a meeting with a respectable reason. Half respectable.'

She laughed. 'That's true, I s'pose. Half true.'

They had sandwiches at a small round table in El Vino's, at Blackfriars. She drank Perrier because she was busy that afternoon, forcing Charles to content himself with a single glass of wine. He told her about Martin's progress in his training and the kind of deployments he might expect, show-ing concern as to whether he was doing enough work to get his legal qualification, and seeking her advice on that. After he had spun it out for long enough to seem like the main reason for their meeting, he asked about her own work.

'I'd like a permanent full-time job with them,' she said. 'Not a partnership – I'm too old to start on that ladder – but the kind of assistant solicitor job in which you can come and go a bit. Trouble is, I never know what we're doing. Whether Nigel's going to leave and go into politics here as he keeps threatening or whether we'll stay in the Foreign

Office and have a posting, or whether he'll run off to be an MEP in Brussels or what. Still, I suppose I'm no worse off than women who run careers with children. At least I don't have them to worry about.'

Did you – do you – want them? he wanted to ask. Are you trying, as the wretched phrase has it? As she sipped her Perrier, he noticed for the first time tiny lines around her mouth. What is life like for you? he wanted to ask. Is it becoming – is it already – a disappointment?

'So, things are sort of permanently up in the air?' he said, intending it as a preliminary.

She shrugged dismissively. She clearly didn't want to talk about it. 'You're becoming bit of a boozer. You've finished your wine already.'

He had noticed recently that his wine glasses emptied themselves faster than other people's. 'Occupational hazard. I had to do a lot of wining and dining in my last job.'

'You're lucky it doesn't show in your waistline. Unlike Nigel's. He's getting really rather fat. All those Brussels lunches. They say it's the best cuisine in Europe.'

'Didn't strike me when I saw him. In fact, I was in Brussels at the weekend and dropped in on his office – what I thought was his office – but couldn't find him.'

'He was there, doubtless in meetings. He didn't get back until late Sunday night.'

'Meetings are bad for waistlines, too.'

She sighed. 'The whole process seems endless. He's been away every other weekend for months now. I'm beginning to wonder if he keeps a mistress there.'

'Europe is his mistress, surely. Will you have a wine if I have another? It might perk you up.'

'Send me to sleep, more like. Sorry to be such a bore.'

'What if I promise to drink half yours?'

She nodded.

'Tell me more about Martin,' she said when he was back. 'I know he works near here but I never run into him. Is he happy with the law? Will he stick it, d'you think? He never seemed the sort to persevere with something that didn't fire his imagination.'

It was obvious that she didn't want to say any more about herself, so he talked about Martin until she had to go.

Matthew Abrahams had access to information on people within the bureaucracy from sources Charles could only guess at. He summoned Charles the following day.

'Point one, it's true that Measures was working in Brussels on the Saturday,' Matthew said. 'His colleagues thought he returned to London early on the Sunday morning, as he told you; but he changed his flights, took a train to Paris and flew back from there on the Sunday night, getting home late, as his wife said. Point two' – he glanced at his notes which were as usual in Chinese characters – 'it is not true that he has had to work in Brussels every other weekend for the past few months. He has worked some weekends – four out of fourteen, counting this last. His wife may have exaggerated how often he was away, but if she hasn't I suspect he was in Paris during the remaining weekends. We might learn something from flight manifests. If we do, it would be careless of him, and them. Meanwhile, keep seeing her, if you can.'

'What do you think he's doing – passing documents?'

'Possibly. Probably. But drafts and copies of drafts are two a penny in the Foreign Office and in Brussels – there's no proper control – and anyway many of them are going to be shown in negotiations. More important is the interpretation he can give them – this is a prime ministerial sticking point, that was put in at the last minute as a giveaway, this is only there because Number Ten wants it but the Foreign Office doesn't, and so on.'

'So what do we do about it?'

Matthew's gaze traversed the south London panorama beyond his window, settling on the two heavy naval guns outside the Imperial War Museum. 'We accumulate evidence. What we have so far is not evidence – a suspicious meeting, an example of his telling his wife one thing, his colleagues another. Perhaps there is a mistress after all. He wouldn't be the first diplomat to play away from home. But even if he admitted contact with French intelligence, that would not in itself constitute treachery. If we refer it to MI5 now, as we should any evidence of espionage, we'd lose control; and they probably wouldn't put resources into investigating it because they've too many other fish to fry. Besides, they wouldn't want to upset their close liaison with the French. Nor would Foreign Office Security Department want to create any waves. Spying revelations always mean trouble and scandal; everyone prefers a quiet life. In this case we're the only ones with an interest in doing something.'

'You said there were other indications that something was going on, with which this fitted?'

Matthew nodded, without lifting his gaze from the 15-inch guns. 'There is a context. It may provide useful corroboration of what Measures is up to, but may not be in itself useable.' He looked back at Charles. 'Meanwhile, the only way to accumulate evidence is for you to go on seeking it. Which means seeing more of him – and her. I can see it may not be comfortable for you but the point is, he might say something – most spies develop a confessional urge at some point – or she might, even if she knows nothing about it. She's already been unwittingly helpful.'

Charles did feel uncomfortable. It was all too convenient, giving him reason to see Sarah and to plot against Nigel. He worried particularly about the latter. Nigel's espionage merited punishment – at least the punishment of exposure – but Charles's personal connection could too easily make it look – even feel – as if he had a deeper agenda. It was true that something made him feel that Nigel was fair game, almost. His relentless self-seeking, his calculated, energetic charm, his unhesitating use of others, the continuous engagement of a colonising personality made him seem not an ordinarily vulnerable human being, but a beast of the jungle. In which case, Charles could not help asking, was he himself not another? His own readiness to strike made him uneasy; he was not used to the idea of himself as that sort of person.

Over the next few months he had occasional lunches with Sarah, hoping to get her to talk about her marriage but unable to ask directly in case she suspected more personal motives. She made oblique references to herself and Nigel, smilingly dismissive of husbands or marriage in general, and clearly preferred questioning Charles about his own life to discussing hers.

'Don't ever become one,' she said once. 'A husband, I mean. It wouldn't suit you, you wouldn't be you. And it would make it difficult for us to meet.'

'No prospect at present.'

'No-one at all? I don't believe you. There must be some-one.'

'Well, I'm not a hermit, I do see one or two—'

She held up her hand and looked away. 'Don't tell me, I don't want to hear.'

Whenever he learned from her that Nigel was to travel he told Matthew Abrahams, who checked with the Foreign Office. As before, Nigel's official itinerary and that given to his wife did not tally.

Charles also called more frequently on Nigel himself, and they drank once or twice in Whitehall pubs. He made a point of referring to his lunches with Sarah, but Nigel seemed uninterested.

'The to-ing and fro-ing must be tiring,' Charles said. 'Even if it is only Brussels.'

Nigel shook his head. The glistening of his dark eyes made it hard to read them. 'Exhausting but exhilarating. We're getting there, you see; we're approaching a real agreement at last despite the damage that that Thatcher woman did.'

The way he said her name had lost none of its venom. Charles sometimes wondered whether it was partly a function of the word itself, particular movements of tongue and jaw being conducive to the energy of hate. In Nigel's mouth it was as if a terrier had learned to say 'rat' and, like a terrier, once started he would not let go, conscripting everything into an anti-Thatcher tirade. Charles used it to bring him out.

'But didn't she start the Single Market project, all those years ago?' he asked. 'Or at least give it early support, as that Bank of England woman at your dinner said? It was one of her things, wasn't it?'

'She was persuaded by us to go along with it, but she had to be dragged kicking and screaming every inch of the way. Every centimetre, I should say. What she didn't realise was that she was getting a lot more than she bargained for in some ways, and a lot less in others. She thinks it was all about business and trade; access for British insurance companies and all that. Typical. Shopkeeper's daughter. What she didn't see was how hugely integrationist it was, how it paved the way for Maastricht and Amsterdam. Major wan't much better, mind you, and despite all their rhetoric New Labour are almost as bad as Thatcher was on Europe. That's why it's exhilarating that Amsterdam's been ratified at last – no thanks to Tony Blair. We've finally got a conclusion that's good for us and good for Europe, and I get a real kick out of playing a part in that. Contributing something, doing my bit for history, not just playing nineteenth-century nationalist games.' He grinned. 'Can't expect you to agree, of course, but that's the modern reality.'

Charles had long since learned the futility of arguing with enthusiasts, political or religious, preferring to regard their enthusiasm as cultural and psychological phenomena. But it was important now to keep Nigel in play. 'Keep trying,' he said. 'Convert me. You never know.'

Later that same afternoon, Matthew summoned Charles again. It was after six, when most people went home, and Sonia was putting on her coat and checking combination locks. She had long auburn hair, long enough for her to sit on. Matthew sauntered from his office, hands in pockets, talked to her about papers for a meeting the next day, waited till she had gone then followed Charles into his inner office and closed the door.

'You should get to know Sonia better,' he said. 'You will, though not in the way you might wish. She's a find. Brilliant linguist: Persian, Russian, Arabic. She was a bored transcriber until I had the headphones plucked off her and offered her a change in career.'

'As your secretary?'

'Temporarily. A tactic to help her subsequent transition to intelligence officer. She'll run operations, man desks, like you. She'll be good. And it will help her on her promotion board if I can vouch for her having valid operational experience. As she soon will have, with your assistance.' Matthew smiled. 'We have action.'

He had wrung permission from the Chief to send a Z Organisation surveillance team to Paris and Brussels when Nigel next travelled, without Foreign Office clearance. 'Normally we'd have to get clearance, of course, but we can't let them know we're looking at one of their own until we've got hard evidence of wrongdoing. Who knows, he may not be the only one involved. We can't even use the Paris station because they're all declared to French liaison, and if any were recognised within a mile of Nigel Measures the French would smell a rat. So.' He held up one long forefinger, his smile broadening. 'I persuaded the Chief through repetition, repetition, repetition, knowing he had a million other things waiting, that we can do it as an exercise. The Z team will be briefed that it is just that, an exercise, and will be given their quarry's description without being told who he is. They'll comprise some of the people Gladiator's been training with, but he can't take part because, of course, he'll know who's involved, and that it's not an exercise. The Paris station will be told at the last minute that there's a Z exercise on their patch – this is just in case they see you there – but that it needn't concern them or the French. By the time they've finished arguing with Head Office about it the whole thing will be over. And we shall, I hope, have proof positive that your friend Measures is doing something clandestine.'

'But what if they are spotted? What if the French have counter-surveillance cover on their meeting?'

Matthew nodded. 'That's where you come in. You'll be there as the fall-guy, the team's notional quarry. You'll be in the vicinity, not close enough for Measures or any loitering French case officer to recognise you, but near enough to be the plausible exercise target if we're caught out. There'll be trouble if we are, of course. The ambassador and the Foreign Office will be upset, the French and the Paris station will be angry, the Chief will deny all knowledge and blame me for thoughtless freelancing, and you'll have a get-out-of-gaol-free card.' He smiled. 'Of course, they may rough you up a bit on the way.'

'You think the French will swallow that?'

'So long as we – you especially – stick to it, they'll have no choice. They're bound to conclude we might be on to Measures and so run the case more tightly. But they won't be sure and they won't drop it. And that's only if you're caught, of course. Which you won't be. Since you mustn't meet the team in Paris, Sonia will keep you informed of what's happening. She'll act as go-between, coordinating the team and keeping you in the picture. Only you and she will know what's really going on. I haven't told her yet; but I'll brief her tomorrow.'

'I use my own name, then?'

'Of course. You're there as a trainer.'

Charles and the main part of the Z team deployed separately to Paris the following Saturday, the other part deploying to Brussels. Nigel's delegation was already in Brussels and due to return on the Sunday, following a dinner on the Saturday night. Charles attended the Z team briefing before they left, so that they would know him if they had to follow him as their stand-in quarry. They were shown photographs of the un-named Nigel, described as their number one exercise target, walking along his Clapham street, emerging from Clapham North underground, walking through Parliament Square. The photos had been taken by Sonia, whom Matthew had sent on a crash course in clandestine photography. Charles was to stay in his hotel unless summoned to meet her.

'If Colonel Sod strikes and you don't hear from me and can't get hold of me, ring the duty officer in London,' she said. 'We'll communicate via him.'

Charles waited all Sunday in his hotel. He had come prepared. Years of loitering in various names in hotel rooms around the world had taught him patience and precaution. He had waited for agents who never showed, for politicians with entrepreneurial aspirations but mercurial temperaments, for scientists who couldn't find the hotel, for officials seeking re-insurance with the other side, or for the coded call from the local MI6 station which meant get out, leave the country, now. Espionage, like war, was ninety per cent waiting.

This time he had come equipped with Proust, begun a year before in Bangkok and resumed intermittently during long hours over the Pacific and Atlantic, during airport delays in Copenhagen, Barbados and Delhi and interminable waits in Rio, Hawaii, Hong Kong, Dar-es-Salaam and Pretoria. If nothing happened – if Nigel didn't appear or the team couldn't find him – he would finish it this trip.

Sonia rang at ten past two to say that 'all but one of the board' had returned to London from Brussels that morning, without the marketing director. It wasn't yet clear what his plans were. She rang again at seven to say that he seemed to be staying put. Charles finished Proust that night.

Sonia rang for the third time before nine the following morning. The Brussels team had seen him leave his hotel early but had lost him. Sonia had sent her Paris team to stake out the station and watch the early trains from Brussels. They were rewarded by the sight of the marketing director walking briskly to the taxi rank with suitcase and briefcase. Two were close enough to hear him ask for the top of the Champs Elysees, following which they had lost him because they were all on foot.

'Too risky to jump in another cab and shout "Follow that cab!"' she said, abandoning veiled speech. 'You never know what they might think, us being foreign. They might just drive us to a police station. But two of the others have taken a cab to the Arc de Triomphe, to see if they can pick him up there.'

Charles, too, abandoned all attempt at concealment; veiled speech was usually a waste of time, anyway. 'Send someone to the rue d'Astorg. It's just off Place St Augustin. At the junction with the rue Roquepine there's a café. Get someone in there with a camera and look out to see if he waits for a pick-up outside the tobacconist opposite.'

It would be careless of them to use the same place again, but convenience, routine, familiarity were ever the enemies of security. On their own ground, with no reason to suspect a threat, they might well be lazy.

Sonia's next call, forty minutes later, was cryptic. 'On my way to pick you up.'

'Everything okay?' He assumed she meant that something had gone wrong and that he had to get to the area in order to be followed.

'All fine, it's happened. Perfect. We got everything. They've left the scene. I'm ringing from the café. I'll come now.'

'Stay there, I'll join you.' As the French had just used the location and moved on, the corner café was probably the safest place in Paris.

She had chosen the very table he'd shared with Martin and was breaking her *pain au chocolat* into small pieces before eating them one at a time. He'd imagined her always calm and undemonstrative, but had noticed recently that she couldn't help smiling when pleased.

'The two in the first cab spotted him crossing the Champs Elysees as they paid off. Fortunately, he had to wait to cross, so they were able to follow him here and saw him go and stand outside the tobacconist over there, just as you said. The team came straight in here. He must've been early because he was there six minutes before anything happened, so they got good shots of him. Then a car drew up and he got in: a green Renault. They got shots of that too. Meanwhile, the other two whom I'd sent on had been dropped off at the junction of the rue d'Astorg with the rue de la Ville l'Eveque. They were just starting to walk back here when they saw the Renault with him in it turn the corner in front of them and stop behind another car, a blue Citroën. Someone got out of the Renault – not him, but a man carrying a briefcase the same as his – and got into the Citroën which drove off. Then the Renault drove off. We lost them both, of course, but they got shots of the whole transaction. Lots of brownie points, d'you think?'

'Brownie points plus more *chocolat*.' Documents, he thought. They were taking them off to copy. They ought to have had facilities wherever they debriefed him, unless they drove him round in the car and debriefed him on the move.

He and Sonia lingered and talked. She had a husband and two young children at home in Hertfordshire. Her mother was Iranian, her father a Briton who worked in the oil industry. She had been bought up largely in the Middle East and had had a partly Muslim education. 'I was lucky to get through the vetting,' she said. 'I wouldn't be where I am now if it weren't for Matthew. D'you know him well?'

'Not as well as I should like. I don't know whether anyone does. He's quite private.'

'I think he has various people throughout the office whom he nurtures. I'm one, you're one. I don't know how many others there are.'

'I'd no idea he did that.'

She sat back, smoothing her hair with both hands. 'I love my husband, I'm devoted to my children – nothing would come before them – but still I'd walk on burning coals for Matthew Abrahams. I think he's just wonderful.'

Some days later Charles was shown the photographs in Matthew's office. They showed the story clearly, from Nigel leaving the Brussels train with suitcase and briefcase, to his standing outside the tobacconist's and getting in the Renault, then his briefcase being carried from the Renault to the Citroën by a man Charles had seen with Michel, his DST contact. The case was unarguable.

'Not enough for a conviction,' said Matthew. 'Not here, anyway. It would be in France, of course. Enough, though, to nail him as far as his Foreign Office career is concerned. I hope to be there when he's confronted with it. You can't, I'm afraid.'

Charles was relieved by that. Slightly to his own surprise, he no longer shared Matthew's relish for the kill. Hearing it said brought home the reality of disgrace and dismissal, the broken bones of ambition, the spilt blood of self-respect. He had never actively disliked Nigel; their pasts were so entwined that like or dislike was irrelevant, almost as if they were siblings. Despite still regarding him as a beast of the jungle, Charles felt no bloodlust, had no desire to watch him suffer. There was also the guilt that Nigel always evoked in him; Nigel had married her when he hadn't. True, she hadn't wanted to marry Charles, but why not? Because of something in himself, some lack, perhaps a lack of what he himself had called emotional incontinence. Emotional commitment, in other people's language. He hadn't wanted her enough, or hadn't shown he did, whereas Nigel had been sympathetic when she needed someone. And he'd been there. Above all, he'd been there. Charles respected and resented him for that, and consciousness of resentment sharpened his guilt.

'He must have taken a late Sunday or early Monday train back to Brussels,' Matthew continued, 'because he was on a Monday evening flight from there to Heathrow. He'd transferred his booking over the weekend, telling his returning colleagues that he was staying on because Sarah was joining him. Could you devise another pretext to see her? It would be useful to confirm that he told her he had to work on Monday.'

Charles had half a reason to see Sarah, about the renewal of the lease on his rooftop flat. He rang her. 'Five minutes of your legal advice tomorrow. In return for lunch, dinner, anything.'

'I'm cheaper than that, I'm afraid. I can do a quick breakfast, just. If it's really quick.'

They met in Daly's, where the Aldwych becomes Fleet Street. It did a steady trade in lawyers' breakfasts and the plain wooden tables were mostly full. Arriving early and seduced by toast, coffee and bacon, Charles ordered for them both and took a *Times* from the rack. She and their breakfasts arrived simultaneously.

'I can't eat all that,' she said.

'I'll eat what you don't. I thought it would be quicker to order than wait till you got here.'

'You'll have to help me.'

Her advice on his lease was much as he expected: he didn't need a specialist lawyer and it sounded a fair offer so long as the terms of the new lease had not changed. 'It will add more to the value of your flat than it will cost you, so long as you can afford it. You're not about to lose your job or anything, are you?'

'Not that I've heard.'

'Nigel might be about to lose his. Give it up, rather, when these negotiations come to an end. He's got the political bit between his teeth again. More talk of standing as an MEP.'

'Well, he's in the right place to fix something. Is he over there now?' It was going to be easy, no pushing or contriving. But the more trusting and confiding she was, the worse he felt.

'He came back earlier this week. Monday, Tuesday – no, Monday – night. He works ever more ridiculous hours, right through till Monday evening. She must be some mistress.'

'Couldn't you go out and join him for a bit of a jolly?'

'Wouldn't be much jolly. He's in negotiations from the time he gets off the plane until he gets back on it. Anyway, my waistline couldn't cope with the Brussels cuisine. Nor with any more of this, I'm afraid.' She pushed her plate away, rested her elbows on the table and cradled her coffee in both hands. 'Sorry.'

Guilt, affection, the desire to protect, the urge to confess, welled up in him. He had no qualms about professional deceit, but practising it on her crossed a line. 'There's something I should tell you,' he said.

She raised her eyebrows.

He couldn't do it. This was a secret that wasn't his, part of the public realm. There could yet be a prosecution: she could be implicated, more so if he told her. There was too much at stake.

She was still waiting. He had to speak but he couldn't tell her that. Instead, he heard himself say something quite different, something unplanned but long anticipated: 'I've discovered that Martin is our son.'

For a few moments she continued to stare, unmoving, then she lowered her eyelids and put her cup on the table. 'How do you know?'

'I discovered it when some late traces came through. They included his birth certificate.'

She was still looking down at her cup, her finger hooked through the handle. 'How long have you known?'

'A few weeks,' he lied.

She looked at him again. 'Are you sure it's him? Are you absolutely sure?'

'The tracing threw up his adoption papers along with his birth certificate.'

'You knew when we last met?'

'Yes. I wasn't sure whether to tell you. Or how. I wanted to tell you.' There was a pause. He feared her silence. 'His adoptive parents were half Irish, half English and he was brought up in Scotland, as you know. A happy upbringing, apparently.'

'Does he know who we are?'

Charles shook his head. 'I don't think he's ever tried to find out. Doesn't seem interested.'

'When exactly did you discover this?' Her tone was colder, almost official.

'A while ago.'

Her eyes continued to rest on his. 'Why didn't you tell me before?'

'I didn't know how you would take it. I've been thinking about it all the time.'

'It's hard to believe, you know. I'm not sure I can. It's such a huge coincidence. Huge.'

'Coincidences happen. This one has.'

She gazed at him for a few seconds more, then a change came over her features like a subtle change of light. She looked decided, resolved. She pushed back her hair and bent to pick up her handbag. 'Well, there's a thing.' Her tone was matter-of-fact. She sat clutching the bag on her lap. 'You really haven't told him?'

'No.'

'Are you going to?'

'Not unless you want me to.'

She frowned. 'Is it possible that he knew all along, that he sought me out? My name is on his birth certificate.'

'Only your maiden name. He's never given any hint that he knows.'

She stood. 'I must go. Thank you for breakfast.'

She left without a glance. He watched until she had disappeared among the Fleet Street commuters. Truth-telling was a fine thing, especially when it made you feel better. But telling it not because it was the truth, telling it in order not to tell another truth, that was not so fine. He wanted to blame the office, to slough off his guilt that way, but it wouldn't do. He felt he had let her down a second time. And the third, the destruction of her husband's career, was still to come.

13

Except that the expected destruction didn't happen, or not fully, not then. A fortnight passed during which Charles heard nothing from Matthew Abrahams and assumed that the confrontation was still to take place. He saw Nigel once hurrying across Whitehall into the Ministry of Defence, and glimpsed him again at reception, but they didn't speak.

One afternoon Matthew rang and suggested a drink in his office after six. He drank little himself but, like most senior officers, kept drinks in his desk drawer; throughout the old MI6, conversations after six were invariably fuelled by alcohol.

'Whisky?' asked Matthew.

'Red wine.'

Matthew smiled. 'This is really more a whisky talk.'

'Whisky, please.'

Matthew nodded and sat. 'The treachery of Nigel Measures is proven. He's been spying for the French throughout these last negotiations, in fact for rather longer than that. He volunteered his services to them for what in the Cold War we called ideological reasons. Or idealistic, like your friend Gladiator. He takes no money save his travel expenses, which are paid in cash. He believes in a united Europe, wants to do all he can to bring it about, is convinced that HMG is holding the entire European project back. He has given them everything, all our position papers, fall-back options, red and not-so-red lines, the lot. And now it's finished. He's being posted to Washington.'

'Has he confessed?'

'No.'

'He's going to be sacked?'

'Not sacked. Rewarded for a job well done, as his immediate superiors and the outside world will see it.'

'The French – are they continuing with him?'

'They'd love to, they're very keen; they value his advice, they told him. They'd like a long-term relationship. But it's all ended in tears.' Matthew smiled and picked up his whisky. 'He said he couldn't do that, because it would be spying, and he didn't want to be seen as a spy. They said: but that's just what you are; what do you think you've been doing? He didn't like that. Broke off contact with them. End of the affair. Have you seen him?'

'Not to speak to. But he rang this morning, which is unusual. He wants lunch tomorrow.'

'Good. Don't probe. Just listen to what he has to say, take his temperature and report back.' Matthew held up his hand. 'I know what you're thinking – why is he being rewarded, and how do I know all this?' He got up from his desk, went to his safe and returned with a folder from which he took a photograph. 'Have you seen this before?'

It was the photograph of Nigel shaking hands with Jacques Delors, the President of the European Commission.

'Yes, in Nigel's house. It's on his mantelpiece.'

'It still is. This is a copy. The original was taken at a secret meeting in Delors's Paris office, arranged at Measures's request by his French case officers. That's probably when he began spying for them. Measures may take no money but of vanity there is no end, as the Preacher tells us.' He put the photo back in the folder. 'And if I say that espionage in Europe is not entirely a one-way street, you'll understand why I can't say more.'

So they – we – had a source, a source who trumped Nigel. A source who had to be protected. 'Human source or technical?'

Matthew shook his head.

'So he goes to Washington and gets away with it, scot-free?'

'It's been decided at a – let's call it a political level – that maintaining good relations with the French is more important than showing we've caught them out. Especially as their source is not continuing, whereas ours is. Also, it's useful to have a card up our sleeve if we get caught out. Tit for tat, we can say, a mark of the maturity of the relationship between ourselves and our ancient enemy. We can both swallow this sort of thing without retching. We get on well with them, we collaborate with them, but we're neither of us naïve, we accept infidelities.'

Charles was surprised how frustrated he felt, now that Nigel wasn't to be confronted with his betrayal. It made him want to tell Sarah rather than spare her.

Matthew topped up their glasses. 'Of course you find it annoying. More than. Measures deserves to be punished. As I said, it's a political decision. At a very high level. Meanwhile, Measures is not a happy bunny, which is some compensation. He suspects he's being manoeuvred against. And the day may come when we are permitted to discomfort him directly. Meanwhile, be careful over lunch.' He smiled again. 'You and your lunches, Charles. You lunch for England.'

Charles shrugged. 'I do my best.'

It was a self-service lunch on trays at the National Theatre, without wine. Nigel seemed hurried and pre-occupied. Uncharacteristically, he chose salad. 'Brussels lunches too much for you?' asked Charles.

'Leaving Brussels. Got a posting to Washington. Out of the blue.'

'Congratulations.'

'I'd rather stay where I am, it's more involving. In fact, I was thinking of leaving altogether at the end of this job for something in politics, as Sarah may have told you. Still, Washington's a good posting. Dozens would die for it. With promotion, too. And Sarah's keen. Says she's had enough of London, doesn't mind about her career. Hard to say no.'

'Why should you want to? Ticks all your boxes, doesn't it?'

'Feels like a betrayal.' Nigel, always a rapid eater, shovelled lettuce into his mouth as if killing it. He looked across at a mime artist in the foyer, who was maintaining a pose before a small, equally motionless, audience. 'I've been doing something I believe in, you see, really believe in. This new job's just clever-dick chancery reporting on the Washington political scene. Interesting, but hardly something to stir one's mortal soul. Anyway, it's perfectly well covered by the serious press. It's not going to change

229

anything. If I accept it I'll be deserting a cause I believe in
to do a job I don't believe in but which others would give
their eye teeth for. So it feels to me like a betrayal. D'you
see what I mean?'

'It wouldn't constitute betrayal in most people's books.'

Nigel nodded vigorously. 'That's it, you see, that's the
point. What constitutes betrayal? Disloyalty, I guess; but
what if you have conflicting loyalties? What then?'

Charles had sympathy for that. 'You have to choose.'

'Not that simple, though, is it? You may be loyal to an
institution, but feel that it's got something important wrong:
something to which you have an equal or greater loyalty,
and which in the long term is in the institution's best interest, only it doesn't see it. Then you're either forced to do
what you know to be wrong or to go against the institution.'

'You can try to persuade it of its error. You don't have to
work against it or betray it.'

Nigel shook his head. 'Doesn't work. Institutions have a
collective mind which it's very hard for an individual to
influence. They don't listen to what they don't want to hear.'

'Then you ask for another posting.' They were looking
directly at each other now. 'Or resign.'

'How would that help what you believe in? You'd be out
of it, powerless, without influence.'

Charles kept his eyes on Nigel's. 'Work for your cause in

a different way. Get a well-padded job with the European Commission, if that's what you believe in.'

'Which you don't, of course?' Nigel raised his voice and sat back. 'I doubt anyone's ever accused you of Europhilia, Charles, as they have me. Or of listening to the arguments.'

'I'm waiting to hear them.'

They continued staring at each other, until Nigel turned to look again at the mime artist, rocking back on the hind legs of his chair, hands in pockets. 'Perhaps I'm not making myself clear. What I'm saying is, how far should the honest believer go in supporting what he honestly believes?' He spoke without looking at Charles.

'As far as honesty permits.'

The remark hung in the air. Nigel shook his head.

'You think that's not far enough?' continued Charles. 'You want to be dishonest?'

'You've never had to make such choices, have you, Charles? You've always been clear about what you wanted and gone for it. Or clear about what you didn't want, and left it, got yourself out of it.' He looked back at Charles. 'And, of course, betrayal's your business, your profession. At least Sarah will be happier in Washington. That's something.'

'Has she long been unhappy here, or is this recent?'

Nigel ignored the question. 'I may as well tell you there

was some stupid business about me getting too close to the French, identifying with the other party's position, going native, time I moved on, all that sort of nonsense. As if understanding those you're trying to persuade and getting on with them is a hindrance to negotiating. Couldn't expect Security Department to understand that. Probably politically driven, some snide ministerial aside, more xenophobic Eurosceptic lunacy. Typical of the office not to stand up to it. I told Sarah all about it. She's furious. Thinks you must be involved.'

'She said that?'

'She did.'

Charles didn't want to believe him. 'Yet they've rewarded you. They can't think you've done badly.'

'Why shouldn't they reward me? I haven't done anything wrong, have I? I've just told people what I think. I tell everybody what I think. Anyone who wants to hear. Nothing wrong with that, is there?' His dark eyes were indignant.

Charles made no reply. They did not have coffee.

During the next year or two Charles heard occasionally of Nigel and Sarah in Washington, he as a rising star, she as an adroit and popular hostess, a particular favourite with visiting British and European politicians. Then came news of Nigel's surprise resignation to stand for the European

Parliament. He got in and they moved to Brussels, intend-ing to divide their time between there and London. Charles heard later that Sarah had resumed working for her pre-vious law firm in their Brussels office. He once sent a Christmas card, but never got one back.

After Martin's Z training finished there was no reason for he and Charles to remain in touch. Charles was posted to Geneva and Martin, as soon as he had qualified as a lawyer, volunteered to be part of the Z section deployment against the Taliban regime and the growing al-Qaeda threat, before looking for a permanent job. At his last meeting with Charles he turned up carrying a copy of the Koran.

'Required reading?' asked Charles.

'Just to show I've made an effort.'

'Your Afghan tribesman won't appreciate it. He'll never have read it.'

'By the time I've finished with him he'll be a holy war-rior. Unless I die of boredom first. It's worse than the bloody Bible. No stories.'

Charles considered the cheerful young man before him, conscious of what he might have called parental concern, if he had had any right to such a claim. 'Watch your step out there. Keep your nose clean.' He would like to have told Sarah what was happening, but there was no chance of that, either. 'Ask your Z people to let me know when you're coming back. We can have a beer.'

'Not much hope of one out there, from what I hear.'

They parted with handshakes and jocular restraint.

During the next two years in Geneva Charles worked mainly on resurgent Russians, part of the time with Sonia, Matthew's former secretary, who had been promoted. Just after 9/11 he was asked to cover for Martin's Islamabad case officer, who had been taken ill. The region was in ferment when he flew out to Pakistan. Martin had extended his Z section assignment and had still not begun to practise as a lawyer.

Going through the file again shortly before his arrest, Charles came across a photograph of Martin he had taken outside Peshawar during that trip. This was a bearded Martin in tribal dress posed against the rugged hills of the border country. Rock-strewn folds of hard, unforgiving land stretched into the blue distance, beyond which was war. It was a landscape of harsh beauty and Martin, tough, spare and relaxed, looked comfortably part of it. His task had been to train and supply arms to the anti-Taliban tribes and to gather any intelligence he could on UBL. He was not supposed to engage in combat, but Charles soon suspected he was doing just that. There was nothing on file about it and he doubted that Martin's regular case officer ever realised.

'You're on your own,' he remembered warning him. 'If you're caught over there no-one in London will acknowledge you.'

'And if I'm killed I'm dead. I sort of guessed that.' Martin grinned. 'But I can imagine no other work. It's not work, it's life, it's being more vividly alive. How's your desk?'

'Less exciting than this, but just as real. More so. Desks win in the end. It's time you came back and got started. Or you'll have to qualify all over again.'

'Thanks, uncle. Give me five years to think about it.'

Peshawar was a Wild West town and they were drinking green tea on the veranda of the place where Martin was staying. It seemed to be part hotel, part trading post and part informal military headquarters.

'Sarah's in Brussels,' Charles said. 'Her husband left the Foreign Office for the European Parliament.'

'Still spying for the French, is he?'

Charles shrugged.

'Landed on his feet by the sound of it. She'll enjoy it, anyway.' Martin gazed at the hills beyond the town. 'Long way from here, Brussels.'

'You'll have to come back one day. Unless they bury you here.'

'Maybe. I'm going over tomorrow. Just a quick in and out to see one of my merry men. Come with me.'

'That's *verboten*. Very *verboten*.'

'Of course, I was forgetting the desk. And the pension. Important considerations at your age.'

They crossed the border together the next day. Charles allowed Martin to assume he had been goaded into it, but in fact it was because he was reluctant to leave the vigorous, likeable and independent young man of whom he felt secretly proud.

They left early in the morning in Martin's battered Toyota Landcruiser, bumping over tracks and non-tracks. It was not until some time after they had crossed it that Martin told him the border was behind them.

'Nothing's changed,' said Charles.

'The border's pretty theoretical in this part of the world. Pretty confusing, too. Nobody knows who to trust any more. Farther in we travel in the dark, on foot.'

Charles had pictured sitting around a campfire and talking late, perhaps telling Martin of his origins, if it felt right. But the reality was a cold, fire-less and sleepless night in the hills, talking until dawn with one of Martin's sub-agents. Or, rather, not talking in Charles's case, since the other two conversed in a local language and Charles was confined to listening, nodding and smiling. The agent, a wiry, wizened man with white hair, treated him with dignified courtesy.

'I told him you're a famous English warrior,' said Martin, 'a great chief in England and that you've killed six Arabs with your bare hands. Most Afghans hate the Arab fighters.'

Charles tried not to show that he was shivering.

The following night, slipping gratefully into clean linen sheets in the head of station's house in Islamabad, he felt for the first time that he must be growing old. Or, at least, that he was no longer young. Roughing it has ceased to be an adventure. In fact, he no longer sought adventure.

He took early retirement in the new century, not very long after 9/11 and the proclamation of the War on Terror. By then he was beginning to feel that he should have gone ten years before, after the fall of the Berlin Wall and the end of the Cold War. That had been his territory. The new war had brought a new world and a new language, exciting because of its urgency and the immediacy of results, but essentially short-term, hectic and – relatively – easy. Results came quickly or not at all. He felt as he imagined a cricketer must feel when playing the twenty-overs game instead of a full five-day Test. It lacked the intellectual allure, the ideological and tactical complexities of the near century-long struggle against communism. Also, his operational appetite was fading. Espionage was still the great game, but he had played enough. It was time to go, before repetition dulled his edge and made him careless. He would write his long-contemplated book on Francis Walsingham.

Matthew Abrahams, by then chief, tried to persuade him to stay. 'The Cold War is over, but some of the eternal verities remain. Russia is still Russia and China is still China. National interests are undimmed. Their missiles still point at us; they're spying as much as ever. You may think yourself an unwanted Cold Warrior but within a few years that's precisely why you – we – will be wanted again. Except that, unless we stay, we'll be forgotten. There's still a lot you can contribute.'

But Charles went. The last he heard of Martin at the time was that he still loved his Afghans and was increasingly involved in tracking down al-Qaeda.

Reading the file, more recently he learned how Martin had set up his own legal practice in England, dividing his time between that and his Afghan work. Charles had accepted, reluctantly, that they would never meet again, as with Sarah. Yet still he carried within him the conviction that somehow, before life ended, all major threads must be gathered for some final account. Who would gather them, and how the account was to be rendered, was something he had no feel for, until that grey day in Scotland when Matthew Abrahams rang.

14

Walking to Pimlico took longer than Charles thought and his attempt to recall everything he might need caused him to loosen his normal grip on time. He ran the last few hundred yards, but she was already there when he arrived. She was texting, and didn't see him until he was at the table.

'Sorry, just a work thing for tomorrow.' She turned off her phone and put it in her handbag. 'You look exhausted. D'you feel all right?'

'Better than I must look. No reason I should be tired. Haven't done anything all day.'

'No, but you've been arrested. You've been done to, which is worse. Now, tell me everything. Why you're back at work, what you're doing, how the arrest came about, everything, all over again if you can bear it. Start from the beginning.'

His story lasted well into their main course. He talked quietly, pausing whenever he noticed that the young couple at the next table had fallen silent. The man kept stealing looks at Sarah, as men had always done. It pleased Charles to think he wasn't alone in finding her still attractive, but fortunately the couple were mainly occupied by their own soulful conversation and did not appear to be listening. The woman did most of the talking and the man most of the nodding.

When Charles finally finished his account, Sarah seemed more curious about him than about what had happened. 'You haven't found or lost any wives along the way in the years since we met?'

'No wives. The odd girlfriend here and there.'

'How charmingly accidental that sounds. More often here than there, I bet. Now, tell me about this Walsingham book. Why – no, your house, your house in Scotland, let's do that first.'

He described his house.

'Sounds worryingly remote,' she said.

'That's why I'm there.'

'But you shouldn't be. Not too much, not on your own. You'll turn in on yourself. And it won't help with your book. You'll be bored.'

'And boring?'

'I never said that.'

When she ordered coffee rather than a pudding he realised there wasn't much time. 'It's good to talk again,' he said, conscious of a change of tone. 'More than good, whatever the circumstance. But there's something that worries me over and beyond what's just happened to me. It's Martin. I haven't seen him since a couple of years after you and I last met. That breakfast at Daly's.'

Her expression did not change but the corners of her mouth tightened, emphasising lines she never used to have. 'I've no idea what's happened to him. He's certainly not been in touch with me. I assumed you would know all about him since he's the case you're investigating.'

'I know only what the file says. After you and Nigel left for America he went to Pakistan and Afghanistan on our behalf. He became a very good agent, did a lot of things, took a lot of risks. He set up a charity – an educational charity – then came back and set up his own legal practice. He raised money for the charity, went back and forth quite a lot and has been peripatetic ever since.'

'He's not married? No children?'

'He's certainly not married, not here, anyway. He may have wives or concubines over there. The file implies that there have been women in his life but no identities or suggestions of anyone permanent. Nor any hint that you and I might be grandparents.' He smiled.

She did not. 'He's been working for you – your office –
Nigel's office – throughout?'

'Yes and no. He continued for quite a few years, even
after he converted. Then there was a long gap, until very
recently.'

'He converted? To what?'

'Islam.' Again he saw her mouth tighten. 'I don't know
why. It's in the electronic bit of the file, which is much less
informative and doesn't go into detail. Just refers to it. The
Taliban were making life difficult for his charity.'

'What sort of charity?'

'Educational, as I said. Not just children. Adult literacy
too, especially women. That's what the resurgent Taliban
didn't like. They targeted teachers, schools, family and
tribal heads. He stuck it out there for a while, but in recent
years he's spent more time in the UK as things have become
more difficult.'

'Doing what? Where does he live?'

'Birmingham. He runs his legal practice from his house,
specialises in Pakistani work, attends the local mosque. He's
well-regarded, apparently. Respected as a good Muslim.'

'Perhaps he is.'

'You're not surprised?'

'I'd never have predicted it, but now you say it's happened I can believe it. He always wanted a cause. I'd have

predicted civil rights, human rights work, that sort of thing. Maybe this is that sort of thing.'

He noticed she hadn't touched her coffee, which was just as well, because he had some way to go. 'It seems that they – the office, the new SIA – picked him up again once we became seriously re-involved in Afghanistan. They wanted to know if he would travel back there, get in touch with his old contacts, report on the Taliban insurgents and AQ in Pakistan. Risky for a Westerner. But his past credentials were supposed to stand him in good stead, provided enough of his old contacts survived.'

'Has he grown a beard?'

'I don't know, I haven't seen him. There's no recent photo.' He sipped his coffee. 'It took months for anyone to contact him. They even had to have a risk assessment for themselves, all the usual modern nonsense. Finally they allowed themselves to go and see him. Martin doubted that his old contacts would be much use now; but he agreed to ask around because he has business in Pakistan, anyway. Travels to and fro, so he could test the water. Well, he went and it worked. Not many of his old contacts survive but those that do are influential and he came back with some intelligence. He always did, he was always a good producer, happy to spy on terrorists. Since then it's become a regular thing, a trip every couple of months or so. Just after his penultimate trip he was summoned back, urgently. This was unprecedented. His case officers didn't think he should go. Neither did he. Then, I believe, Nigel went to see him, alone. After which he did go, and hasn't been heard of since.'

'Nigel – are you sure? He never said anything to me.'

'I'm not absolutely sure, no. There's nothing on file about it. But I do know he got Martin's current address and telephone number and can't think of any other reason he'd want them. He'd have seen him during the weekend before Martin left. Since then, ever since Martin's been missing, there've been indications of attack planning by two extremist groups in this country. The groups don't know each other – one's in Birmingham, the other in High Wycombe – but they're both in touch with a mysterious individual who seems to be coordinating them. No-one knows how he communicates but the groups refer to him between themselves as al-Samit – the Silent, or the Silent One. Presumably he communicates only face to face or by courier. Nigel has put something on file about that, saying he thinks it might be Martin. He reckons he's been turned and is now working against us.'

She stared. 'Is that possible? Surely Martin wouldn't do such a thing? Do you think he would?'

She had raised her voice slightly and the man at the next table glanced at her again. Charles lowered his own voice.

'I don't, no. I'd be very surprised. But I do know that the way al-Samit communicates – avoiding everything techni-cal – is how I trained Martin, helped train Martin.' He paused. 'Did you ever tell Nigel who Martin really is?'

She shook her head. 'There's been no reason. I would have if there had, but there hasn't. We never talk about all that. Haven't done for years. Not that we did much, anyway, even then. It's all past, water under the bridge, there's been – too much else.' She shrugged. 'Life, you know. Accretion of.'

But no more children, he thought, searching her face as he always did. He was thinking again of their last conver-sation, that breakfast in Daly's when she had got up and left. What he was about to say might prompt the same reac-tion, perhaps making this definitely their last conversation. But it had to be done.

'I think Nigel does know,' he continued slowly. 'There's a restricted annex to the file in which it was recorded at the time, by me. It gives Martin's real birth identity and your and my relations with him. I was asked to record it. I didn't like doing it without you knowing. I felt as if I were betray-ing you. But I did it. Nigel has that annex in his safe, now.'

She stared at him. It was impossible to tell whether she was plumbing her own feelings or assessing his.

Eventually she said briskly, 'Well, he's said nothing to me

245

about it.' She picked up her coffee. 'But then he's said nothing to me about you being back or having seen Martin or his changing sides or anything. Why would Martin do that – change sides and become a terrorist? I don't get it.'

'Belief, conviction, disenchantment, resentment, lack of purpose in life, desire to do something, be someone, the influence of others – though I can't see him falling for that, he's more likely to be the influencer. You can't know without talking to him. If it is him.'

'I find it very hard to believe. Except his desire for a cause, his sense of justice.'

'So do I. Which made me wonder why Nigel might want to persuade people that he has.' It was time to cut to the chase. Charles folded his arms and leaned forward. 'Nigel never wanted Martin brought back onto the books. It's implied in the file, though never spelt out. But I've talked to Martin's recent case officers who are quite clear about it: the initiative to bring him back came from them, the operational section, and it was only when it reached Nigel that everything slowed down. Each time they overcame one reason against it, he – not directly but via a quiet word with the controller – ensured another was produced. But in the end he failed, as we know. Then he saw Martin himself, alone – most unusually for someone as senior as Nigel – and then Martin disappeared.

'Nor did Nigel want me brought back to investigate the disappearance, despite what he now says. He tried to stop it but Matthew Abrahams insisted. Then he put it about – it's his theory, no-one else's – that Martin is al-Samit, is very dangerous and has to be found at all costs, taken alive or dead, preferably dead.'

'Nigel said that? He actually said it?'

'So I've learned. Anyway, there I was, back on the case, and what does he do then? He has me arrested.'

Her eyes widened. 'Nigel? How do you know that? How do you know it was Nigel?'

'The police. They said that's where the suggestion that I was the source of the leaks to James Wytham came from. They came from Nigel.' He paused while the waiter offered more coffee. Sarah refused but he accepted, to make it more difficult for her to leave before he finished.

'You asked them?' she continued. 'And they said it explicitly? They said it was Nigel?'

'They named him.'

There was a pause. She seemed to be staring at the rings on her finger, the rings Nigel had given her. She looked up. 'I mustn't be late. Shall we get the bill?'

'I'll get it.' He waited because the couple at the next table got up to go and were standing close to them. After they had gone he still made no effort to get the bill. 'What's striking, of course, is that the two people Nigel didn't want back in the SIA, both of whom he seems to have got rid of one way or another, have something in common in relation to him.'

'Me, you mean?' She smiled, more sadly than humourlessly.

'Well, yes, you too. But that's not it. It's that business with the French years ago, remember? Just before you went to Washington?'

'That business? You mean that nonsense about him being indiscreet, being their spy? That was just jealous colleagues teasing. Nigel wouldn't spy for anybody. He doesn't approve of spying. To be honest, he doesn't approve of you, really.'

'Not only for that, I'm sure.'

She took no notice. 'It was all so exaggerated, such a lot of idiotic malice. People envied him because he speaks such good French and got on so well with his opposite numbers. I was so angry when all that was flying around. It damaged his career, you know, I'm sure it did. It's partly why he left.'

Her cheeks had coloured. Charles had rarely seen her indignant. But there was no way back now.

'Nigel did spy for the French,' he said, with quiet deliberation. 'I know he did. I saw him do it, in Paris, during one of those weekends when he'd told you he was in

Brussels. So did Martin, who was with me. He was doing it for years and stopped only when he left the Foreign Office. It's all recorded in that secret annex which he now has in his safe, if he hasn't destroyed it. I don't know whether he ever suspected that I knew about it, let alone whether Martin knew, but he certainly knows now. Only two other people still serving know, one of whom is Matthew Abrahams. The file shows that. But Matthew is dying and Nigel probably doesn't realise the other is still serving.'

For the first time since the months before Martin was born, when their relationship was falling apart, Charles saw hostility in her eyes. 'Aren't we all spies?' she said sharply. 'Isn't that what you used to say when you were trying to justify yourself? That it's only human, just a question of context?'

Another, older, couple were being shown to the next table. Charles turned away from them. 'I guess some of us are more human than others.'

'So during all those times when we used to meet, you knew what Nigel was doing but you never said anything?'

He nodded.

'And I thought we were meeting because you wanted to see me.'

'I did. I did want to see you. I've always wanted to see you.'

'But you were spying on me? That was why you used to see me, to find out what he was doing?'

Her voice carried. He hoped it would be covered by the scraping of chairs at the next table. 'Only partly.'

'Partly? Partly? God, you're so controlled, Charles. Can I believe anything you say? Yes, it's true – but. That's how it is with you, always a but, always some other reason, some other motive which makes it not true after all, because it's not the whole truth. It never is with you, is it? Never the whole truth about anything.' She thrust herself back in her chair. 'And so this is supposed to be why Nigel doesn't want either of you back in the SIA and why he's tried to get rid of you both? And I suppose it's him who's causing Matthew Abrahams to die of cancer, too?'

Despite the table between them, Charles felt as if he were physically fighting with her, holding her down. He controlled his breathing, speaking slowly and quietly. 'Sarah, you must know it means a great deal to Nigel to be chief – CEO – of the SIA. It's what he gave up Europe for. He knows that if this episode of his past – however it's interpreted – gets out, even a whisper of it, it would scupper him. They'd sack him or, if they were merciful, retire him early. I can't be certain that he's done what I think he's done, but from where I sat in that cell today it looked pretty damn like it. And you know – you saw for yourself – that there was no case against me. It was contrived, all contrived. The whole process was skewed, none of the usual procedures, warnings, anything.'

Unasked, the waiter appeared with the bill. Charles ordered two more coffees. He couldn't let it end like this. 'I'm sorry, Sarah,' he said, 'but that's how it looks. If I could find a way of resolving it that doesn't involve you, I would. But I can't see one. All roads lead back to you. They always have.'

She stared at him. He half-expected her to do something violent, but after a few seconds she sighed and sat forward again. 'Supposing you're right,' she said slowly. 'What do you want me to do about it? Help you destroy my husband's career and reputation, because of some equivocal episode years ago that everyone's forgotten about and which never harmed anyone anyway? You want revenge, is that it?'

'Not revenge, and not for what he did years ago. It's because of what he's done now, to cover it up. I want you to help me establish whether he really did what I think he's done and then to help me confront him with it and persuade him to go quietly. No fuss, no scandal, no humiliation.'

She stared at him, then laughed briefly and mirthlessly. 'Isn't that what we now call a big ask? It is revenge, isn't it? Whatever your reasons now. You never did like him, you were always jealous. It's personal, isn't it, Charles? In the end it's personal.'

'I've never disliked him, it's nothing to do with all that.'

'And if he didn't go quietly you'd do it the other way, wouldn't you? You'd expose him. And you'd want to use me to help you end my husband's career, ruin his chances of another job, ostracise us from all our friends, the life we've built for ourselves. Quite a lot to expect of me, don't you think?'

He nodded.

She pushed back her chair and picked up her handbag. 'I was happy to help you today, pleased – I don't mind admitting it – to see you after all these years. I often think of you, I really do. But I'm not prepared to blow up my life – our lives – just to give you the satisfaction of getting your own back on Nigel. After all, what if everything you say is true? What terrible things would happen as a result of it? Martin is either lost and there's nothing anyone can do about it or he survives but doesn't want any more to do with your office. You're a free man and when your contract ends you can go back and sulk in Scotland and get on with your boring book. Nigel stays and does a good job – as he always does, wherever he's been, I don't think anyone would deny that – and where's the harm? What's history is history, Charles, it can't be rewritten.' She stood up. 'Thank you for dinner. I'd hoped we might start seeing each other again. But not with all this. I'll try to make sure the partners don't bill you too fiercely.'

He watched her walk out, aware of other diners staring, and no longer minding.

He paid and left. The pavements were wet and the street lights showed an uncertain thin rain. He chose to walk again, turning into Belgrave Road and crossing the railway bridge towards Victoria; walking was better for ruminating and he didn't mind getting wet. In one respect – probably only one, he conceded – she was wholly wrong, one hundred and eighty degrees wrong: history could be rewritten. History was the record and the record was the only thing about the past that could be changed. That's what Nigel would be doing: destroying or doctoring the secret annex. Then any allegations made by Charles, Martin, Sonia, even the dying Matthew Abrahams, would be neutered, the unsubstantiated grievances of the discontented and rejected. There might be fuss but without evidence it would be difficult to remove him, and he'd have had no need to try to get rid of Charles and Martin.

But he had, so bringing upon himself the very fate he feared. Why? Failure to think it through? Panic? Indulgence of a long-nursed enmity, his judgement warped by malice? Charles wished they could sit down together and talk about it. Imagining that, as he walked, was easier than facing up to the rest of what Sarah had said.

It was as he came off the bridge towards the traffic lights on Buckingham Palace Road that he noticed them, the younger couple who had been at the next table and had left before Sarah. A pair of thirty-somethings, the man slim with short brown hair, jeans and a fleece; the woman also slim with close-cropped black hair, jeans, a dark jacket and shiny, black, low-heeled shoes. Like him, they had chosen to walk although not dressed for rain. He wouldn't have noticed them if they hadn't stopped to cross Buckingham Palace Road, then stayed on the kerb when the pedestrian lights went green. They stood with their heads cocked very slightly to one side, as if listening. After a few seconds they turned to their right, as one, and walked rapidly towards Victoria Station, looking straight ahead.

Charles at first assumed they were lost or had been somewhere else since leaving the restaurant, given that they were only twenty or thirty yards ahead of him. He didn't think about surveillance until, coming into Sloane Square, he glanced at the trees and paved area in the middle and saw the woman walking ahead of him, alone. She carried an umbrella now and wore a headscarf and a lighter jacket – possibly the dark one reversed – but he knew her by her busy walk, tight-fitting jeans and those shiny, black, low-heeled shoes. They were unusual: comfortable walking shoes with an almost patent leather shine. She crossed the square and disappeared behind the far side of Peter Jones. As he entered the King's Road she emerged onto it ahead of him, out of Cadogan Gardens. She still walked briskly without looking back, drawing farther away until pausing at a shop window, her umbrella shielding her from him. She would have been given that and the headscarf in the car that must have picked them up out of sight, along Buckingham Palace Road. That's why they'd paused at the crossing, listening for instructions. The car must have just dropped them off ahead of him, someone else having followed him meanwhile. Her slim companion was presumably nearby, but Charles was careful not to look round.

His surveillance-spotting skills were rusty but something of them survived. Those unusual shoes were a give-away; careless, or a sign of unpreparedness. To have sat at the next table and then reappeared on the street afterwards suggested that the team was too small to do the job properly. Presumably they had wanted to hear what he and Sarah said in the restaurant and perhaps the older couple who had taken their place were doing the same. He had been too taken up with Sarah to heed what went on. Unprofessional, he would have conceded in earlier years. But so were they; it must have been a rushed job, mounted at the last minute when they discovered he and Sarah were meeting.

But how? By intercepting his phone, or simply because Sarah had told Nigel? He hadn't asked whether she had. It wouldn't have been police surveillance – they'd have had no reason to do it and it would have taken too long to set up if Nigel had requested it. Deploying the SIA's usual resources would also have taken time to set up and justify. There were laws these days about following people, laws Charles had disapproved of when they were introduced, but useful now. Most likely Nigel had rapidly called in part of Martin's old Z organisation, if it still existed.

But why, to what end? There was surely nothing Charles could do that Nigel couldn't discover simply by asking Sarah, or the police, or Charles himself. Unless it was something that Nigel badly wanted to know and couldn't get any other way, something perhaps that Charles didn't yet know himself.

A taxi disgorged a couple of drunks whom he presumed to be British bankers until hearing them arguing in Russian. Time was when they'd have been the quarry on a Chelsea street, not him. He ambled on towards the Boltons while his surveillants presumably scurried around him. What Nigel most wanted, surely, was for Gladiator never to be found. Or, if found, to be found only by him, Nigel. What he did not want was for Charles to find him. That was why he had had Charles arrested and taken off the case, and why his SIA pass hadn't been returned with his possessions. The reason for following him now must be that Nigel feared he would continue his search for Gladiator, perhaps all the more determinedly. And would perhaps even find him.

He was right, Charles concluded as he turned into Bolton Gardens. More right than he knew.

15

The SIA switchboard answered promptly the next morning. Nigel was not available and the operator couldn't say when he would be. Charles asked to be put through to Nigel's secretary. This was not possible, either. He asked why. The operator, sounding more awkward as she became more formal, said: 'I have to tell you, Mr Thoroughgood, that that is all I am authorised to say.'

'To anyone or just to me?' He knew the answer.

'I'm sorry but I can't say any more.'

'Could you put me through to Jeremy Wheeler instead, please?'

There was a pause. 'I'm sorry, Mr Thoroughgood, but Mr Wheeler is not available.'

'Could you pass him a message, please? Could you—'

'I'm sorry, I'm not authorised—'

'—tell him that if he doesn't ring me in the next half an hour I'll call at the front door of the office. That's all. Thank you.' He put the phone down.

He was fairly sure that Jeremy would not call his bluff. He had no intention of humiliating himself by trying to gain admittance without a pass, still less of creating a scene and risking further arrest. But he thought he could reckon on Jeremy's fear of fuss. Ten minutes later Jeremy rang, sounding his most pompous.

'Charles, before you say anything I have to tell you that I am unable to discuss or comment on the situation in which you now find yourself and am authorised only to hear and if necessary note anything you may say.'

It was important to remain polite, albeit easier with blameless switchboard operators than with Jeremy, whose features would be swollen with self-importance.

'I quite understand, Jeremy. Thank you for ringing. I appreciate it. I was just wondering whether I'm expected to come into work and if so how I get my pass back.'

Jeremy couldn't resist the bait. 'Of course you can't come to work, you're suspended. Didn't anyone tell you?'

'No-one's spoken to me apart from the police, and presumably they can't suspend me as they're not my employers.'

'No-one's sent you a letter? Someone should've. I'll organise it.'

'Bit late now.'

'We have to. Employment law.'

'For how long am I suspended?'

'Until the police have completed their investigation and decided whether or not charges are to be brought.'

'I see. Well, thanks for making that clear, Jeremy. It's very kind of you. I appreciate it.'

'You realise that I can't comment on your case.'

He was weakening. Charles smiled to himself. 'Of course, of course, I fully understand your position. You have wider responsibilities.' Jeremy always responded to anyone using phrases similar to his own. Flattery could not be overdone so long as it was shameless, which for Charles meant ignoring his own embarrassment. 'A man in your position has to consider the interests of the service as a whole, as well as important legal aspects. Not to mention the interests and well-being of individual members.'

'Indeed. One has also to take into account actual or potential reputational damage.'

'Indeed. And with the new SIA, all such considerations must have a more complex context requiring far more interpretation, inter-relation and inter-disciplinary aware-ness than before. But if I can just step outside my own case for a moment, I'd like to say how beneficial it is for all concerned that you are where you are, Jeremy. People must be very grateful. A relief, too, for Nigel to know he's got a rock to lean on.'

'Well, he's – you know – one does one's job.'

'I was just wondering whether it's okay for me to speak to one or two friends in the office. Purely socially, of course. Not about my case.'

'Friends? In the office? Who?' Jeremy sounded genuinely surprised.

'One or two. It's just that I wouldn't want to put anyone in an awkward position.'

'An instruction's gone out that no-one is to speak to you. What friends have you got? Who are they?'

'Don't worry, it's okay. As I say, I wouldn't want to put anyone in an awkward position.' He knew now what he needed to know. However, it was important to part on a good note since he might need someone to take his calls later. 'But I fully understand, Jeremy, thank you. I'm glad you're there.'

'As I said, I can't discuss your case but you're welcome to ring again and talk about anything else. Anything at all.'

'Thanks, I shall.'

'I can't meet you, of course.'

'Of course not.' He put down the phone with a purifying surge of energy. With every door that closed, he felt more determined and more confident.

He next rang Matthew Abrahams at home. There was no

answer and no answerphone. He assumed that calls from his own flat were being intercepted but this was one he made no attempt to conceal; they would have expected him to contact Matthew. He put on a suit and took his umbrella, hoping for rain. He walked to South Kensington underground with *Jane Eyre* tight in his jacket pocket. If he ever had another suit made he would specify larger pockets. Or buy a Kindle.

Nigel would lack resources for twenty-four hour cover without going through normal procedures, but Charles still could not afford to assume he was clear of surveillance. It was important to appear unaware, to encourage them to relax. He took the tube to St James's Park – imagining their urgent messages to the effect that he appeared to be making for Head Office with the possible intention of forcing entry – then crossed Victoria Street and walked down Horseferry Road to Marsham Street, by the Home Office. He asked the porter in Matthew's apartment block if he could leave a message.

'You're very welcome, sir, but I'm afraid Sir Matthew was taken to hospital yesterday.'

'Was he – did it appear that he might be there some time?'

'Impossible to say, sir. St Thomas's, over the river.'

Charles retraced his steps along Marsham Street, detouring through Dean's Yard in Westminster Abbey because he liked it, then crossed St James's Park to the Duke of York's steps. As he reached the top there were a few introductory drops of rain, which was perfect. He turned into Pall Mall and shortly after entered his club. That would set them a problem. They wouldn't be able to follow him in, wouldn't see who he met there, wouldn't know whether he made any calls on the club phones or whether he emailed anyone.

In fact, all he did was have a club lunch of fish and a glass of wine, catch up with the papers and sit by the fire to read a chapter of *Jane Eyre*. Rain was by then beating against the tall windows giving onto Pall Mall. There was only one entrance, so they'd have to watch from somewhere along the street, since it would be hard to linger in a car in that area. They'd be having a miserable time of it. He ordered tea.

When the wet November afternoon faded into dusk, he took his umbrella from the cloakroom to the corner behind the porter's box where the club and any stray umbrellas were kept, substituting it for a large green golfing one. Then he crossed the deserted dining room to the door opening onto the unlit gardens at the back of all three adjacent clubs. From the bottom of the steps he headed for another set that led down to the basement of the Athenaeum, but the door was locked. Climbing onto the terrace and getting in that way was too risky, so he crossed to the plane trees, bushes and shrubs at the rear of the garden. From there he could watch unseen any activity in Carlton Gardens Terrace. The parking places were fairly full, which would partly shield him. Three men stood talking outside the Royal Society until a taxi drew up. As they were getting in Charles reached through the black iron railings to put his umbrella on the pavement, then set about scaling them.

The effort proved another unwelcome reminder of age. He used a diagonal as a foothold but the railings were high and when he heaved himself up to the spikes he found them too close to get his foot comfortably between them. It was a struggle to get both legs up and swing them over while turning and jumping. He landed heavily but, so far as he could see, unnoticed. Opening the umbrella and holding it so that he was shielded from the left, he walked rapidly towards Trafalgar Square. At what appeared to be the dead end of Carlton House Terrace were steps down to Spring Gardens and the Mall, which formed a useful surveillance trap. Unless a team was already deployed ahead covering every option, anyone following would have to come down the steps to see which way he went, while he watched un-observed from the underground car park. No-one came and so, still shielded by his borrowed umbrella, he headed for Charing Cross underground.

At Euston he bought a return ticket to Milton Keynes, the stop beyond Tring, Sonia's station. She normally reached it at about seven, he remembered her saying. He got off at Tring at six-thirty. It was easy enough to wait in the dark as if for his lift home, while watching who came and went in the car park. At least he could be sure that everyone who got off with him had left the station.

She drove a Toyota Landcruiser, used for transporting children and the generations of rescued dogs she and her husband collected. When Charles had worked with her on the Russian desk, after their operational outing to Paris and following their postings to Geneva, he used to confuse the names of dogs and children, but now the children had left home. He had called on her shortly after starting with the SIA but couldn't remember what she'd said they were doing. Something professional, both of them; she had steered them away from the re-shaped intelligence profession.

There were two Landcruisers in the car park, one of them new. He stood behind the other and watched the next train disgorge its hunched figures, picking her out as, head down, she hurried through the rain towards him. When she unlocked the car he jumped in the back, crouching on the floor by the seat.

She gasped.

'It's okay, it's me,' he said. 'Just drive on. I'll explain when we're out of the car park.'

Once they were clear and the interior lights had gone out he sat up.

'God, you made me jump', she said. 'I'm getting too old for this sort of thing and you'll be covered in dog hairs. What's going on, what are you doing? Where've you been the past two days? I tried ringing your flat and then a notice came round saying that anyone who had contact with you was to report it.'

'Nigel Measures had me arrested.'

'What for?'

'Allegedly for leaking to the press. In fact, to stop me finding Gladiator.'

They drove to a pub where, over her mineral water and his Guinness, he explained.

'Measures must be off his head,' she said. 'Manic. Getting Gladiator to go back was a death sentence. But if he is here now – regardless of whether he's al-Samit or not – why would Nigel want to find him? I can see why he'd want you off the scene but better let sleeping dogs lie, surely? If Gladiator's never heard of again, so much the better for Nigel.'

'Of course. But his removal of me only half worked, and now I'm out of his control and with more reason than ever to want to find Gladiator. That must be why he put me under surveillance, and it's why I didn't ring you. Also, he might suspect that I suspect he's the source of the James Wytham leaks. As I do.'

She glanced round the near-empty bar. 'You're sure you're clean now?'

'Sure as I can be.'

'What d'you want me to do?'

'Have another drink.'

'I can't, I'm afraid. Stephen's away and I've got hungry dogs to feed.'

'I want you to find things out for me. But it could cost you your job.'

'Maybe I will have that drink.'

He described what he wanted. She was silent for a while, then shrugged and said, 'Well, early retirement beckons and if there's a chance of nailing Measures after all these years it's worth it. Anyway,' – she toyed with her empty glass – 'I want to help.'

He was surprised by the depth of his own relief. He wouldn't have been able to do it without her. 'I don't know that I can ever adequately thank you. You do appreciate the risk? It's more than just your job, if Nigel's behaviour so far is anything to go by.'

'Of course I do. Just thank me. That'll be enough. Come on, I haven't much time. What do you want and how should we communicate? This is fun. Like real spying again.'

16

They communicated during the following fortnight mostly by dead letter box, meeting only once in the flesh. Both knew enough of intercept capabilities not even to consider electronic means. Despite her defiant willingness, Charles was as keen to spare her the taint of friendship with him as to hear what she could find out.

'The office has changed so much, it's not at all the organisation I joined,' she said when they met. 'Loyalty, care of agents, care of staff used to be paramount. Now it's all targets and timelines, health and safety, performance measurement, obsession with process and management dross.'

'We're getting old. They've changed, we haven't.'

'Maybe, but we used to ask ourselves whether something was right or wrong. Now we just ask whether it's legal. Instead of a belief and ethic we have a target culture and monitoring. They've tried to turn intelligence into a business, and the thing about business is that everything's for sale. Now we've a salesman in charge. You're right, we're old. I'm sounding like my father before he retired from the railway. Time I went.'

They were in the Fox and Hounds at Christmas Common, not far from Frieth, the Chiltern village where Charles had been brought up. It was after lunch on a Saturday of sleet and intermittent early snow. Sonia was to visit her mother in Watlington, at the foot of the hills. Charles's sister and her family lived in his parents' old house, which was his cover reason to be in the area. He had signalled this to anyone listening by ringing his sister and proposing he join them for dinner after a solitary pub lunch and an afternoon walk. He had parked the Bristol prominently in Turville and walked up to Christmas Common along woodland paths he knew well enough to be confident he brought no surveillance with him.

His and Sonia's clandestine communications had worked so far. They used a hotel not far from the SIA office. In the act of picking up a *Times* from the coffee table, she dropped her spare Landcruiser keys into his open briefcase by the armchair, which he had left for the gents just before she entered the room. He arrived nearly an hour before and left half an hour after her, having ordered tea for two and evidently, as he repeated to the waiter, been stood up. He spent the time reading the papers and watching the beguiling harpist, a young blonde woman in a long green dress whose fingers seemed to caress rather than pluck sounds from her instrument.

They had arranged that Sonia would regularly have a sandwich lunch there, usually alone, sometimes with a colleague. Charles would go for tea in the afternoons. If, in the corridor leading to the lavatories, he saw the first picture on the left slightly tilted he would correct it, go to Euston, get a return to Milton Keynes, check for surveillance, then take a London train back and get off at Tring after dark. He would unlock the Landcruiser and take from beneath the previous day's *Guardian* on the seat whatever note she had left for him. When he had anything to communicate, he would leave his note there.

He learned from her that the search for al-Samit was intensifying, although his identity and whereabouts remained unknown even to the young plotters he coordinated. Contact was only one-way, which – helpfully – led them to complain amongst themselves. A joint SIA/police operation was launched, unsurprisingly named Op Silence, with almost all surveillance resources diverted to it. Sonia's friend in the legal department told her that the police had been briefed that they need not hurry their investigation of

Charles because current operations should take priority; investigations of any further James Wytham leaks should be put on the back burner. There hadn't in fact been any leaks since Charles's arrest. Is there any way we could ID Wytham? he had asked Sonia in his message.

Before she had time to reply he had signalled for the Christmas Common meeting. Most of the lunchers had left and they got a table by the fire. Two men at the bar were complaining about the damage caused by muntjac.

'I've told Stephen I'm seeing mum,' she said, 'but not you. I would have said but then I'd have to start explaining and I'd end up telling him everything. Quite a treat, a weekend pub lunch. Stephen and I got out of the habit about fifteen years ago. What's the news?'

'I'll tell you in a moment. Anything on Wytham?'

'Complete blank. He appears to have written nothing beyond the leak articles, doesn't have a blog or website, doesn't feature anywhere. I didn't run a trace on him because that would have alerted the office to my interest and they must've done it themselves, anyway. Also, your police interviewers would have known about it if they'd come up with anything. So, next best thing, I talked to old Ronnie Westgate. You must remember Ronnie? Great expert on the Russian intelligence services, especially the GRU.'

'No-one wants to know now, I s'pose?'

'Exactly, though they're spying as much as ever. Anyway, Ronnie's been retired and re-treaded as a reviewer of archive files for release to Kew. What a waste. But he sits with our brand new PR department, alongside the bright young things who talk about image creation and mission statements and deal with the press. He says none of them knows who James Wytham is. They assume it's a pen-name. They even asked Headington, the editor. Got nowhere, of course.'

Charles put his hand to his head. 'James Headington, of course. I'd forgotten.'

'You know him?'

'I knew him a bit at Oxford. Haven't seen him since.' It was obvious, almost childishly obvious. 'Stupid of me. I should've realised. During the year we lived out of college he shared a flat with – guess who? Nigel. He had a wealthy aunt and it belonged to her. It was in a priory outside Oxford, in a place called Wytham. And Headington, his real name, is another part of Oxford. Easy transposition. That would appeal to Nigel.'

'So Headington the editor is James Wytham? Being leaked to by his old flat-mate?'

'Either that or Nigel writes it for him and he edits it. At Oxford he edited *Isis* and Nigel used to write stuff for him then, anonymous gossip-column stuff. He used a pen-name for that, too, but I can't remember what it was. So they've done it before, and they're bound to have kept up with each other. Nigel wouldn't let successful friends lapse.' He hadn't meant to sound resentful. 'Stupid of me. I knew Heading-ton was the editor but just never thought about it.'

'If we could prove the leak we could nail Nigel on that alone.'

'There's more. The reason I wanted to meet.' He paused as two couples noisily moved two single tables together. 'Sarah rang me.'

'Rang you? When? Where?'

'Here. I mean, at home. Yesterday morning.'

Nervousness, or excitement, had made Sarah loquacious. 'Martin's just rung me,' Sarah had said, speaking quickly. 'At home. He was lucky to find me, I've got the day off and I was waiting in for the annual gas inspection, of all things. That's not the only reason I've got the day off but it's why I was in rather than out doing something else. I don't know how he got our number. He was ringing from a phone box, I think. I thought we were ex-directory. Perhaps we're not. Or perhaps he'd had it since – since when we knew each other. Unlike almost everyone else, we've never moved.' She paused, then resumed more deliberately. 'He rang because he wanted to speak to you. Or said he did. I offered to give him your number – assuming that was all right because you were trying to find him – but he said he didn't need it. Just wanted me to pass a message. It's a strange message, just one word. Presumably it will mean something to you. I asked him how he was, but he obviously didn't want to talk. He just said he was surviving and hoped I was, too. That was all.'

Charles waited. 'What was the word – the message?'

'Oh yes, sorry, stupid of me. It was a word, just one word. Templewood. That was all. He said, just tell him Templewood.'

'Templewood.' Charles nodded to himself. It was the exercise name for the hide by the farm in Shropshire where Martin had completed his rural surveillance training years before.

'D'you understand it?' Sarah continued. 'Does it mean anything?'

'I know what he means.'

'He didn't say any more.' She sounded deflated.

'Does Nigel know he rang?' He would soon, assuming they were still tapping Charles's phone.

'I haven't told him. It's only just happened.'

'May I come and see you?'

She hesitated. 'Well – of course you could, but is there really any point? We can say anything we have to say over the phone, can't we? Besides, I'm just about to leave. I've got to go down to our house in Oxfordshire. There's a shoot this weekend. Nigel's invited some people to stay. He's coming down later.'

Charles related all this to Sonia. 'It means Martin wants to meet there,' he said. 'At Templewood, assuming it still exists. And that he fears interception. He took a big risk in ringing Sarah, must be pretty desperate. I'll go to Templewood, if I can find it again, but I wanted you to know where I'm going in case anything happens.'

'Is that likely?'

'No, it's unlikely, always. But I don't know what's happened with Martin, so I wanted you to know.' He described the farm and hide as best he could. 'The map references and directions are near the back of one of the early volumes of the Gladiator files.'

She paused while the barman brought her sandwiches and Charles's pie and beans. 'Do you think he could be al-Samit?' she asked. 'Is there any chance that Nigel could be right?'

Charles shrugged. It had occurred to him – Martin had, after all, converted – but he couldn't bring himself to believe it. 'Only in the sense in which anyone's capable of anything. I can't see him plotting to kill us all; he'd just reject us, want nothing to do with us. Unless he's playing some very long double-treble-double sort of game that I can't fathom. And because I can't, I'm not going to waste my time trying. Next thing, can you find out where Sarah's and Nigel's Oxfordshire house is? First I've heard of it.'

'You're not thinking of dropping in on her, are you? Just for old time's sake?' She looked at him. 'Are you quite clear about what you want from Sarah?'

'Not what you might think.' He shrugged again and smiled. As former keeper of the secret annex, Sonia knew his whole story. There was no-one apart from Matthew himself he would have trusted more. 'At least, that's not what I'd be dropping in for.'

'This time.'

'I want her to help me threaten Nigel with exposure in order to force him to resign. If he knows it's not just me he's more likely to go.'

'But you've tried that with her already, haven't you? Two weeks ago, in the restaurant? You got your answer.'

'Yes, but this time I shall have seen Martin, so I'll know what's been going on. If I can convince Sarah that Nigel tried to get Martin killed, she might be more persuadable.'

Sonia looked steadily at him. 'You have a ruthless side, don't you? It doesn't often show.'

'But this is serious, isn't it? Trying to get someone killed, getting someone else arrested. It deserves exposure

277

at the very least. Quite apart from what he did with the French.'

'I agree, it is, it does, it should be exposed. But do you see what a huge step it would be for Sarah? If there's a row it's not just her husband's career and reputation she destroys, it's her own life, their friends, their standing in the world. The mud splashes over her too.'

'Not if he goes quietly.'

'What he's done so far doesn't suggest a man who's prepared to go quietly. He might do something really desperate if you try to force him. No-one could blame her for not going along with you.'

'I wouldn't blame her, either. I'll just try to persuade her.'

'Is that all? Honestly? You'll stop there?'

'Honestly. I'll see Martin and talk to you again before I do anything. But I'd still like the address.'

The following Tuesday afternoon the painting in the St Ermin's Hotel needed straightening. With luck, that would mean she had left the address in her Landcruiser that morning. He was almost sure he was not being followed but nevertheless he stayed for tea with the harpist, with whom he was now on chatting terms. Any surveillance might conclude she was the reason he visited.

Sonia's note included more than Nigel's Oxfordshire address and telephone number. She had added: 'Al-Samit

suspected High Wycombe area as from last Friday. Surveillance deployed in strength. Think before you act.'

They were still tapping his phone, then, and must have
heard Sarah's call. Although they wouldn't have been tapping hers, they would know when she took Martin's call
and would have traced it back to a call box in the High
Wycombe area.

The following morning Charles headed west just after
five. At that time it was possible to enjoy the journey. The
first part took him in the direction of High Wycombe,
which would have excited his surveillants if they were on
to him, but he stayed on the M40 at a law-abiding seventy
miles per hour. He wanted to give no-one any excuse to
stop him. After a breakfast at a service station he cut across
country and through Kidderminster towards Ludlow.
With no sign of surveillance, the drive from then on was
pure pleasure. The countryside was beautiful, the car
handled as it should and the big V8 breathed deeply and
effortlessly. Perhaps, he thought, he should sell Scotland
and buy Shropshire. Perhaps Sarah was right to say
Scotland was too remote and to warn of the dangers of
contraction in solitude. But he would miss the sea and
would still be alone. Without his intending it, being alone
seemed to have become his future, wherever he lived, the
sum of dozens of disparate choices made throughout life

without any thought of what they might add up to. He didn't mind, he thought.

In Ludlow he checked into the Feathers. There were doubtless cheaper places, possibly better, but he had stayed there long ago during his earlier Templewood mission. That time he drove an office Vauxhall, rendezvousing the next day with the SAS to pick up Martin. Carefree days, in retrospect; one of the secrets of life, he now thought, was to know them at the time.

In the afternoon he set off towards Leintwardine, motoring slowly through hills and hangers that inevitably recalled Housman, in mood if not in fact. After crossing the River Teme he turned right towards Brampton Bryan and Bucknell, heading from there up into the hills through narrow high-banked lanes laced with grass in the middle. He remembered it better than he had thought. Nothing seemed to have changed, apart from some of the larger farmhouses, which looked smarter and richer, indicating owners whose income did not depend on land. He parked at the pond where two lanes met, not far from the pick-up point where Martin had jumped into the Land Rover. From there he would have to footslog it across the fields and up the hill, hoping memory would still hold.

Pretty soon it was less his memory than his heart and lungs that preoccupied him. He reckoned himself fit for his age, still ran regularly, still enjoyed long walks, but didn't remember these hills as so steep. Nor did he remember the route once he reached the final crest. The sky was grey, a damp wind buffeted the grass and there was snow on the Welsh mountains to the west. In the deep valley to his right a red Dinky-toy tractor was carrying hay to sheep, white blobs on a green handkerchief. A hawthorn hedge marked a gentler slope to his left but there was no sign of the gap he sought, only a sheep's skull and rabbit holes in the bank. He followed the hedge down the other side of the hill until eventually he saw a rusty metal gate and in the grass beside it a broken and faded footpath sign.

From there he followed a thinner and more neglected hedge across two fields. Eaten out by sheep and worn through by their tracks, it was decades since it had served any purpose. Probably not since the days when farms had workers whose winter jobs were hedging and ditching. Those might also have been the days when the single-roomed ruin they called Templewood had functioned as – as what? A shepherd's hut during the lambing? Too substantial for that and, anyway, they would have lambed lower down or in the barns. Something to do with the water supply? He recalled an iron relic in the stone floor. Or someone's folly, a summerhouse for picnicking and enjoying the views, built during a burst of prosperity and romantic naturalism. Whatever its origin, the overgrown ruin had provided a good hide from which to log the comings and goings of the unsuspecting Valley Farm below. That it was also cold, wet and hospitable to vermin was so much the better. Train hard, fight easy, the army used to say. He wondered when MI6 had last used the place. The new SIA would find it incompatible with health and safety.

But he had yet to find it at all. From the end of the hedge he could see the farm, a scattering of grey stone buildings in varying states of disrepair, roofed with slate and corrugated iron and surrounded by the scruffy detritus of old working farms – tyres, rusty implements, bits of tractor, discarded axles, fence posts, wire netting, the skeleton of a van, dilapidated hen-houses and a moss-grown caravan with an incongruous blue roof and dirty net curtains. A few chickens were scratching about and a collie was sniffing a pile of logs. The only change was that they had started to convert one of the barns to accommodation, and then abandoned it.

The ruin must be nearby, since it offered virtually the same view, but the wind-warped undergrowth looked too sparse to conceal it. Charles began circling the rim of the valley from the field side, peering down into twisted thorn and stunted scrub oak. Thinking it must be lower than he remembered, he made his way down through the trees. As he slithered and caught himself on a branch he heard a man's distant voice, a single gruff shouted word. The dog turned and trotted back to the house. He froze: they wouldn't spot him among the trees but they might notice movement.

It was as he stood holding the branch that he became aware of the hide above and behind him, to his right. He must have moved below and across it after entering the trees. Dug into the hillside and facing across the dell, it was concealed from above and on both sides by undergrowth, concealed also from the dell by tree growth. There was an entrance with no door, a rotting door frame with the lintel missing, the stonework around it cracked and sagging. The windows were dark misshapen rectangles, sprouting weeds, and the tiled roof was holed and uneven, its timbers exposed.

If Martin was there he would have seen Charles arrive, but there was no sound. Charles remained still, neither frightened nor uneasy, but wondering if he should be. Martin was an unknown quantity now; what he was doing, what he thought, what he wanted was a mystery. It was possible he had returned to kill his former case officers; Charles had once run an agent who had done just that to the officer of a liaison service. Perhaps he really had become an extremist as Nigel Measures wanted everyone to believe, or perhaps he wanted to revenge himself on anyone from the service that had sent him back to Afghanistan. Well, he could do it here and now easily enough. The only sound was the cawing of rooks.

Treading carefully on the loose earth, Charles climbed the few yards to the hut, stepped in and paused to let his eyes adjust to the gloom. It felt damp, there were leaves on the broken stone floor and weeds coming up through the cracks. In the middle, about knee-height, was the iron relic he remembered. It looked like the remains of a water pump. He had forgotten there was a boarded ceiling, sagging and holed in places. Some of the boards had rotted and fallen to the floor.

'Welcome back to Templewood. Glad you came alone.'

17

Martin spoke quietly, from somewhere very close. Charles felt a slight spasm in his throat.

'Don't worry, I'll come to you,' said Martin.

There was slithering and creaking overhead. Charles remembered now that the actual hide was between the roof and a reinforced section of ceiling, entered from the bank behind via an enlarged hole in the tiles, hidden by bushes. Martin would have slid in on his belly from the field and could be heard now, pushing his way back out through the thicket.

Charles stepped outside the door to await him, shielded by branches from the farm below. After a minute or so Martin appeared without a sound from the other side of the hide, a tall man with reddish-brown stubble. He wore camouflage kit and the kind of green woollen hat the army used to call a cap comforter. He carried a green rucksack in one hand and held up his other like a policeman stopping traffic.

'Come no closer. I probably smell worse than the last time you picked me up from this place.'

Charles stepped forward. 'We can chance a handshake.' Martin's grip was strong and his hand hard. His face was dirty and his green eyes looked tired. 'How long have you been here?' asked Charles.

'Long enough. Sarah passed the message, then? She assured me she could. Mrs Measures, I should say.' He laid heavy emphasis on her married name. 'How is she?'

'Well, I believe. I saw her a couple of weeks ago.'

'Still married?'

Charles nodded. 'Where shall we talk?'

'Here. Nowhere's safe.'

'From what?'

'From your friends. Your employer, if you're still employed. From the organisation you got me into many years ago and which right now is trying to kill me.'

They squatted on the earth, leaning against tree trunks. Martin's speech was quiet and controlled, as if long thought about, or even rehearsed. He would have had time to rehearse, thought Charles, lying day and night in that damp hide.

'You sent me to Afghanistan to target the Taliban. Or al-Qaeda. It wasn't clear which, but that didn't matter. No longer the PIRA, anyway. I'd done that crusade. I was keen and d'you know what? – I loved it, every frozen, boiling, tedious, gruelling, exciting, awful, wonderful, boring minute of it. Away from my own country, I found I loved war. It surprised me, I thought I'd be appalled by the suffering and want to help but instead I found the struggle of man against man the most exhilarating thing I knew. Better than sex, religion, climbing Everest, better than anything. It may seem a dreadful thing to say, but I never felt more fully alive than when killing. I did a lot more of that than I ever let on to you or your successors.'

He paused, looking for a response. This was a more expressive Martin than Charles remembered. He's been saving it for a long time, he thought. He nodded. 'I always suspected you did.'

'That wasn't why you sent me, I knew that. But they were so appealing, those Afghans, it was impossible not to get involved. Their fierce simplicity, their courtesy, their manners, their pitilessness, their fantastic loyalty and treachery, their bravery. I love them for it. I know it's said that you don't buy an Afghan, you rent him, but that doesn't make him any less brave or even less loyal, provided you know the rules he lives by. For him, life is fighting and striving; for us it's security and comfort. Colours are vivid for him, for us they're blurred. Life for him is crueller, and clearer. I couldn't be with them and not be one of them. I was young, I guess. That's why I stayed on after 9/11.'

'You found a cause.'

'I found a mission. I stayed to help. Schools, medicine, roads, whatever I could. Mainly schools, because without education you can't do anything; but if they've got that they can do the rest themselves. For a while it was fine; so much to do, and no-one seriously trying to stop you. But when the security situation worsened and the warlords fell out with one another everything changed. I became a Muslim, as perhaps you know. That kept my head on my body, at least. It also helped my education mission. It was never a question of belief – I no more believe in the Prophet than in the Pope or the Reverend Ian Paisley, for Christ's sake. Not that there aren't some fine things in Islam. Like most religions, it's a good enough way to live if you don't believe very much, or take it literally. It's just that accepting faith means giving up on questioning, which is how we learn, how we move on. So I pretended.'

'You had a lot of time for thinking,' said Charles.

'A lot of time sitting cross-legged and talking. Conversion was not only a way of showing where my sympathies lay, it was also a way of getting beneath the skins of a people and culture that intrigued me. Not that the Afghans are very religious, most of them. Unlike AQ – which I could've joined, by the way, if I'd sworn allegiance to UBL and all that.' There was another shout from the farm below. He glanced down the hill towards it. 'Going deaf, that dog. But love dies, doesn't it? That's the trouble. Dwindles, fades, anyway. I fell out of love with the office and in love with the Afghans, the non-Taliban ones. But when the stability they were promised after 9/11 never happened, it became more and more difficult for me to do my work. Down in the south where the Taliban were regaining control the only way for me to survive would have been to join them, and I didn't want to kill my own. At least not then.'

'You do now?'

'Don't worry, not you. So far as I know.' Martin's smile showed a broken tooth and made him look younger than his thirty-five years. 'So, I moved back here full time and built up my practice, my legal practice, largely in the Pakistani community where my languages help. I travelled out there quite a lot. I kept my hand in with Afghan work, when I could, though there wasn't much scope for legal process there.'

'But you were still an agent, weren't you, still working for the office?'

Martin picked a strip of bark from the ground and turned it over the fingers of both hands, his arms around his raised knees. 'Off and on, gradually more off than on. We sort of drifted apart. It was mutual, I guess. They used to be pretty good at keeping in touch in your day, didn't they? Just that – keeping in touch, we're here if you want us, we haven't forgotten you. They'd never forget; and if you were ever lost they'd always, always find you. That's what you felt. But not nowadays. It's changed since your time. Now everything's immediate, current; either a quick win or forget it, waste of time. I did get in touch a couple of times because I came across people in my charity work. People who might have been useful in future, with a little cultivation, gentle and early. But no-one's got time for that now, it's all wham-bam-thank-you-ma'am. You miss a lot of good agents that way.'

Martin broke off a small piece of bark and flicked it away. 'And then one day the phone rings again. What about getting back into harness for a while, scouting things out, re-visiting some old contacts who might help us win the great War on Terror without their knowing it? Only this time I had two case officers, younger than me, which was a first, a man and a woman. Nice couple, good, keen; didn't know much about Afghanistan but that's not their fault, they'll learn. So I did a couple of trips to Pakistan for them, which I could combine with genuine business, and I made contact with one or two people. Came back each time with a few snippets which they raved over – and which suggests to me the SIA doesn't have much coverage out there these days. Does it?'

Charles shrugged. 'I don't see current stuff. They asked me back to find you.'

'Tell me about it. In a minute. So, after the last trip I get this summons to go back in a great hurry. It came by an unusual route, suggesting there was something urgent they wanted my help with. Looked fishy to me, not the normal way of my friends over there. They like to play things long – if it doesn't happen this time, then next if Allah wills, and if he doesn't it still doesn't matter, because their timelines are millennial. No performance indicators for them. The office took its time to decide, of course, but my young minders were wary and in the end I sent a holding reply. Can't go now, court commitments, that sort of thing.

'Then, out of the blue, our old friend Mr Measures comes knocking on my door. We hadn't met since dinner at his house years before, he kept telling me. So pleased I was back in harness, wanted to thank me himself. Of course, I didn't let on I'd seen him in Paris after that dinner, playing away from home, doing what he shouldn't. His little

291

indiscretions there didn't harm his career, obviously. Desperate for me to go back immediately, he says; the service needs me, the country needs me, world peace and Christians and Muslims everywhere need me. Information urgently required on someone called al-Samit, who's apparently over here coordinating the troops. But no-one knows who or where he is: could I go back there and find out?'

Charles held up his hand. 'Nigel called on you? Alone? Unannounced? In your office?'

'At home.'

'And he said al-Samit was already here? He definitely said that?'

'Yes. Why – isn't he?' He smiled, slightly.

'Go on.'

'Seemed pretty dodgy to me, going back, not only for the obvious reasons but because of our mutual friend's unexpected visit. Last thing you want to do with that bunch of conspiracy theorists out there is to go round asking questions. But that's what he wanted. He gave me a name, someone I'd never heard of but whom I should meet. Also a few titbits, so I had something to talk about. If I didn't go, the streets of our cities would run with blood, all that sort of crap. He's persistent, I'll say that for him. Anyway, it was good to feel wanted again, to be useful. I agreed.'

'What kind of titbits?'

'Nothing much. The main one was something about CIA saying they had no agents in AQ core, their cupboard was bare. I was supposed to have seen that in court transcripts. I got a flight next day.'

'Without talking to your case officers?'

Martin paused while breaking another piece of bark. 'I assumed they knew all about it. Didn't they?'

Charles shook his head. 'He did it off his own bat. What happened when you got there?'

'I went to Peshawar as per normal but when I called on my usual contact I was welcomed by the very man Mr Measures had kindly recommended to me. Only he wasn't the great facilitator I was promised. He was a nasty bit of work from Yemen with a visceral suspicion of Western converts and a reputation for sniffing out and snuffing out spies. I knew in about sixty seconds that this was a one-way trip, but I sort of didn't believe it at first. In the way that things can seem too good to be true, they can seem to be too bad to be true, too. You can't believe it, you think there must be some mistake, you're misreading the signals. So I went along with it, playing the innocent abroad, feeding my titbits to him and the others.'

'Then we left the others and he took me to what was meant to be a safe house, a compound in a village over the border, about a day's drive. It was safe, all right, a regular meeting place for AQ and Taliban heavies. Also pretty handy as a prison and interrogation centre for people like me. That was where I finally accepted that this wasn't just a cock-up but that Measures, your very own Measures, had deliberately sent me to my death. Is that how the SIA gets rid of its old agents these days?'

'They don't. But Measures does.'

'Why did he do it? What's the point? All he needed to do was leave me alone and never contact me. I'd never have gone knocking on his door.'

'Because he's chief now, or virtually, and because you know about his treachery in Paris, and he doesn't want anyone associated with the SIA to know that. He wants to get rid of us both. He had me arrested.'

Charles told his story. By the time he finished Martin had no bark left to break and sat motionless, his hands clasped over his knees. The light was fading and Charles was cold.

'Must be off his head,' Martin said.

'There may be other reasons, emotional reasons of his own, that feed into it.'

Martin put his head on one side. 'Been a naughty boy with Sarah, have you? How is she? Sounded strained on the phone.'

'Haven't seen much of her. But—' He hesitated. Their temporary physical removal from the rest of life made it feel like a time for frankness. But again he stalled, as he always had. Having no feel for what Martin's reaction might be, he feared it. Sarah's reaction was not an encouraging precedent. He was reluctant, too, to confront his own guilt again. Anyway, it would take too much time, time that should be spent deciding what they were going to do. They could talk later. 'But I get the impression things aren't that great between them,' he said. 'She must have been pleased to hear from you.'

'Maybe. He couldn't have done it all on his own, though, could he? There must be others in on it with him. Just getting you arrested and your pass withdrawn, for example, he couldn't do that on his own. There must be others who know about it.'

Defending colleagues still came naturally to Charles, even if it was the SIA. Maybe it wasn't what the old services had been, maybe it was less than the sum of its constituent parts. But, like monastic ruins, it still stood for something. 'He did it all on his own. You and me both. Agents and staff are never sacrificed or betrayed. Ever. That is the sin against the Holy Ghost. Nigel is manipulating the service for his own ends. He's got away with it so far because it's become bureaucratically flabby and has lost its rigour. But tell me what happened to you. What did they do to you, how did you get back?'

Martin was feeling among the leaves for another piece of bark, but found none. He clasped his hands again. 'I was lucky, dead lucky. They didn't get the chance to do much. What they would've done doesn't bear thinking about. Fortunately – praise be to Allah and Uncle Sam for working together – we were blown up. A US drone strike. Half a dozen heavies killed, along with the Yemeni and some nearby women and children. Plenty wounded. I was knocked out, came round and got away in the confusion. Took me nearly a week to get back to Peshawar, living on nothing, almost freezing to death. Then I had to get back to Islamabad and get out. I daren't go to the High Commission for help because that might have given Measures another chance to do me in. I had to go black, as I think your CIA friends put it. Luckily, I still had contacts who do passports, credit cards, that sort of thing. They obliged because they thought I was working against you, not for you. Things have changed out there.'

'But Measures must know you're back, or believe you are. From before you rang Sarah. That's the only reason he would have put me under surveillance, to lead him to you. And he's telling everyone you're al-Samit.'

'I'm the Silent One?' Martin shook his head slowly. 'I should've been, I should've stayed silent. If I had I wouldn't have had to move in here. I'll tell you what happened. I travelled back under alias with no problems, cleared out everything I needed from my office and home and went back into hiding, where I've been ever since. I reckoned I had a while before they'd find out I was missing, not dead, and that contacting you was my only hope because I knew you were out of it. I tried old numbers, addresses, everything. Eventually, I got a fix from a database on some place up in Scotland, but no response. So I rang Sarah. Last resort. I knew that would put Measures on to me but reckoned by then he must suspect I was back. It was the only way I could get a message to you. I actually had something to report, quite apart from what happened to me. Still trying to help, you see. Pathetic, isn't it?' He grinned. 'Because I did learn something about al-Samit, an overheard bit of conversation. Guess.'

'It's Nigel Measures.'

'Not bad. Try again.'

'We haven't time. Who is he?'

'*She*.'

'It's a woman?'

'Good to see you're still on the ball. I was going to keep it to myself, because I don't reckon the bunch of fruitcakes she's dealing with here are up to much. And of course it wasn't exactly safe for me to ring my case officers and report. But then there was that cinema bomb a few weeks ago, remember? Nutter blew himself up. I don't know whether that was them or not but I thought, blood on the streets and all that, innocent people, I can't risk it. So I rang my old agent number, got an answerphone and just said, "al-Samit is a woman", nothing more. Didn't leave my name or anything, but I guessed they'd work out it was me. Voice recognition?'

'It was a dedicated number. Only you had it.' The red tractor entered the farmyard below, accompanied by two more collies. Charles got to his feet. He felt damp, stiff and cold. 'Let's go over all that again later. We need to work out what we're going to do. We could chance dinner, if there's somewhere you could get cleaned up. Where are you staying?'

'Here.'

'You can't.'

'I can but I shan't. I have been, but I'll move on tonight, walking cross-country, lying up during the day. I've got enough rations to get me back.'

'Back where?'

'If I tell you, it's a burden. Someone might get it out of you. Need to know, you always used to say.'

'High Wycombe?'

'Don't want to risk getting a good Muslim family into trouble.'

'I'll book you into the Lion at Leintwardine. In my name, my credit card. I won't stay, but we can eat there. Then you can go black again.'

Martin was reluctant. He didn't want to appear any-where in public, especially with Charles. Charles argued that the chances of his having brought surveillance with him were negligible. If they didn't plot Nigel's downfall now, they'd have to meet again to do it another time, which would be more dangerous.

'Convenience and comfort are the enemies of security, you always used to say,' said Martin. 'What's changed?'

It was almost dark by the time Charles prevailed.

'It's the thought of a bath, really,' said Martin, getting up and brushing himself down. 'Getting soft in my old age.'

He gathered his kit and they walked together back up the darkening hill and then down to where the car was parked, taking care not to be silhouetted against the stip-pled western sky.

When they reached the Lion, Charles went in and paid while Martin took his time unloading his kit from the car.

'Wait till I open the fire escape for you to come up that way,' Charles had said before he went in. 'If they see you looking like that, let alone smell you, they'll say they're full.' He waited downstairs while Martin changed into his reserve shirt and trousers.

They ate a leisurely dinner of local lamb. Martin described the slaughter and preparation of sheep and goats, which he'd learned in Afghanistan. A shave, a bath, a comb through his hair and a change of clothes took five or ten years off him, though he still had to wear his boots. As they talked Charles wondered yet again at the mystery of his own flesh and blood, at those lips, those teeth, those eyes, those hard but now clean hands moving with the easy grace of youth; all conjured unknowingly during a few moments in the dark. As before, he waited to feel some tug at the solar plexus, some lurch in the heart, some intimate stab of recognition. But none came: instead, there was the old incredulity at the astonishing matter-of-factness of it, of this man eating and talking before him. It was knowledge that made the difference, he told himself again. Had he not known, he would never have wondered at the creation of this being, would never have watched his expression for flashes of likeness to Sarah, fleeting as shooting stars, would never have taken any more interest in him than in any other likeable man in his thirties. Blood, he concluded, as he had before, knew not itself; but knowledge of blood was all.

Martin talked about his charity in Afghanistan and the work he hoped, one day, to do again. More than once Charles was on the point of telling him. He wanted to, wanted him to know. But he remembered what Matthew had said about not putting himself first, thought of what Sarah might want, and held back yet again. If he took that step he wanted to take her with him.

He came closest when Martin said: 'I just don't understand why Measures should be so frightened. If no-one cared enough to sack him years ago, they're hardly going to now. And who's going to blow the gaff, anyway? Not you, you're too loyal to your old service. Not me, I've no interest. Not Sarah, she's got too much to lose. Not this Sonia you mentioned, she's probably like you and anyway, he doesn't know about her. No-one would tell his dirty little secret, if he hadn't had you arrested and tried to get me killed. He knows I'm not al-Samit. Is he just crazy or is there something else?'

'When I was a student I read a judgement by a fourteenth-century judge on *mens rea*. He said, "The devil alone knoweth the heart of man." We're no farther forward.'

'That was when you knew Sarah and Measures together, wasn't it? When you were students? I keep forgetting that. She told me once, or maybe you did.'

'We all knew each other, yes.'

'Maybe lifelong jealousy on his part, then. It was obvious you always carried a candle for Sarah.'

'It was, was it?' Now, he thought, right now.

But Martin went on. 'Anyway, it's the future we need to worry about. What are we going to do? Apart from get another bottle.'

They plotted that Charles would confront Nigel, with Sarah's help, if she agreed. Martin would go back into hiding but with contact arrangements in place; Sonia would act as go-between and cut-out. If Nigel refused to resign at Charles's first attempt, then he and Martin would confront him together, threatening to go public.

'And if he still refuses?' asked Martin.

'He won't.'

'But if he does? Going public would have consequences, especially for me and my practice.'

'If we say it, we've got to mean it. But you'd have more to lose, of course.'

'Not as much as he has. Besides, there's always the memoirs.'

After dinner they walked out into the car park and stood gazing at the Teme where it rippled around the garden and under the bridge. It was a moonless, cloudy night with few stars.

'You must be over the limit,' Martin said.

'Maybe.' It wouldn't be the first time. He could book himself in for the night, which would mean paying for two hotel rooms – three, with Martin's – and doing without his clean clothes and shaving kit, which were in the Feathers. A slightly greater security risk, from Martin's point of view. Anyway, being a few points over the limit didn't worry him as much as most people he knew might think it should. He put that down to his generation. Across the road, where a lane ran parallel to the river, he glimpsed a figure move between two parked cars, a white Mondeo and a Range Rover. 'This was a Roman settlement,' he said. 'They built the first bridge here.'

'Here? Where this one is?'

'I'm not sure. The original might've been downstream.' They sauntered over to his car to get the rest of Martin's gear. Charles opened the boot and passed him a webbing belt and pouches. 'Anything else?'

'Just my sticks.'

Charles handed him the two metal telescopic walking poles and shut the boot. Someone shouted from close by. There was more shouting, but he couldn't distinguish what was said except for the word, 'police'. Martin moved and said something. Afterwards, and for the rest of his life, Charles would struggle in vain to recall what it was. There were several sharp cracks and he felt a shocking blow to his left shoulder, as if someone had hit him with a cricket bat. He staggered to his knees, then was knocked flat and winded, his right cheek and ear hitting the tarmac hard. A great weight fell on him and he saw and felt no more.

Later, in his hospital bed, he tried to get his memories into chronological sequence. It was difficult, because his only connected narrative was what people told him had happened, and he couldn't always distinguish between what he remembered and what he imagined as a result of being told. He definitely remembered the ambulance interior, but not whether it was as he was taken in or taken out. He remembered more shouting but not by whom, when or what. He remembered bright lights and a man's voice saying, 'We can't leave them like that, we've got to turn one over.' He remembered pain around his eye and in his back but not whether it was at the time or afterwards, when he came round and had thought he must have been playing rugby again.

Then there was a pleasant, timeless period, a dreamy state in which he drifted in and out of consciousness, couldn't concentrate on anything and didn't mind. It was like floating. Another voice, a woman's, said, 'Tell the police they'll just have to wait. He's not ready yet.'

Next came the long monotony of consciousness, discomfort and weakness. He was by himself in a white room overlooking the hospital car park with houses beyond and hills in the distance. By resting his eyes on the hills he could almost persuade himself he was in them, or forever approaching them. He couldn't get Housman's line about blue remembered hills out of his head, but nor could he remember the rest of the poem. Everything else in his head was bad. Mostly he thought about Martin.

Various doctors came and spoke to him and, one day, the police. On another day the door opened and instead of food or a change of dressing – an uncomfortable procedure – it was Nigel Measures. He wore a green tweed jacket, with green jumper and brown corduroys. He looked unconvincing in country clothes. He was smiling.

'Just popped up to see you, Charles. Didn't take long. Wanted to see how you are, how you're getting on. And to thank you.'

Charles began the slow business of sitting up. 'Thank me?'

'For tracking down al-Samit. Gladiator. Pity it ended in his death. But at least you're okay, thank God. Ricochet, wasn't it? Nothing broken, they tell me. Didn't penetrate too deeply because of the splayed-out shape. Is that right? Plus your black eye, of course. Quite a shiner you've got there.' Still smiling, he pulled up the chair. 'Apart from that you're looking well. You were lucky. We all were.'

Charles controlled himself. 'Except for Martin,' he said. He managed to make it sound almost jocular.

'Gladiator. Yes, well, most unfortunate, as I said. Under-
standable, from the police point of view. Dark night, him
holding what looks like a gun; then when they challenge
him he doesn't drop it but turns towards them with it.
They're entitled to shoot if they think there are lives at stake,
including their own. There'll be an enquiry, of course. Police
Complaints Commission and all that. Always is when they
shoot someone. They'll want to talk to you, find out what
happened from your point of view. What d'you think you'll
say? Hard to remember clearly, I suppose?'

His energy was as relentless as his smile. Charles let him
talk, feigning greater weakness than he felt and watching
the play of Nigel's ceaselessly mobile features. Now was not
the time; but it would come. He pictured Nigel skewered
against the white wall, writhing silently. He didn't argue
with anything, not even the identification of Martin with al-
Samit. Especially not that.

'Must be upsetting for you,' Nigel continued, 'given
Gladiator's origins. I know your relationship was purely
professional, and that he knew nothing about it, about your
being – about your relation to him and all that. That's right,
isn't it?'

It was the first time Martin's paternity had been mentioned between them. Possibly Sarah had told him. More
likely, he had read it in the file, in the secret annex that

recorded his own dealings with French intelligence. Charles replied slowly, as if with difficulty.

'No, he never knew. Makes me sad to think of that.' He paused, then added. 'You knew all about it, of course.'

'God, yes. I was briefed on it ages ago by Matthew Abrahams. He thought I should know about it when I was saying I wanted you back on the case, to find Gladiator.'

Another lie, as pointless as it was ineffectual. The man inhabited a web of lies. Charles wanted to ask what he'd done with the secret annex but it was more important to appear unthreatening. He nodded.

'You heard he'd died, Matthew?' Nigel continued. 'Two days ago. Not unexpected, of course. But sad all the same, very sad.'

Charles stared. 'I didn't know that.'

'Nice obituary in the *Times*. What he deserved. But well done to you, Charles, with Gladiator. Very proper. Must've taken a great deal of self-discipline not to tell him. Very professional of you. I wonder what made him turn against us. Any ideas?'

Charles was still thinking about Matthew. Hardly un-expected, as Nigel had said, but the permanent loss of his friend, that wise and playful mind, would take him a while to absorb. However, there was no time now for the luxury of private indulgence, as Matthew himself would have put it. 'I wasn't in touch with Martin when he converted,' Charles said. 'How was he when you saw him, just before he went back?' That was an unnecessary pin-prick, but he couldn't resist it.

Nigel folded his arms and glanced out of the window. 'Fine. Quite calm and collected, determined to go. He said nothing about his motives when you were with him last? Nothing religious, no ideological confession, no outpouring of hatred of us or the west or anything? No hint of why he'd become al-Samit?'

Was Nigel always this good an actor? Charles asked himself. He thought of their late-night conversations in Oxford, the early morning encounter on the Cherwell bridge, that awful dinner at the Elizabeth. Self-dramatising, perhaps, like nearly everyone at that age. But the Nigel of those days had not acted to deceive. Well, he wasn't the only one doing it now. It was essential that he should think that his invented identification of Martin with al-Samit was unquestioned. 'Nothing much in the way of outpourings,' he said. 'Not that I remember now, anyway. Mind you, I seem to have forgotten a lot, from what people tell me.'

Nigel brightened. 'You trained him well, I'll say that for you. Too bloody well.' He laughed. 'But I was so relieved when I heard you weren't seriously injured. Not only for your sake, I admit, but for all of us. Mine as well. Even more explanations to the Police Complaints Commission if you'd died too. Now you can tell them the whole story yourself, as I'm sure you will, very competently.' He paused and then, as if flicking a crumb from his sleeve, asked: 'What d'you think you'll say to them?'

He is transparent, Charles was thinking, clear as water. Perhaps he always had been. The puzzle was not so much how had he got away with it, but why had he not done even better for himself? People so often took you at your own evaluation; you could get almost anywhere by flattering and smiling. But the most adept were often also the most vulnerable to the same tactic. Charles forced a weak smile.

'Just pleased I didn't let you down,' he said. 'My first thought when I came round was that I'd cocked it up. I thought Martin must've attacked me. He wasn't always an easy man to be with. As for the PCC, I'll confine myself to what happened that night, what little I remember of it, just as I did when the police interviewed me.'

'They've spoken to you already, the police?' Nigel's tone was sharper.

'Yesterday or the day before. Can't remember which. I had the impression their main concern is to avoid blame for shooting another unarmed man. They're not interested in the background or anything in the past. Especially the deep past.'

Nigel relaxed and nodded encouragingly. 'The deep past. A good phrase for all that's dead and buried.'

Like Martin, Charles thought, thanks to you. Except that Martin was not yet buried but lying chilled in a mortuary drawer, a piece of evidence. He couldn't help picturing it; the more so because Martin had been such a warm and vigorous presence.

Nigel left with the assurance he wanted, knowing nothing of Sarah's visit the previous day. It was that which had given Charles the strength to hold back what he had most wanted to say. Self-control had always come naturally to him, perhaps too naturally; but this time she had provided crucial, if unintended, reinforcement.

He had been dozing when she arrived and had awoken to see the door closing behind her. He struggled to sit up, embarrassed by his awkwardness and his black eye. She was wearing jeans with long brown boots and a suede jacket.

She smiled and laid some flowers on the bedside table. 'Don't. Stop it, Charles.'

'Stop what?'

'Trying to sit up. Just keep still. You're all right as you are. I was warned about your black eye.'

'Tea?'

She shook her head and pulled up the blue plastic chair. 'How do you feel?'

'Fine. I could go home, really, as soon as the anaesthetic wears off completely. Keep falling asleep. I'll go as soon as I feel I can drive.'

'Don't even think of it, it's too far. Anyway, your car needs repairing, Nigel told me. It was hit by bullets and the police have taken it away. Nigel says the office will get it back and repair it for you.'

It hadn't occurred to him that the Bristol might be damaged; nor had he realised until then that he no longer had the keys. 'How bad is it?'

'It'll be fine when it gets over the anaesthetic.'

There was a pause, which for him was filled by the presence of Martin. 'You heard what happened?'

She nodded.

'The police firearms team thought he had a gun,' he said. 'They'd been briefed that he might have. But it was his walking sticks, which he'd just taken out of the boot of my car. Most of the people they shoot seem to be unarmed. There was that man in London who came out of a pub carrying a chair-leg in a plastic bag. They shouted at him from behind and he turned round. To see who they meant, presumably. It's what people do. I expect that's what Martin did.'

He saw her eye caught by the small misshapen lump of metal on his bedside table.

'My bullet,' he said. 'They dug it out of my shoulder. Hit the wall first, they think.'

'Just as well. Horrible thing. You were so lucky.'

'Martin isn't – wasn't – al-Samit, the one who's allegedly coordinating terrorists here. Nigel knew that when he persuaded him to go back to Afghanistan to find out who the real al-Samit is.' He spoke slowly, watching the effect of his words like an observer noting the fall of shot.

She stared. Her features showed nothing except concentration.

'When Martin got there he realised he'd been set up, betrayed,' he continued. 'They were going to kill him, but he escaped. He went into hiding when he got back here but he did ring the office and tell them the only thing he knew about al-Samit. She's a woman. Nigel would have known that when he told the police that Martin was al-Samit, and probably armed.'

She continued staring.

'His body fell on top of me, apparently. Knocked me flat. Gave me my black eye.'

'Perhaps you should keep that, too.'

Her words were muffled as her face suddenly crumpled, almost as in laughter. She bowed her head and opened her handbag, her shoulders shaking. He struggled to sit up further and touch her but she waved him away, holding a tissue to her face and repeating that she was sorry. When he eventually got himself upright he leaned forward. He couldn't reach her hands but could just touch her knee.

She was sobbing wholeheartedly now, hiding her face in both hands. 'If I'd known he was the only baby I'd have – I'd have – I'd never have—' She let the tissue fall and clutched his fingers with one hand, pressing them to her knee.

A nurse holding a tray and tea-cups opened the door. 'Cup of tea, anyone?'

'Thank you, just—' Charles tried to indicate with his bad arm that she could leave the tray with them but she backed out, saying she would come again later.

Sarah bent to pick up the tissue, then let go of his hand and stood to repair her face in the small wall mirror, working deftly with aids from her bag. 'Sorry about that. Took myself by surprise.' She made it sound as if she'd spilt something on the tablecloth.

'Does Nigel know you're here?'

'No.'

'May I come and see you when I'm out?'

She nodded and turned from the mirror to look at him. 'He loves me, you know. Nigel. He still loves me.'

'I don't doubt it.' She turned back to the mirror. 'Nor do I blame him,' Charles said.

A different nurse knocked and entered with tea. Sarah sat again to drink it while they briskly discussed the practicalities of his discharge, how he would return to London, how helpful the police had been in getting his possessions and his bill from the Feathers, what the PCC inquiry would involve, how fortunately limited was the press coverage.

She put down her cup and stood. 'Sorry I was so pathetic.'

'You weren't.'

'I came here to cheer you up. Didn't do a very good job.'

'You did.'

''Bye, Charles.' She bent swiftly and kissed his forehead, leaving him in a waft of perfume he thought he knew, or should know. But he thought that about most perfumes.

18

Sonia drank green tea, barely separating cup and saucer when she sipped. The faint click they must have made when she reunited them was inaudible because of the hotel harpist.

'Fancy her, don't you?' said Sonia.

Charles looked at the harpist as if noticing for the first time her long hair, strong slender arms, graceful figure and young face. He and Sonia had agreed that the risk of surveillance was negligible now that its purpose had been so definitively achieved, so far as Nigel was concerned. 'Haven't thought.'

'Come off it, you've hardly taken your eyes off her since she started playing. Always a harpist or pianist or waitress or something for you, isn't there? In the background. God, it would be awful to be married to you.'

'Helps me think.'

'About what?'

A friend in Ops had told her that the real al-Samit was still active and that Charles had been under surveillance throughout his trip to Shropshire. The SIA had concealed a beacon in his car one night. 'Apparently Measures ordered it because he was sure you'd eventually lead them to Gladiator,' she said. 'And the police firearms team was briefed that he was likely to be armed and would resist arrest. In Ops they all thought – still think – it was being done with your cooperation and that the beacon was back-up in case something went wrong. The theory now, they're told, is that Gladiator was the real al-Samit and that his predecessor and successor is a stand-in.'

'But what about Gladiator's call telling them it was a woman?'

'That was a ruse to put us off the track. According to Measures. The irony is that nothing much is happening, quite genuinely. The real al-Samit, whoever she is, doesn't seem to be getting it together with the aspiring martyrs. It's all talk. Nobody's actually doing anything concrete. They're a lot of adolescent wasters who need to grow up. Which makes it easier for Measures to say that Gladiator was the al-Samit who mattered, and that now they just use it as a codename for any messenger from AQ.'

The harpist finished to restrained applause from the dozen or so tea-drinkers. She executed a half-curtsey and left. 'What are you going to do now?' asked Sonia.

'She'll be back. She's only gone for her tea.' He moved his leg out of range of her kick. 'Recruit Sarah. It's the only way.'

'D'you think she's recruitable?'

'Maybe.'

'D'you really think you should?'

'I do, yes.' He sat back carefully, twiddling the spent bullet between his fingers. He had carried it since leaving hospital. His shoulder was still giving him some pain. 'I know you think I shouldn't, and you might be right. But Nigel getting me arrested was one thing. Getting Martin killed was quite another. She's upset in a way I've never known her before. She might do it. Or at least not prevent it.'

'You're so detached. You make her sound like a case you're running.'

The bullet slipped through his fingers and he bent slowly to pick it up. 'I am behaving as if detached. Doesn't mean I feel detached.'

'Sure you're not just a sentimentalist? Keeping the past alive to stop it becoming past, fending off eternal extinction? Like what Shakespeare says about lust in age: a little

317

fire in a dark field. Are you sure that's not really why you're so determined to involve her?'

'I can't be sure there's nothing of that. But it's not the main thing.'

She looked seriously at him. 'Do you love her, Charles?'

He was struck, as always, by the confidence with which women spoke of love, as if they knew exactly what it meant. 'I did.'

'Still?'

'She's part of me. I'd like to be part of her, if that's an answer.'

'And here's your harpist again. With her tea.'

'Little fires in dark fields.'

She smiled. 'We all need something to keep us warm. If your plan works it will have been right. If it doesn't, it will have been all wrong. Just like the office.'

'I need to know when she's likely to be alone in their house in Oxfordshire.'

Sonia sipped her tea again. This time the clink of cup on saucer was audible. 'I'll see what I can do.'

It was another week before the Bristol was returned, valeted and as near gleaming as its faded paintwork permitted. It was delivered by an SIA driver who enthusiastically described the invisible repair of the aluminium boot-lid and the expensive replacement of the rear window.

'Minus the beacon, I assume,' said Charles.

'Not my department, sir. Lovely motor, though.'

Some days after that Sonia – free to use the phone now – called to suggest a drink. They met after work at an hotel not far from Matthew Abrahams's Westminster flat. Charles had been to his funeral in Cambridge that morning and was grateful for company, and a drink.

'Sorry it's taken so long,' she said. 'The CEO – as Measures insists we now call him – has an intranet calendar, but it doesn't show his private engagements. So I contrived some business with his secretary and discovered he's host-ing Whitehall bigwigs for Sunday lunch in Oxfordshire this weekend. A couple – one from the Cabinet Office and a junior minister – are staying on the Saturday night, *avec* spouses. Sarah's going down on the Friday. Apparently she doesn't work on Fridays. How was the funeral?'

'Good, as funerals go. It was in King's, his old college. They did him proud; a lot of people. Restrained emotion, dignified and moving. I talked to Jenny and his sons. They all coped very well. But this is the send-off he'd want, bringing this to a close. Didn't see Nigel there.'

'He was lunching the Foreign Secretary. Far more important. Says he'll go to the memorial service.'

Charles set out again on the M40 on the Friday morning, this time in a downpour that overwhelmed the windscreen wipers at anything over fifty miles per hour. The rain was forecast to continue through the weekend. He took the ring road around Oxford, then headed west along the A40 until Burford. The hill was awash with water gushing from the drains and the gutters on the stone roofs were overflowing. He stopped for coffee in the Lamb, to give himself more time to think.

In fact, he didn't think constructively for more than about ninety seconds at a time, distracted by memories until driven out by a cleaner who set about the stone flags with a noisy floor-polisher.

There was a lull in the rain, so he wandered down the high street to the Windrush. It was heavily in spate, barely contained by the arches of the stone bridge, and the fields upstream were flooded. Downstream, it did not yet threaten the high grass bank around the church, having free run across the meadows below. He walked through the churchyard, pausing as always when in Burford by the church door to acknowledge the grave of John Meade Faulkener, neglected author. Climbing the bank to watch the grey torrent, he took out the pay-as-you-go mobile he had bought and dialled Sarah's number.

'It's Charles. I'm in Burford. May I come and see you?'

'Now? Well, yes. I'm a bit busy. We've got people this weekend. I'll have to go out later.'

'Just a coffee.'

'That's fine, it would be lovely to see you. What's that noise?'

'It's the river.'

'Mind the Swinford bridge here. It floods easily.'

The road to Swinford ran parallel to the Windrush. The river's course through the fields was marked by willows flooded up to their branches. He turned left past the not-yet-inundated cricket pitch and paused on top of the narrow bridge to stare again at the swirling spate. The bridge was smaller and lower than that at Burford, the road on either side under greater threat. As was, he thought, the nearby pub, which had a catering van parked outside. He drove on up the hill to the house she'd described. It stood behind a stone wall with a freshly painted green gate and her sky-blue Fiat in the drive.

The rain had resumed and he was drenched between the car and the porch, where he stood shaking water from himself. His knock provoked a dog's bark and Sarah's reproving voice. She opened the door while struggling to restrain an overweight black spaniel. 'Don't mind Milly, she's harmless. Come in. Isn't it awful. I've never seen so much rain.'

Her struggle with the dog meant they didn't have to

decide whether to greet each other with a kiss on the cheek or a handshake, or nothing. From the kitchen at the back a sodden garden descended in levels to another stone wall, beyond which was the meadow and its flooded willows. The river surged through the midst of the flood, a giant grey snake of water. The spaniel sniffed Charles's legs. Sarah put the kettle on the Aga.

'Milly, stop it,' she said. 'Sorry, she won't leave people alone. I hope you don't mind dogs?'

'Not at all.' Milly continued her devoted sniffing. 'They always like corduroys.'

'Milk, sugar?'

'Just milk, please.' He waited for her to hand him the mug. 'Interesting how little we know of each other. Whether either of us takes sugar, whether I mind dogs.'

'Have we ever been together in a kitchen before?'

'Shouldn't think so.' They had been in bedrooms, restaurants, pubs, parties, college balls, her Dublin study, her London house, the nursing home, his room in the Chesham and the police station. As students they had walked miles together in the country, yet had remained domestic strangers. 'Domesticity might be a real test.'

'It certainly might. I'll remember sugar if you remember Milly's name.'

He sipped his coffee. Given what he was about to say, it

was important not to be too chatty. 'You can probably guess what I've come for. I've come to ask for your help.'

She looked sharply at him. 'It doesn't seem to me that you need my help. You're quite capable of destroying my husband's career by yourself.'

'If I cause his ship to run onto the rocks and capsize, you go down with him. But if he can be persuaded to disembark quietly at the next port – health reasons, another job, anything – then you'll be okay. He wouldn't even need to know that you would back me up. I could do it without telling him, just as long as I know you would.'

Milly forsook Charles's corduroys and began an inspection of her empty food bowl. They both watched her, then Sarah turned and stared out of the window, cupping her coffee mug in both hands. 'D'you get pleasure from being ruthless?'

'No, but it would give me pleasure if Nigel resigned, because of what he's done.'

'Would it give you pleasure to bring him down anyway, if he didn't resign?'

'Sarah, he's committed a crime; two crimes – three, counting my arrest – the second tantamount to murder. If with your help I can force him to resign – just resign – he'll have got off very lightly.'

'But if I don't help you'd do it anyway?'

'Yes.'

'So you would do it to me, too?'

'I don't want to do that. That's why I hope you'll help me. I hope not to.'

'You hope.' She emphasised the word, still staring out of the window. Milly stood mournfully with her nose against the back door. The rain had almost stopped. 'You hope.' She repeated it slowly, with greater emphasis.

'Sarah, it was your son, our son, whom Nigel caused to be killed.'

She put down her cup and turned to face him, her arms folded.

'He knew it,' Charles continued. 'He knew what he was doing, and he did it without compunction. Whatever his reasons.'

She stared at him for a few moments more, then turned back to the window. Milly scratched softly at the door. 'I'd give anything for a cigarette,' she said.

'I didn't know you smoked.'

'I don't.'

'Why don't we take the – Milly – out into the garden. It's stopped raining. She wants to go out, look. It might be good for us to walk.'

She fetched a pair of Wellington boots from the utility room. 'You can borrow Nigel's if you like.'

'I'll be okay in my shoes.'

To his surprise, she smiled. 'Of course, your everlasting brogues.'

'They wore out, the old ones.'

'I didn't know they did that. I thought they were supposed to see you out. That's what you used to say.'

'These will.'

It was better in the open, discussion no longer confined and intensified by walls. Milly ran about, peeing and sniffing. They walked down the pebble path, through a lopsided rose arbour and down the stone steps to the lower level. Charles had to walk on the grass to stay beside her, the lawn squelching at each step. Unbroken grey cloud moved seamlessly and rapidly. Beyond the wall lay the flooded meadow with its sinister grey surge.

'What would you do if I said yes?' she asked.

'I'd confront him.'

'Where? How? What would you say?'

'Anywhere, anyhow, by phone if necessary. I'd say, either you resign or I write to the cabinet secretary, the permanent secretary at the Foreign Office and the parliamentary oversight committee, the latter to make sure it leaks. That way I stay within the system, break no rules, remain legally watertight. But they might be persuaded to ignore me – disgruntled old hangover from the old regime, congenital boat-rocker, impossible to prove; bad time for this to come out, bad for morale in the new SIA, reflects badly on the government that only recently appointed him. Better have it investigated at leisure by someone who'll establish nothing. But if I can say that his wife will support me in vouching for his treachery and is prepared to appear before the oversight committee herself, they'll cave in. They're bound to.'

'He's due here this afternoon.'

They leaned against the wall. It was easier to stare at the flood than face each other. 'And if I say no?' she asked.

This time he did not reply. He heard a car on gravel, voices, a door banging.

'You would, wouldn't you?' she continued, still staring at the river. 'You'd do it for the pleasure of getting him.'

'Not for pleasure. For Martin, for what he did to Martin.'

'Martin's dead.'

He looked at her face in profile. She had aged, of course, her cheeks sagged a little and her lips were compressed, but it was still the profile he remembered.

'You must think I'm hard,' she said. 'Perhaps I am. But, you see, he's always been dead to me. He had to be. It was how I coped.'

'You regretted giving him away?'

'Now, yes. At the time, yes. In between, no.'

Charles spoke softly. 'But he wasn't dead, was he? Until Nigel got him killed. He could have been here now, with us.'

'You knew who he was, for all those years, and you never said, you never told me.' She spoke flatly, still staring at the river.

'What if I just tell Nigel I'm going to do it, but don't? Would you help by persuading him that I would?'

She turned to face him, the tears standing in her eyes. 'God, you're remorseless. You never give up, do you? It's always what you want, isn't it? Isn't it, Charles? Always has been.'

'There you are!' Nigel shouted from the kitchen door. Milly barked and ran back up the garden. They both started and moved a step apart.

She wiped her eyes with her hands and turned away. 'Well, now's your chance.'

They walked up the garden together. Nigel stood before the door, hands in pockets, legs astride, confident, proprietorial. He was wearing a dark suit with no tie and the jacket buttoned on two buttons. He spoke again as they emerged from the lopsided rose arbour.

'Knew it was you from your car, Charles. Did a good job on it, didn't we? Looks spotless. You must be very pleased.'

'No complaints about the car,' said Charles.

327

Sarah walked quickly ahead of him.

'Got Roger to bring me down early, darling,' Nigel continued. 'Thought you'd appreciate my presence in advance of our guests. Bit worried about getting over that bridge in these floods, to be honest. We should keep an eye on it and send them the long way round if it gets any higher. You didn't notice whether Roger got back all right?'

She shook her head as she disappeared into the house.

Nigel turned to Charles. 'Roger's my chauffeur. Great guy.'

Charles stood back to allow him to follow Sarah into the kitchen. He wondered when guys had replaced chaps or blokes in Nigel's vocabulary. Probably quite early and quite unconsciously, as soon as he sensed the way the world was going. The world except for Charles, that was, to whom guys still sounded affected in any but a North American accent. He wondered, too, about his penchant for irrelevant thoughts at times of crisis or decision; mental displacement activity, presumably. He once unwisely gave voice to it in front of his headmaster, and was caned.

'So, what brings you here, Charles? We're expecting company later.'

'I came to see you.'

Milly was sniffing Nigel's travelling bag and his office security briefcase, which were on the floor by the dresser.

Nigel took up position beside them, hands still in pockets. Sarah had left the room.

Charles closed the kitchen door and for a moment didn't know what to do with his own hands. It was like being in the army again, where there was often no obvious task for an officer's hands. He stepped towards the table and gripped the top of one of the kitchen chairs.

'Nothing I can do to hurry up the police process, if that's what you're after,' said Nigel. 'They've got half a warehouse of hard drives to go through following those arrests a few months ago, so yours is at the back of the queue, I'm afraid. It'll come through all in good time. Nothing to worry about.'

'And, of course, you must be very busy trying to find the real al-Samit.'

Nigel's brusque bonhomie gave way to defensive determination. He pulled back his shoulders and pushed out his chest. 'The so-called al-Samit remains a problem, certainly. It's possible we got the wrong one with Gladiator, though I think the investigation will show that we didn't, or not exactly. For my money, there's no single al-Samit. It's just a name they use. Gladiator may have used it – probably did, if you ask me – just as someone else must be using it now. Unless they just say it to make us think there's someone else.'

'I rather thought you had got the right one with Gladiator. By which I mean, the one you wanted.'

Nigel's features did not move. 'Well, we didn't, as you know. All very unfortunate.'

Charles leaned forward, pressing on the chair. 'But he was the one you wanted, Nigel, wasn't he? The one whose secret annex you've got, the file which will come in handy for refreshing your memory when you visit your opposite number in France. The one which told you that Martin was Sarah's son. My son. Unless you've destroyed it?'

There was a pause. Sarah returned quietly and stopped in the doorway, her arms folded, head bowed.

'I don't know what you mean,' said Nigel.

'I think you do. So does Sarah. And not only us. There's someone else.'

For an instant Nigel looked bemused, as if about to protest that Matthew Abrahams was dead or ask who Charles meant, but he controlled himself. Charles had expected anger, indignation, outrage, a scene of some sort, but they were all too well behaved for that. There was a faint creaking as Milly curled up in her basket.

'What are you really after?' asked Nigel, as if merely curious. 'What do you want?'

'Your resignation.'

Nigel raised his eyebrows. 'Oh, really? Is that all? You

don't want my blood or a couple of million pay-off? You just want me off the scene, do you? Got your eye on my job, perhaps, the promotion that always eluded you? Must be something like that. How else could this benefit Charles Thoroughgood?'

'It's not for my benefit at all, which you may find hard to understand. It's because of what you did years ago with the French and what you've done recently to cover that up. It's because you tried to send Martin to his death, then had me arrested and finally got Martin shot.'

'Oh, I did all that, did I? I'm the villain of the piece, the all-powerful arch-conspirator?'

'And you're James Wytham, aren't you? The source of all those timely leaks arranged through your old friend, the editor. It was you that persuaded the police to arrest me, you that got Martin to go back to Afghanistan, you that ensured the police were told he was armed. Most of it's provable, Nigel, quite apart from your flirtation with the French. If you go quietly, I shall stay quiet. Otherwise, I shall report it.'

Nigel glanced at his wife. She still leaned against the door post, arms folded, still looking at her feet. Her silence was helpful to his cause, Charles felt. He sensed that Nigel felt it, too.

Nigel took one hand from his pocket and rested it on the dresser, as if relaxing for a long talk. His fingers almost touched one of their wedding photographs. 'You're jealous, aren't you? You always have been, jealous that I took Sarah from you and stood by her when you didn't. And because of that you want to destroy me. Us.'

'That's precisely what I'm trying not to do. I'm giving you the chance to go quietly, to remove yourself, so that you're not destroyed.'

'You can remove yourself, Thoroughgood. Now. Right now. Get out before I call the police.'

Charles stared at him. The rain began again, spattering on the windows.

'Right!' Nigel slapped his palm on the dresser, rattling crockery and startling Milly. He strode out of the kitchen, brushing past Sarah, and clumped noisily up the stairs.

Sarah looked up. It was, Charles thought afterwards, her remaining, and her silence, that gave him confidence to continue.

They heard Nigel coming down the stairs, more deliberately than he had gone up. His footsteps sounded magisterially in the hall, then he entered the kitchen holding a double-barrelled twelve-bore shotgun at waist height, pointing it at Charles. Sarah's mouth opened and she moved a step back, away from him. She said his name. Milly got out of her basket, wagging her tail and looking up at him. Charles did not move.

'Out,' said Nigel, moving the barrels from Charles to the door. 'Now.'

Charles remained as he was, hands still on the back of the chair, the table between them. Incredulity kept him motionless, but Nigel interpreted it as refusal.

'If you don't go, Thoroughgood,' he said, 'I shall shoot you.' He spoke as if threatening a child with some minor domestic sanction.

'Nigel, for goodness' sake,' implored Sarah, softly.

He glanced at her, then slowly pointed the gun at the tall metal waste-bin in the corner, and fired. The noise filled the room. Milly scampered and whimpered, there was a muted cry from Sarah as she put her hands to her face and a physical spasm ran through Charles's chest, leaving his ears ringing and his hands clenching the chair. The waste-bin was flung into the air, rebounded from the kitchen wall and came to rest on its side, rocking. It was crumpled in the middle and had a jagged, fist-sized hole right through it. The kitchen cupboard behind was holed and splintered. The room smelt pungently of exploded nitrocellulose.

Nigel pointed the gun back at Charles's midriff and advanced slowly round the table towards him. Firing it had changed something in him; his face seemed somehow more full, his dark eyes now calm and self-absorbed.

'See?' he said quietly. 'I mean it. I'll do it.'

Charles believed him. Nigel's expression was thoughtful, almost remote, as it was that morning years before on the bridge over the Cherwell when Charles had briefly thought he was going to throw himself in, and had facetiously said so. He watched Nigel approach, the twin black holes of the barrels coming closer. The muscles of Charles's arms and legs quivered but part of his brain was remembering, calculating, planning. Keep coming, he was thinking, closer, come closer. Still he hadn't moved.

He was remembering the unarmed combat instruction from Little Stevie on the training course. SAS Stevie, the short, wiry ex-Para, gentle in manner, brisk in execution. What's a gun for? he used to ask. For killing at a distance. So if anyone with a gun gets close to you he's thrown away his advantage. And if he's close enough for you to grab it, you can move faster than he can pull the trigger. You can even, if you're quick, get your thumb between hammer and firing pin. They'd practised and proved it. With a long-barrelled gun like a shotgun it was easier. You just had to tempt him close, make him think you were no threat.

Charles let go of the chair and turned to face Nigel, holding his hands just above waist height, palms forward as in surrender. Concentrate on the weapon, Little Stevie used to say, it's the weapon you're after, not him. The dark blind holes of the barrels drew closer until they were touching Charles's jacket, just below the centre button. Nigel would almost certainly have fired the right barrel first, leaving the left still loaded. Charles knew what to do, but it had to be done fast.

Nigel prodded him with the gun. That was perfect. Charles's reactions were not what they were, but presumably neither were Nigel's. Charles lowered his hands and raised his eyes to Nigel's as he began to speak. 'All right, I'll go, I'm going. I just want to—'

He knocked the barrel aside with the edge of his left hand, then gripped it as he swivelled and stepped backwards into Nigel with the full weight of his body. With his right hand he grabbed the butt and yanked it free of Nigel's grasp. As he did so it jumped in his hands and there was another concussing roar. He felt the sudden heat in the barrel and saw the fridge in the corner shiver and buckle. With the gun now entirely in his hands, he stepped quickly away with it and turned to face Nigel, holding it in what the army used to call the high-port position, ready to butt-swipe him if he attacked.

But Nigel was far from attacking, or even struggling. He had fallen back onto one of the kitchen chairs, knocking it over. As Charles turned to face him again he scrambled to his feet and ran out of the room, past Sarah. Milly ran with him, barking.

For a second or two Charles and Sarah stared at each other. The room still seemed to be ringing from the explosion. 'Are you all right?' he asked.

She nodded and swallowed, still holding her hands to her face. 'Are you?'

Charles broke open the gun, the spent cartridges ejecting against the wall behind him. Keeping it open, he laid it carefully on the table. A boxlock Gallyon, he couldn't help noticing, a handmade English gun, 1920s or 30s. A good gun.

From outside came the sounds of a car starting and a spurt of gravel. 'I think he would have done it,' he said.

She nodded, lowering her hands to pick the fallen chair. 'Where on earth is he going? What's he going to do?'

Charles indicated the fridge. The door of the freezer compartment was holed and sagged open, spilling some of the contents onto the floor. 'Gone to buy a new fridge, perhaps.'

She replaced the chair and mechanically pushed the others into line. 'How can you joke at a time like this?' She was smiling nonetheless.

'How can you not?'

He picked up the freezer contents and pushed them back into the compartment. Surprisingly, with a bit of lifting and pushing, the door closed. There was a hole in the top of the fridge but it was still working.

Sarah picked up the waste-bin and stood looking at what had come out of it. 'We've got two couples coming for dinner this evening. They're staying the night. More tomorrow.'

'Ring and put them off.'

'I can't. It's been arranged for so long.'

'You can't not. You can't possibly explain all this. Or Nigel's absence.'

She put down the bin and fingered the splintered kitchen cupboard. 'D'you think he won't come back, then?'

'I've no idea, but I doubt he'll be host of the year if he does.'

When she tried to open the cupboard the door fell off. 'I was thinking of some new kitchen units anyway.' She seemed unnaturally calm, like a sleepwalker. 'I can't put them off. It's so late. I can't think of a reason.' She peered into the cupboard. 'It's got the saucepans, too.'

'Say he's had an accident, not seriously injured but bruised and shaken, a bit sick. I'll ring them if you like.'

She smiled again, shaking her head. 'And who would you be, Charles?'

Milly reappeared and made for the contents of the waste-bin. It felt to Charles as if they were both acting in a slow-motion film, or underwater. It was necessary to return to normal speed, or normal something. 'You ring them, then. I'll go and see if there's any sign of him.'

The front door was wide open and rain gusted into the porch. He closed it as he stepped outside. Nigel had taken Sarah's blue Fiat, leaving traces of its paintwork on the gatepost. Charles walked a few yards up the road, then turned back. He wasn't thinking straight; there was obviously no point in walking after a car. As he turned he found he could see over the wall and down the hill to the rear of the pub and the stone bridge. Little of the bridge was visible since the water had risen to the top of the arch and spread over the road on either side. The meadow was completely flooded now, which meant there was no way out of the village in that direction. Nigel must have gone up the hill the other way.

But then he noticed something blue in the water and a knot of people on the road this side of the flood. It took a second or two to realise, then a further few seconds to decide whether to go back and tell her, to take the Bristol or to walk. He ran.

There were two men and three women, plus a couple of children, all standing by the pub, away from the torrent. There were unfinished layers of sandbags by the pub door and the adjacent cottage. The catering van was still there.

'Doing sixty if he was doing anything,' one of the men was saying. 'Christ knows what he was on. Came round that corner like a bat out of hell, skidded all over the place, hit the side of the bridge there and bounced off into the water. All four wheels in the air at one point, just before he tipped over. He was flung about all over the place, couldn't have had his belt on, but I saw his face. He was that bloke what bought old Mrs Hillier's house. Then he went into it on his side, with the current turning him over and over.'

The rear of the Fiat was jammed against the underside of the arch. They'd rung 999 but it would take hours for emergency services to get there; they were flooded out with calls, they said – one of the men laughed – and they'd have to go the long way round. There was no hope for him anyway – he never got out of the car. Dead before he hit the water, most likely, the way he was thrown about. Married, wasn't he, but no children so far as anyone knew? Wasn't he that secret man, head of MI5 or something?

Charles went to the water's edge. 'You sure we can't get him out?'

The man who had laughed shook his head. 'Forget about him, mate. It's all over for him. It's you what won't get out if you put a foot in that current. Nor will the car till the level drops. Look how it's wedged. Poor bugger.'

He was right. The car was wedged like a crushed cigarette-packet against the bridge, its roof flattened almost level with its doors. Nothing of the interior was visible. In no hurry now, Charles walked back up the hill in the rain.

19

Nigel had no religious beliefs that anyone knew of. He was cremated on an oppressive grey day that was like so many Oxford days, a speciality of the Thames valley. During the service Charles distracted himself from the effort of more appropriate reflections by trying to work out why this should be, but his thoughts kept returning to Nigel himself. Despite it all, he had found it hard to dislike him until the end. In fact, he had respected him for his love for Sarah. He may even have been a faithful husband. And, he had never seemed to resent the fact that Sarah had had Charles's baby but not his. Not openly, at least. Thinking this made everything that had happened seem so profoundly unnecessary. Nigel could have lived a fulfilled and successful life without doing anything of what he had done. But the devil alone knoweth the heart of man, as the old judge had said. And, anyway, life itself was as profoundly unnecessary as anything that happened in it.

Such thoughts led nowhere, Charles well knew. He looked around. All the seats were taken, which he hoped might please Sarah, if she were in a state to notice. She wore a sharp-edged, shapely black coat with a black hat and half-veil. She and her sister were the only women wearing hats and he could not help musing on what a hat could do for a woman, the right hat anyway; nor, as he looked at her, on how from his early youth smartly dressed women in church had aroused in him the most unchurchly thoughts. He hoped they would never cease. He thought too of Martin's still-unburied body, chilled in the mortuary, pending the inquest. He would attend that funeral, too, come what may.

Nigel's friend Valerie Hubbard, the junior security minister, delivered an elaborate and meandering oration. Hymns were sung, the clergyman led prayers and Nigel's brother – of whom Charles had never heard – read the first eighteen verses of John's Gospel. Sarah did not participate.

Charles kept to the back as they filed out, at the cost of having to talk to Jeremy Wheeler. There was a queue to shake Sarah's hand.

'Tragic, absolutely tragic,' said Jeremy, adopting a stage-whisper undertone. 'Very personal for all of us. Real cat-fight over the succession now. The smart money's on Morley, the outsider, the thinking general. Surprised you're here.'

'Why?'

'You were an Abrahams man. Suppose you went to his, too? I was busy, unfortunately. But you knew Nigel at Oxford, of course. Poor Sarah, she's taken it very well, very dignified. You were rivals over her, weren't you, you and Nigel? He pinched her off you or something?'

'It was more complicated than that.'

Jeremy grinned and lowered his voice further, which somehow made it louder. 'Now I see why you're here. Don't blame you. Attractive woman still.'

In fact, Charles had kept to the back precisely to avoid meeting her. He didn't want to force her to smile, shake hands, make conversation. He had thought constantly over the past three weeks about how he had affected her life, and could see nothing good. Everything bad that had happened to her – except perhaps for her inability to have more children, though possibly even that, somehow – had been as a result of knowing him. He kept returning to the remark she had once made about his lack of joy, which still hurt and puzzled him. Perhaps she was right, if not quite

343

accurate, mistaking it for the baleful consequences of know-ing him.

The wake was at the Studley Priory hotel, where he had taken Sarah on their first date. Jeremy said he would go, to see who was there. There was talk of a memorial service in London. 'Should be settled by then, the succession. I've decided not to allow my name to go forward, by the way.'

'Why?'

'D'you think I should?'

The idea was preposterous. But perhaps no more so than Nigel's brief tenure. 'Most definitely.'

Jeremy's round face filled with emotion. 'Thank you for your endorsement, Charles. I wasn't going to say anything but if you really think I should—'

'I do.'

He solemnly shook Charles's hand, then looked over his shoulder. 'There's Morley. Better go and make my number with him. See how the land lies.'

Jeremy's eager departure enabled Charles to slip away from the queue before Sarah. Outside in the car park mourners for the next funeral were arriving. Many of Nigel's had already gone. Charles walked about for a while, reluctant to drive straight home but equally reluctant to do anything else. He didn't want to go to the wake and be sociable and force himself upon Sarah, yet he felt the need to mark the occasion, not simply to leave it. If Sonia had been there he would have talked to her. He hoped there would always be Sonia to talk to.

He noticed Nigel's official Jaguar and saw Sarah now walking slowly towards it, talking to Roger, the driver. Decent of the SIA, he thought, to chauffeur her on the last day of her semi-official life. He had no idea what a wholly private, single existence would hold for her, where she would live, how good her friends were, whether her work was something she could throw herself into. Whatever her future, there was no room for him in it. He could hardly complain.

He was parked not far from the Jaguar, so he stepped through a gap in the hedge into another section of the car park and walked three times around that to give her time to get away. They had spoken only twice since Nigel's death, the first time when he rang to see if there was anything he could do. She thanked him but said no, the arrangements seemed to be proceeding normally, there would be an inquest of course but the office was being helpful with the official side of things, it was kind of him to ask. A couple of days later she rang and left a message saying she had told no-one about what she called 'Nigel's scene in the house' and hoped he hadn't either. He left a message saying he hadn't and wouldn't and again offered help, but heard no more.

The sounds of departing cars faded. He stepped back through the gap in the hedge. The Jaguar and the remaining mourners were gone, but standing by the Bristol was Sarah. She had her back to him and was looking the other way across the car park. For the first time in his life Charles felt something approaching an epiphany. It was some seconds before he spoke.

Author's Note

The Single Intelligence Agency, the combined intelligence service described in this book, is an imagined institution. Neither it nor the fictional characters portrayed are intended in any way to represent the three separate British intelligence services. In particular, the invented character, Nigel Measures, has no connection whatever with any head of any British intelligence agency, past or present.

The story of Measures's espionage on behalf of the French is, however, based on what is reportedly a real case. On pages 118–119 of his book, *Friendly Spies* (Atlantic Monthly Press, 1993, ISBN 0–87113–497–7), Peter Schweizer quotes a retired French intelligence official as describing how a 'junior aide' on the British Foreign Office European Community negotiating team spied for the French between about September 1985 and the June 1987 EC Brussels summit.

During this period, which included the Single Market negotiations, the official allegedly passed 'invaluable' intelligence
to the French on the British negotiating positions. He also,
like Measures in this book, reportedly had his photograph
secretly taken with the EC president, Jacques Delors.

I have no idea how true this story is or what happened to
the alleged spy – whether he was discovered, whether he is
still serving or whether he lives in honourable or dis-
honourable retirement – but I can say that Measures and
what he does in this book bears no relation to any official
whom I have known or heard of.